BLOOD TIES

A Novel by

Marjorie Tursak

© 2012

Marjorie Tursak

Karen,

thank you for being
such an amazing hostess
and cook and for becoming
a part of our group. I
hope this book gives you
some enjoyment.

Many Blessings
Marj

ACKNOWLEDGEMENTS

Many thanks to Tricia Honsaker for her proofreading skills. She saved the book from a multitude of errors.

Also, much appreciation to Patrice Martin for manuscript assistance.

CHAPTER ONE - KOHLER

John Kohler finished the cut for the inlay in the maple cabinet and switched off the whining router. He bent backward with his hands on his hips to crack his back, then brushed his arms swiftly to dislodge the fine particles of sawdust. He glanced at the clock on the workshop wall. The mail should have arrived by now.

He was tired, and decided to fix himself a cup of coffee. Kohler had slept poorly the previous night; the dream had disrupted his rest again. The dream. Always the same. He found himself deep in the forest, with the virgin white pines towering nearly forever into the crystalline blue sky above him. Sunlight filtered into thousands of thin shafts of light, striking the bracken fern. His vision blurred, clarified, blurred, and the crowns of the trees rotated above him, or was it he that was turning around and around, like a dizzy slow motion child's ride at the playground? Then he was running through the woods, tripping and stumbling and falling, and scrambling to regain his footing, desperate to escape the sound that seemed to come from all around him. His blood coursing like liquid fire through his veins, and terror and disgust, like a thick smoke, choking him, permeating his very mind, and the sound, foreign, yet familiar, that spurred him on until, groping rapidly through the ferns on all fours, he can see the sunlit clearing in the distance. But the sound is louder and louder, shaking and rattling. Is it the Terror crashing through the brush of the under-story forest? And the rhythmic beat, stronger and stronger, and so familiar, yet terrifying; and he can't reach the clearing... and suddenly finds himself bolt upright in his own bed.

He had looked at the clock. It was 2:00 in the morning, and his heart was hammering in his ears. Sweat poured down his face and his bedclothes were soaked through.

The nightmare had followed him since his youth, recurring perhaps twice a year, but it was always horrible. He never knew what set it off, nor why it occurred at any particular time.

He shook himself like a dog trying to throw off water, and entered the kitchen through the enclosed breezeway that connected the house and his woodworking shop. After turning on the flame beneath the teakettle he flexed his frame once more and headed out to see if there was anything in the mailbox, which stood by the road. He was expecting a check from the young Lansing couple who had purchased a china cabinet earlier in the spring. He had allowed them to take it with half down and the rest to be paid in two months. Most folks said that it was a poor business practice, but Kohler thought that the couple seemed trustworthy. *Besides, their folks have a cottage up here on the bay*, he thought. *It's not like they won't be back around.*

The mail yielded the check, the L'Anse Chronicle, and a letter. The return address of Saginaw indicated that it was from his sister, Grace. He was always glad to hear from her; they had not seen each other regularly in the past fifty years.

He could still distinctly remember the day of their Dad's funeral, though he had been only four years old at the time, and Grace seven. She stood at the graveside weeping inconsolably, with the neighbor ladies trying to comfort her. After the graveside ceremonies they returned to the house of John's godfather, Merle Nyberg. John had refused to allow Merle or the ladies to remove his overcoat. He stood at the long floor-to-ceiling windows in the parlor and stared through rivulets of rain at the darkness descending upon the field across the road. There were people moving about the house behind him, a few women in the kitchen cleaning up dishes and packing the remainder of pies and sweet breads away, and some men sitting in the parlor chairs, silently smoking their pipes.

"When do they expect William's sister?" One of the ladies had entered the parlor, wiping her hands on her long flowered apron.

"Tomorrow, probably," Merle replied. "It's a shame she couldn't make it here for the funeral, but it's trip way up here, and on the short notice, too."

"Is she taking Grace back with her? Mrs. Lehto said so."

"Yah, she will be here to put things in order as best she can, maybe stay a few days. Then they will leave."

"It's a shame they have to split the brother and sister up like this. It's not good."

"She can't take both the children, she's got neither the room nor the money, as I understand it. And I want to take the boy. His daddy was my best buddy, it's all I can do now."

"It won't be easy, raising a child. How are you going to bring this little boy up, with no woman around?"

"We'll manage," Merle answered.

So Grace went to Saginaw with Aunt Eva, lived her life there, married and bore her children. There was no reason for her to return to the Upper Peninsula. Merle had raised John in the old Finnish farmhouse outside of L'Anse. After he was old enough to write, John had corresponded with his big sister at least once a month throughout his life.

Kohler re-entered the house and waited for the water to boil. When it did he shut off the flame and made some instant coffee before reading Grace's letter.

"Dear John," it began, "How are you doing. We are having a dry spell down here, and the bean farmers are worried that their crops won't do so good, but we being in town don't notice it so much. Just water the garden and lawn, but they say the lake levels have dropped.

"I am writing to say hello, and that we miss you, but also I would like to ask a favor of you. Rachel is at the end of her junior year at Central Michigan and she's been studying such stuff as anthropology and archaeology, and has gotten herself interested in Indians. She has been doing quite a bit of study with the Chippewas down here at the reservation by Mt. Pleasant, but I guess that there is more action, as she says, in the U.P. She says that it would be a golden opportunity for her to get firsthand knowledge about the Indian rights battles, and that sort of thing, if she could be up there by you. So anyway, I was wondering if you would be kind enough to let her stay with you for the summer? You have the spare room at your place, and she will give you money for groceries, and do as much as she can of the cooking and cleaning.

"Well, she's stewing because she wanted to write herself, so I'll let her add on her lines. She fancies herself to be an adult because she's twenty years old, and she says she should be allowed to write her own letters. Take care and let us know. Love, Grace."

The last page of the letter was written in the flowing script of his niece.

"Dear Uncle John, I do hope you are well and that your business is booming! Mom thinks she still has to take care of me, but I had really intended to take responsibility for my own matters and write to you myself. I do hope you'll forgive her for her interference!

"As she said, I'll be a senior at Central next fall and have been studying anthropology and archaeology. I hope to go on and obtain a Master's Degree in the former subject. You can't believe how interesting it is to me! At the present time I have been tracing the history and customs of the Ojibwe (Chippewa) people in Michigan. I find, though, that some of the most recent developments have really captured my attention, particularly the battle for treaty rights, such as the fishing rights controversy, and the resurgence of traditional Indian religion. I've heard that both are prevalent at the reservation by L'Anse, and I'd really like to spend the summer interviewing people from that area. I plan to use the information for a paper next year in one of my classes. And who knows? Maybe I can continue the study and use it in pursuit of my Master's.

"Oh, and there's another thing. Mom said that you have most of the information about our family history that Grandpa William kept. I'd really like to see it. Being raised without grandparents on your side of the family has left me feeling somewhat rootless. It would mean so much to me if you would show me the old pictures and letters you have.

"Please do let me know if I could spend the summer with you. As Mom said, I will do my share of the work, and I will contribute to the finances. I usually work over the summer, but my folks are willing to let me take the time off for this project, and they said they'd help me financially. (But I bet they're glad I'm the last one they have to raise!) I also have an old VW Bug that I drive around, so you need not worry about having to provide for my transportation. Thanks for considering this favor. Write soon! Love, Rachel."

Kohler threw the letters down on the kitchen table and ran both hands through his hair.

Stupid girl! He thought angrily. *Stupid, stupid little girl, she worries about not having grandparents, but she can thank her stinking red friends for taking care of her grandmother.*

He sat down at the table, which was dominated by his fly-tying paraphernalia, and stared at the small vise, hackle pliers, and vast array of silks, furs, feathers and threads that were used in his hobby. He tried to push the missives from his relatives aside and concentrate on a trout fly, but the letters insisted on a hearing. He felt a constriction in his throat and stomach as he mentally reviewed Rachel's note.

He had not had much opportunity to spend time with his sister's children while they were growing up. He left for Oregon to follow his lumberjack dream when the oldest boy, Roger, was only two. The second child, Rory, was born while Kohler was in the Northwest. Rachel was the latecomer, the unplanned child arriving when Grace was already in her late-thirties and not looking for more diapers and sleepless nights. By then Kohler was back in Michigan and established in his woodworking business. He was able to take the long trip down to the Lower Peninsula only once a year to visit his sister and her family. The result was that Rachel became his favorite, and the boys never seemed to mind that she received his attention more than they. And though her mother tried to dress Rachel in frilly, delicate dresses, she stubbornly gravitated toward blue jeans and ball mitts, and when she was old enough, would beg Uncle John to tell her about his adventures in Oregon. When Kohler took off a week to stay in Saginaw with Grace, Ralph and the kids, it seemed that most of his time was spent with Rachel at his knee, she sitting in rapt attention as he told her about the magnificent splendor of the old growth forests west of the Cascade Mountains. It was Kohler who had first read the old Michigan staple of *Paul Bunyon* to her.

After she became a teenager he saw much less of her. Even if his visit to Saginaw was in the summer, Rachel was busy with the activities of her peers, and unable to pay her uncle much mind. Nevertheless, he still felt close to her, and that was why her letter made him so angry. What was she getting herself into, anyway? *Study history, if you want*, he thought. *Read about the Indian wars. Let it be entirely academic, but why involve yourself with these people in the present? It could only lead to trouble.*

Kohler's day was disturbed, so much so that returning to his work was impossible. A grieving anger smoldered inside and, rather than drink the coffee he had fixed, he sat at the table, staring at the fly-tying equipment and brooding. After some minutes he rose abruptly, made two bologna sandwiches and removed some fishing tackle from the living room closet. He was nearly out of the door with his rod and reel when, as an afterthought, he put the stuff down and went into the bathroom. Taking a bottle of Maalox from the cabinet above the sink, he took a long swig. He wiped his mouth on the sleeve of his flannel shirt.

"Indians. Filthy Chippewa!" he said out loud.

Everything else he would need for an afternoon and evening of fishing on the Sturgeon River was already in his pickup, a testimony to how often Kohler fished. Indeed, from the opening of trout season near the end of April to its sad conclusion at the end of September, he was often found in waders and his best fishing hat, casting for Brook or Brown trout.

Kohler's home was located in the tiny village of Wolf Lodge, which had boasted a rip-roaring lumber camp at the turn of the century. Now it was eclipsed by L'Anse, which was located eight miles north on the main highway. When Kohler stepped outside of his house there were no other neighbors about. Only his house and four others were still inhabited. The Post Office had closed years earlier, and the dirt main street was unkept. The forest, fecund and primeval, was reclaiming the territory, with young trees sprouting where sidewalks once ran smooth. Kohler was glad. There was a certain justice about it, in his thinking, the repossession of the land by the woods. It had belonged to the trees and rivers and wildlife for millennia, then the silence was interrupted by the havoc of the European. Now, at least in a few areas, the forest was reasserting its domain.

For Kohler, the trout was a part of the celebration he felt in all things distant from man. The use of the fly rod, with its need of precision and grace, was a part of the age-old dance of the forest. It eased his mind, relaxed him, and swept from his consciousness worry and anxiety. It had been so since his first trout expedition in his sixteenth year.

He stashed the gear in the back of his red Ford and headed south toward the Sturgeon River. The late May day was sunny, but still very much early spring in the north country, cool and breezy, with the leaves not fully developed on the hardwoods. He drove on the dirt road for three miles, to an obscure opening in the woods on the right. It resembled the beginnings of a U.P. bush road, but was overgrown and sprouting bracken fern and saplings. Here he turned in and pulled the vehicle off the road just far enough so a person traveling by would have to turn their head and look in to see the truck. Rather than carry his waders, he donned them. They were not the article of clothing to be tramping through the woods in, but with the creel, fly case and rod, he had quite enough to haul. He shoved the sandwiches and a quart canteen of water into the front of the wader bibs and set off along the overgrown path.

About half a mile into the forest, he found an aspen sapling bent to the right. He tied it that way several years before. He turned in accordance with the maturing young tree and began to walk in the general direction of the river through the thick woods of yellow and paper birch. There was no established trail, nor did Kohler want one. It is said that a true trout addict is a furtive, closed-mouthed man, who asks no secrets and gives out none. Kohler had no desire to broadcast the location of his favorite trout spot, and he made certain that only an expert woodsman could have found his trail. Not even most of the Indians could, with the exception of maybe Sam Whitefeather, Kohler smirked to himself. *They are highly overrated, those savages*, he thought. *At best they're a bunch of drunken sots who know nothing more than how to live off the government dole and complain about the so-called injustices against them. Ha. The only injustice done was that they talked some stupid white man into sparing their good-for-nothing hides when they should have been wiped off the face of the earth*! Kohler ground his teeth, and then remembered that he had come to the woods to keep from thinking about the Indians, and Rachel, his own sister's kid, involved with the foul beasts… Enough! Enough! He concentrated on the forest, and took note of the trout lilies, trilliums and wood anemone that carpeted the sun-draped forest floor.

Presently he bore hard to the right and after another seventy-five yards, emerged from the wood at the edge of the river. The shrubs and birch grew in profusion close to the bank and he waded directly into the shallow water, quietly, careful not to splash about and betray his presence. The black flies were swarming around his head viciously, so he removed a small bottle of Muskol from the zipper compartment of the waders and lavished the repellent around his ears and neck. The heavy flannel shirt would suffice to keep the voracious insects from chewing his arms off.

Kohler's first official angling act was to go carefully downstream and sit upon a large boulder protruding from the water. From here, a spot shaded by a large black spruce overhanging the stream, he was able to observe the one hundred yards of river running upstream to the southwest. At the far end of this stretch was a waterfall. It cascaded with a great roar from a shale ledge about eighteen feet high, creating a deep and unusually still pool at the base of the falls. Twenty feet from the falls the river once again assumed its normal depth and flowed downstream towards Kohler's boulder. Between his rock and the pool the river boiled and swirled around outcroppings and snags, the water crystal clear in some sections, and in others a current running the color of root beer from the cedar swamp drainage. Sometimes it was a foot deep, and sometimes it fell into potholes of three feet. The air near the river was saturated by the rich, pungent odor of a stand of balsam fir that occupied the left bank near the thundering waterfall.

As he studied the scene, Kohler began to relax. He carefully observed the areas close to the banks, trying to spot any telltale clouds rising from the water. A hatch. That was what he wanted to see, though he knew that he might sit for a time on his rock before any insects emerged and swarmed out over the rushing surface of the stream. It was nearly 2:00 in the afternoon, not a good time to be fishing for brown trout anyway, since they were fonder of the evening hours. But he knew that there were some brookies here, too, and he had caught a few of them. While he sat, he dressed his leader, applying the greasy substance carefully with his fingers, massaging it into the line. Still he waited. Finally he stood up and began moving cautiously upstream, paying close attention to areas behind large boulders. He chose a fly of his own creation, one made to resemble a caddis fly, and began to gingerly cast. He chose as his first target a boulder just a few yards in front of him. He dropped the fly into the water upstream of the rock; it spun briefly, picked up the current, drifted, drifted, down and over, then right into the space below the boulder. It sat there quietly. Nothing. He knew if there were an interested party, it would have struck the fly within seconds of its arrival in the pocket. He kept casting and no longer thought about anything. Rachel, Indians, the maple cabinet in his shop awaiting completion. Nothing. He became part of the river, casting, working the current, breathing in the balsam-laden breeze, full of the rippling water and sunlight and shiny-wet rocks and boiling cascading waterfalls.

Then, at about 4:00, a dense cloud rose from near the left bank, about ten yards from the deep pool. It swirled crazily out over the surface of the river, close to the clear water, but not quite touching, like some strange plague out of the movie The Ten Commandments. Immediately he began to hear the slurping and popping of hungry trout as they rose to feast on the new hatch. He moved closer, excitement tingling in his stomach. Kohler never ceased to thrill at the moment of the hatch, for he knew that the greedy fish would begin to strike his fly, also. He ascertained that the hatch was one of caddis flies, and that his present offering would be sufficient for his purpose.

He began to cast, and his arm and the fly rod were one instrument, a living-mechanical device, moving the line and fly out over the water to a specific area his eye chose. The fly landing, floating, straightening its trajectory down the stream, farther, farther, buoying up on the current, jiggling as the water boils near the boulder, slipping over into the shadow land behind the rock.

Strike! His rod was bent nearly double as the fish realized its error in judgement. Kohler played the fish, and the fish played Kohler. But the man won, and brought the brown dripping from the water, all shiny and sparkling with its handsome spots. Kohler judged its length. The legal size for browns was ten inches, but Kohler never kept anything under twelve. He placed the fish in his creel and his rod and arm joined again. Strike! The fight, the play, the victory, time after time, as the shadows on the river lengthened, and until he had his creel limit of five. It was supper and breakfast, he thought, and Kohler finally broke away from the trout-river-balsam breeze trance, and with a sigh, began to pack his things.

Kohler realized that the sandwiches were still in his waders; he had forgotten all about them. But it had been good fishing, and he was perfectly relaxed and calm. He waded to the shore and trekked back through the darkening woods toward his pickup. He didn't fully return to the world of mankind until he opened the door of his truck and the dome light popped on.

The letter from Rachel suddenly forced itself into his mental field of vision and a spark of ire bolted through his blood, but it passed in the calmness that he still experienced. *Let the girl come*, he thought, *and do her silly studying. It's no business of mine to tell her how to run her life, nor with whom she should associate.*

After cleaning the fish and icing them down at home, he wrote and told her to come north.

CHAPTER TWO – AN INCIDENT

On the first of June, Kohler received a letter from Rachel and another note from Grace, thanking him for his hospitality. Rachel would arrive within the week.

Two evenings later he felt lazy, and unwilling to fix himself supper. He decided to drive into L'Anse and have his meal at the Iron Pine Restaurant. The establishment was owned by Kohler's godfather, Merle, until he retired in 1972. Since then the restaurant had been operated by Paul and Elsie Jarve, but the locals could barely tell the difference. People in the area were sentimental and not much given to change, and the Jarves had kept the Iron Pine looking much the same as it did for the forty-odd years that Merle had run it.

So it was that when Kohler stepped through the door, he was taken back to his younger years, when he had spent so much time at the restaurant. Each day after school he would go there, where he sat reluctantly at the southwest corner table and did his homework. When he reached the age of twelve he was required to help out in the kitchen, emptying the garbage or washing dishes.

"How you ever going to learn to be responsible," Merle would say, "unless you work?" Gotta work, boy. It's a fact of life."

The tablecloths and curtains were still red and white gingham, and the old pine panels on the walls remained a glowing golden color. Suspended above the door was the head of a moose with an enormous rack, and the heads of deer and elk hung along the south wall. Beneath the trophies were the implements of the old logging days, peaveys, crosscut saws, and axes. And though the Iron Pine was primarily a family restaurant, there was a heavy oaken bar along the north side of the room. It wasn't separated from the restaurant in any way, but no one seemed to care. Those who came to have a drink, drank quietly, and usually had a meal too.

Kohler seated himself at the bar and the tall, blond Jarve turned from wiping a glass.

"Evening, Paul."

"Evening, John. What'll ya have?"

"How about the pan-fried steak and a glass of milk?"

"Coming up."

While Jarve went for the milk, Kohler studied the objects behind the bar, placed there by Merle when he opened the restaurant. There was a huge cross section of white pine, three inches thick and four feet in diameter, fastened in the center of the wall. Mirrors ran along the rest of the length of the bar on either side of the pine. Beneath the slab of wood was a softball-sized chunk of hematite taken from the mine where Kohler's father had worked. The ore registered seventy percent pure iron content, and weighed over ten pounds. More than once Merle had swatted the young Kohler's behind because the boy had lifted the sparkling grey stone from its resting-place and carried it precariously to the window to be examined more closely. He loved to watch the light play on a thousand tiny crystals on its surface, and to cover his fingertips with the glittering granules. Because the hematite was so crumbly, Merle had a rule against touching it, let alone carting it across the room with the possibility of dropping it.

The Jarves had kept the memorials to what had made the Upper Peninsula great, the iron and pine. It was all history, now, Kohler mused. By 1900 the big pines were about finished, and they started on the hardwoods. Then came the miners. North and west of Baraga County it was copper, but to the east, and extending back into Baraga, it was iron. It was all played out, now. The iron, the pine, the copper; the economy sagged, and it was rough times for the "yoopers".

The opening of the restaurant door interrupted Kohler's reverie. He turned casually to see who was entering, and immediately tasted a rush of anger. The customers were Sam Whitefeather and his wife. Whitefeather, a member of the tribal council, was a tall man about Kohler's age, with hair the color of the hematite and combed straight back on his head. His wife was short and slightly paunchy, and was smiling at something her husband had said as they entered the restaurant.

Why ,they walk in here looking all dignified, as though they belonged here, thought Kohler. He slapped his palm down on the bar in disgust. Jarve was bringing the steak and looked warily at Kohler as he sat the food before him.

"I didn't realize you allowed such trash in the Iron Pine, Paul. Merle would never have put up with such."

"Well, I ain't Merle. Here's your food. Enjoy."

Kohler turned again to look at the Indians, who were seating themselves at the corner table.

"By the great jumpin' Jehoshaphat, they're sitting where I used to sit to do my homework all those years! Whitefeather even looks sober. Don't he look sober to you, Paul?" Kohler said in a loud voice. "Must be the world's only sober Chippewa."

Jarve leaned across the bar toward Kohler. "Keep your comments to yourself, John. We've known each other a long time, but I'm not going to let you disturb my other customers, hear?"

Kohler threw six dollars on the bar and rose from his seat. "And I ain't eatin' in the same restaurant with Indians!" He shoved the barstool violently and stalked out of the building.

The sun was far in the west and the air had a late afternoon tinge of coolness as he began walking fast down Main Street. He was still in the throes of anger and revulsion, and suffered a sort of blindness and deafness to his surroundings. His pickup was parked at the Iron Pine, but he did not think about it; he just felt like walking and walking, empowered by the inward heat of his mind and soul.

When Kohler reached Skanee Road, he turned north and followed it, past the Superette market and the Post Office, and up the hill through the small north end residential district. Soon L'Anse was behind him. He walked a mile out of town before some dark faces in a passing car reminded him of where he was. The road ran twelve miles through the reservation before it emerged at the south end of Huron Bay. The realization sent a thrill of panic through him. *It was true that racial violence in the area, was rare, but if they could only sense how he hated them, and God knows they probably could, they could sense everything else,* he thought, *those redskins... Good Lord, I'd better get out of here, turn around and hurry back to town. I don't even have my truck!* The truck had always kept him safe when he had driven through the reservation on his way back to trout fish at Big Eric's bridge, but now!

As he walked rapidly back toward L'Anse his mind began to clear and he thought about the incident in the restaurant. His fear gave way to confusion. "Why did I treat Paul that way?" he wondered aloud. "I have nothing against him." Whitefeather's face rose before him. It was always like that. If there was an Indian involved, it was easy to lose control, forget where he was, what he said, and be completely given over to the hatred. But they deserved to be hated! They deserved worse! Yet it bothered Kohler that he totally lost all restraint, that he became another person, unable to think or reason, but only to feel the fire flowing through his mind and body, burning and burning, until he thought he would scream. It was as though a darkness descended upon him, or that he descended into a darkness.

His contemplation brought another face before him, one that even now caused a soreness. "Darkness". That was what Anita had called it. He kicked angrily at the gravel by the side of the road.

It was the spring of 1960 when he met her at a dance. He was twenty-four and had been back from Oregon for three weeks, done with logging and the constant dreary rain of the Northwest winter. He sought escape from that, and the strange uneasiness that pervaded his life.

The Finnish Club held a dance every Saturday night at Chassell, and he drove north to the small town to attend. Though the dance was primarily an ethnic event, the Finns wanted to attract the dollars of the general public, and the band played some Elvis Presley songs along with the Scandinavian music. The hall was brightly lit and effused a lively spirit. As John stood watching the participants on the dance floor, he noticed an attractive girl in her early twenties, paired with a gawky-looking fellow. She had fine auburn hair and a creamy complexion, and exuded life with every move of her body. He decided that the gawky fellow couldn't possibly be such a girl's date. When the music ended he moved through the crowd toward her.

"Excuse me, could I have this dance?" he asked her.

The girl appeared to be somewhat taken aback.

"I'm sorry. I guess it would be more proper of me to at least introduce myself first. My name's John Kohler, originally from L'Anse, more recently returned from a very rainy Oregon. Is that fellow you were dancing with your date?"

She recovered her poise and laughed. "No, he's not. Just an acquaintance, Mr. Kohler. And thank you for your invitation to dance. I accept."

The music began and they moved off over the floor.

"My name is Anita Perkins," she said. "I live in Houghton."

"Perkins? Not a name common to this area of Scandinavians."

"Well, Kohler isn't, either! I'm a transplant. My parents were both born in Lansing, but my father is a professor at Michigan Tech."

"Well then, we have something in common. Your father teaches at a mining school, and my father was a miner."

"Oh, really?" she said. "Is he retired now?"

"He was killed in an accident at the Glover Number Two when I was only four years old."

"I'm sorry. I didn't mean to bring up something like that."

Kohler was immediately chagrined that he had mentioned the mining accident. "No, I apologize. I was the one that brought it up, and here it looks like I'm trying to play on your sympathies. Let's start over again."

"All right, but you needn't have apologized. I didn't think you were trying to make me feel sorry for you. You really don't seem the type. So, what were you doing in

Oregon?"

"I was a lumberjack."

"How romantic!"

"Not really. The days of the old ripsnorters are long gone, I'm afraid. My great-grandfather was a logger back in the times when they were still taking pine from the Lower Peninsula. Now, those men were real lumberjacks! Everything is pretty much automated today. Nobody goes into the woods with an ax or crosscut saw, and the bunkhouses are nice clean affairs that look like your mom is keeping it up. Actually, very few logging crews ever stay in bunkhouses anymore, just drive in from town, cut, and go back to wives at night. Not much romance to that."

"So you came back to Michigan to find romance?"

"Not unless you call working at Kellen's in L'Anse romantic. They make skids. But that's not forever. I have a little money saved from my job in Oregon, and I'm buying woodworking tools. I want to open my own shop and make furniture. I figure it'll take me at least a year to get everything set up exactly the way I want it, but it's coming along all right. I could get started on some things as early as this fall. But enough of me. Tell me about yourself."

John and Anita talked and danced most of the night, and at the end made a date to see each other again. She wanted to learn how to fish, so he found an extra rod and reel and took her to Otter Lake the next Saturday.

He rowed around the shore in a boat borrowed from Merle, and for several hours they laughed and talked. Toward evening he said they needed to start to do some serious fishing since the bass would begin biting at dusk, so they settled down to their daredevils and jitterbugs, casting in earnest.

The northwestern sky began to cloud over, with towering thunderheads that were blue-black against the light. The wind ceased, the atmosphere was oppressive, and the darkened waters of the lake became very still and glassy.

"John, it looks like it's going to storm. Maybe we should go in."

"Yup. This is the best time for bass, take my word for it. They'll start biting like nobody's business before bad weather. Best to stay."

"But we might get wet!"

"Do you want to fish?"

"Yes, but …"

"Then fish!"

Kohler was right. All around them the snouts of fish feeding voraciously broke the surface of the lake. It created hundreds of circular patterns that undulated across the water toward the shore. Anita resignedly cast her jitterbug as far from the boat as she could and began to slowly reel it in. Suddenly the lure was hit hard, and she nearly dropped the rod. The reel buzzed urgently as the fish darted away from the boat. They nearly tipped the craft over before they were able to land the glistening bass.

"A monster," Kohler told her. "A real prize!"

Soon the first few raindrops began to pelt the lake, and they rushed to reach the shore, John pulling on the oars for all he was worth. They were still several yards away when the skies opened and poured forth their fury. By the time the couple wrestled the boat back onto the top of the '53 Dodge, they were both convulsed with laughter at their drowned-rat appearance.

As the spring weather began to warm into full summer Anita suggested they plan a picnic. Kohler chose Second Sand Beach; if it got hot enough they could swim in the waters of Keweenaw Bay, and if not, the scenery was lovely to view. It was their fourth date, and Kohler was looking forward to seeing Anita each time. She was special, funny, and willing to try doing the activities he liked. He reviewed her fine hair, sparkling hazel eyes and petite figure, and considered that it might be a good thing to include her in his future.

The Saturday afternoon of their picnic at the beach was warm and sunny, with a few clouds floating lazily in the blue sky. They sat together on the sand and gazed at the calm water. It reflected the clouds and the pines near the shore, but melted into a uniform silver toward the opposite shore a mile away. On the horizon the Huron Mountains rose in indistinct and uneven ridges of blue-grey.

Anita leaned her head on Kohler's shoulder and he put his arm around her. Lifting her face with his other hand he kissed her gently. She drew away, then pulled him back for a longer kiss.

After they parted, Kohler sat back and gazed out at the bay. "Say, lady, what do you have planned for tomorrow, anyway?"

She answered playfully. "Oh, I don't know. I was hoping for a prince on a white horse to come along and take me for a ride."

"What year does the horse have to be?"

"What year do you have?"

"Will a '53 be all right?"

"Oh, I suppose so," she laughed.

On the fourth of July they went to the Houghton City Picnic, held on the banks of Portage Lake. All of Houghton and its sister city of Hancock seemed to be present, in addition to people from other parts of the Keweenaw Peninsula. The crowds were thick.

John and Anita were walking along, arms linked, talking, when someone coming from the opposite direction bumped into John. Kohler turned and began to apologize until he saw the dark, broad face and black hair of an Indian before him.

"I'm sorry, mister, I didn't mean to..." the Chippewa began.

"Why don't you watch where you're going, you filthy red bastard? What do you think you're doing here, anyway? Go back to your reservation, or better yet, just go to..."

"John!" Anita tugged at his arm insistently. He turned and saw an expression of shock and disbelief on her face. His last word froze in his throat. The Indian took the opportunity to place distance between himself and the white man.

The young woman stared at Kohler for a moment. He could feel his face burning, and the blood was rushing through him so quickly that his skin tingled. His fists were clenched, and he slowly released them. He tried to take Anita's arm, but she drew away in a quick little movement and began walking. He hurried to catch up to her, and they strolled in silence for some time. Finally she spoke.

"One question. Why? Just make me understand why you behaved like that."

"I don't know." Kohler felt confused, yet the memory of the Indian's face, the sensation of his body jolting against Kohler's right arm, still caused anger to rise into his throat.

"You must know," Anita said. "That man didn't do anything to you. With the crowds the way they are here, it's a wonder we haven't been knocked over."

"He's an Indian. He shouldn't be here."

"There's no law against an Indian being at a Fourth of July picnic. I just don't understand why you lashed out at him like that. What on earth do you have against Indians, anyway?"

Kohler laughed a bitter little laugh that had to squeeze itself from his constricted throat. "Oh, maybe it's a family affair, or something like that."

"What is that esoteric statement supposed to mean?"

"Well, I told you how my father died, but I didn't tell you about my mother."

"Yes you did. You said she died in childbirth having you."

"Yeah, that's right. And the one responsible for her dying was an Indian midwife." He turned to Anita and clutched her arm. "An Indian killed my mother! I think that gives me reason to hate every one of the savages."

She drew him close and put her arms around him. "Honey, I'm sorry." She smoothed his hair from his forehead, much as a mother would have in trying to comfort a small child. "Sit down over here." They sat under a large maple near the bank of the lake, and she held his hand.

"Now John," she began in a soothing voice, "it may not have been the woman's fault that your mother died. She managed to bring you through it, and I'm rather thankful to her for that."

"It was her fault! Merle told me so. Merle tried to get Dad to have a white woman in; I don't know why he chose a savage." Kohler thought his argument seemed weak, not current enough to help Anita understand why he felt the way he did, and he had to make her understand!

"Besides," he continued, "They're just a menace to society. To good people, I mean. Don't you know what they're like? Haven't you heard of some of the things they've done? I was over at the restaurant the other day and heard a couple of guys talking about how a white man and his wife from down below were camped over at Brevort Lake, near the Straits, and two Indian bucks came into the campground in the evening. They were drunk, naturally, and they kept driving past these people's campsite, several times. Just driving and looking. I guess this guy's wife was an attractive woman, and they were looking at her. And pretty soon they start making comments. I suppose this man thought that if they just ignored them they would go away, and after a while it seemed like they did. But along about dusk the bastards came back, and they had a gun and some rope. They grabbed the woman's husband and tied him to a tree, and took her into the tent and raped her. Can you imagine being tied to a tree and hearing your wife's crying, knowing that she was being raped by a couple of filthy animals? And you not able to move or do a thing but listen? Just listen?" Kohler gritted his teeth and clenched his fists. "That guy should have hunted the sons of bitches down and killed them. If he was a real man, he would have!"

"John, you mean to tell me that there wasn't another person in the entire campground that knew what was going on and could have gone for help?" Besides, you weren't there, you didn't see the incident. How do you know it even happened?"

He looked at her in surprise. "You don't believe me?"

"It's not a matter of believing you. I just don't know if these men were giving a trust-worthy account of what happened. It could have been secondhand, or even third-hand knowledge. And things get exaggerated so, moving from mouth to mouth…"

"But these things happen all the time! You aren't still in Lansing, you know. You're in the north woods, living near a reservation of Chippewas. They're different from white people, Anita. They're a lot worse. Just read through the L'Anse paper sometime and see how many of the drunk and disorderlies are Indians."

"Oh, never mind. I can't see arguing over something that doesn't really affect our relationship, anyway. We don't live with them and they aren't a part of our lives." She rose, straightened her skirt, and took his hand. "Come on. We came to have a good time, and I don't want it to be entirely ruined."

The brief northern summer continued, and the incident was forgotten.

In August the nights became chilly and the skies changed. The light angled differently through the trees, and the clouds floated lower and darker, scudding by on a brisk, no-nonsense sort of breeze. Autumn was approaching. Kohler had fallen in love with Anita, but was just beginning to admit his feelings to himself. He thought of how he had nearly all of the tools that he would need to start his woodworking business, but what of a place to live and have his workshop? And, perhaps, a place for a wife? He stared at the calendar and tried to work it all out in his head. Time. He tried rehearsing a proposal. Maybe in a few weeks he'd be ready to ask her, then by spring ... *This all has to be proper, and thought-out*, he told himself.

One bright Saturday before the month was out Kohler took Anita on a waterfall tour. They left early in the morning and drove around Baraga County from north to south, viewing the area's most beautiful falls. They lunched at Big Eric's Falls on the Huron River, and then drove back through L'Anse and out 41 to reach the Sturgeon River Falls near Alberta. It was mid-afternoon, and unseasonably hot when they arrived.

They sat holding hands on the shelf rock that stretched out from the bank. The spray from the roaring water drifted onto them when the wind blew across the cascades. Other young people, seeking refuge from the heat, arrived and stripped down to bathing suits and plunged into the dark, boiling rapids.

"Is that safe?" asked Anita. "The rocks look so slippery."

"It's harmless. Watch. They'll go right up to the falls."

Two teenage girls, one in a robin's egg blue suit, and one in a flowered pink garb, waded with difficulty into the white water and carefully worked their way around the boulders until, waist-deep, they cavorted in the pounding, wild chaos at the base of the falls.

"Would you like to go in?"

"I don't have a bathing suit on, John. It does look fun, though."

"Come on," he said, standing up and drawing her to her feet.

"All right, just to wade a little, but that's all."

The couple climbed down from the ledge and onto the rocky bank along the edge of the river. After removing their shoes and socks and rolling up the legs of their slacks, they entered the water.

"A little further," Kohler urged the girl.

"I'll get my clothes wet!"

Yet he led her by the hand toward the rushing falls until the water surged to her knees.

"John!" She pulled back suddenly, and he tugged at her hand with a strength that caused both of them to lose their balance and plunge into the rapids. They came up sputtering with laughter.

"And now what? I'm soaked!"

"And now we might as well enjoy it," John said with a grin. He splashed more water into Anita's face, giving rise to a vicious water fight that lasted several minutes. They emerged from the river dripping and laughing and attempting to wring as much water from their clothes as possible. John spread a blanket across the front seat of the car.

"I suppose we had better go before it turns cool and we both catch our death of cold," he said.

"Yes, and it's a long drive to Houghton, you silly. You may have to use the heater before I get home."

As they climbed into the car, John watched the girl for a moment. *She's so perfect*, he thought, *so beautiful, and it's been such a great day*. He determined to ask her to marry him soon.

They returned to the highway and headed north.

"Ugh. I hate feeling drenched like this, it's so uncomfortable. I wish I were home in dry clothes."

"I'll drive just as fast as I can, honey. Hang on, it won't take long." Suddenly, from the right, an old green pickup pulled out onto the highway, spewing dust and gravel from the shoulder. John slammed on the brakes and careened around the vehicle to avoid hitting it in the rear.

"Stupid idiots!" he yelled. "Trying to get someone killed?"

He looked up in the rearview mirror at the three occupants of the truck, which was still just a few feet from his rear bumper.

"Oh, that figures, Filthy brutes! They think they still own the country so they can rule the road, too."

Anita grasped Kohler's arm. "What's the matter with you?"

When he turned toward her, he saw fear in her eyes. But he was already oblivious to everything except the green pickup and its dark occupants. He began to drive erratically, swerving from one side of the highway to the other in front of the other vehicle. Then he slowed to twenty miles per hour, forcing the pickup to slow, also, or hit the Dodge in the rear. Anita turned in her seat and looked at the passengers in the truck.

"John, not again. You and your Indian problem. Now stop this and let them by, or just keep on driving normally. They didn't mean to pull out in front of you, they just didn't see you coming."

"Sure," he said in a low growl. He stuck his hand out the window and motioned the pickup to go around. It swung into the passing lane and pulled ahead of him. When it was thirty yards away, Kohler stamped the gas pedal and drove within inches of the pickup's bumper. He began honking his horn, then stuck his head out of the car window and shouted, "Filthy bastards Get the hell off the road!"

"Stop! Stop this!" Anita screamed.

Kohler, blind angry, looked at her, but saw nothing. With a great push he thrust her off him. Her body slammed into the door. "Shut up! Just shut up!"

He swerved closer to the pickup, forcing the driver to ride part way on the berm of the highway. Anita cowered in the seat, her face a mask of terror and disbelief. Kohler was laughing maniacally, his face damp with perspiration. He edged still closer to the Indian's vehicle, which had slowed in a desperate attempt to make the white man pass them. The truck was traveling entirely on the dirt and gravel of the shoulder. Kohler was close enough to see the occupants of the pickup, an old man, a woman of similar age, and a girl in her early teens. He glared at them and continued to move the Dodge to the right, staying always within inches of the pickup. The two vehicles had slowed to ten miles an hour, but the old man seemed to panic and suddenly increased his speed. Kohler reacted by plunging his accelerator to the floor.

"I'll show you!" he screamed. Cutting the steering wheel quickly to the right, the fender of his car smashed into the pickup's fender with the grinding and scraping sound of metal meeting metal. The truck left the berm entirely and crashed into the saplings at the edge of the forest. Kohler stomped on the gas pedal and left the scene in a spurt of gravel. A car passed them coming from the opposite direction and slowed to a stop near the pickup, but by that time the scene was small in his rearview mirror.

He continued north on the highway, slowly feeling his body relax. He ventured a glance at Anita. She was still huddled by the passenger door, staring at him wide-eyed in fear. He quickly returned his eyes to the road and was overcome by confusion. It seemed to him that he had been dreaming. Nothing had happened, right? And yet, he knew it had. The bitter taste of hatred and fear was still in his mouth. He gripped the steering wheel tightly, until his knuckles turned white. His mind raced. He knew he had been rough with Anita in his blind rage. He hadn't known what he was doing! No. No he couldn't say that. It sounded too much like he was crazy. There were reasons for his reactions. Good reasons. Against the Indians ... but he had been cruel to Anita! He had shouted at her, hadn't he? And even pushed her? He was boiling inside, confused thoughts and feelings all bumping around and rushing to reach some order. But he must apologize. He must make it right!

They reached L'Anse and drove around the south end of the bay, and still he was unable to decide what to do, what to say. There was a death-like silence in the car all the way to Baraga, when he finally reached his hand toward the girl.

"Listen honey, I'm sorry. It won't happen again."

Anita shrunk from his touch, attempting to roll herself into a tiny ball against the car door. "Just take me home." Her voice was strained, tiny, a cartoon voice.

"But, come on, really…"

"Take me home, that's all I want." Kohler removed his hand from her shoulder and his stomach tightened into knots. Perspiration broke out again on his forehead. He had to say something to make this all right! But they drove the rest of the way to Houghton without speaking.

When they arrived in front of Anita's house, she had the door open almost before the car came to a halt. As she exited, Kohler leaned over on the seat and called, "I'll talk to you tomorrow, give you a ring, o.k.?"

She turned toward him, her eyes still frightened animal eyes. "Don't call me tomorrow, John, please."

"The next day, then?" I'll call after I get off work Monday."

She shrugged her shoulders. "I don't know." Then she turned and hurried up the sidewalk to her door.

He tried to call her on Monday. Her father said she wasn't in. Tuesday and Wednesday she wasn't available, and she did not return his calls. The letter was waiting for Kohler when he came home from work on Thursday. It read: "Dear John, I am sorry I haven't returned any of your calls, but I just couldn't. I have just tried to think these past few days about what happened on Saturday, and about the incident a few weeks ago, and what it means for me, and for our relationship.

"I'm sure you know that I care for you very deeply. How I want you to realize that! And, I suppose if we were to continue, something more permanent would have developed.

"John, you are such an enigma to me, and I'm in such pain over you right now! On one hand you are thoughtful and kind, so witty, and strong and interesting, and so much fun to be with. And I love all those qualities in you. But there is something else in you, a bitterness of soul, an overpowering hatred that, when it rises up, destroys every good thing in you. And to be in the presence of that force is to place oneself in the presence of destruction.

"What I saw in you Saturday afternoon frightened me very badly. It made me wonder who you were, and question why I was in the car with such a madman. Seeing you was like watching a great darkness well up from some foul pit and spill out over everyone and everything in its path. I just can't place myself in that kind of jeopardy. You could have easily gotten us killed, not to mention those poor Indians.

"I have to admit that I am still feeling very uncertain inside, and I suspect it shows in the incoherence of this letter, but I have made a decision, and I feel that I must stick by it. I just don't think it would be a good idea for us to see each other anymore. Perhaps I'm weak; I really would like to help you, because I think you have a problem that you need to face and resolve, but I'm not going to try and fool myself. This thing is bigger than me, and I'm afraid that if I continue with you, I will simply be washed away in the destruction, too. When you go into one of your rages you recognize no one, and nothing means anything to you.

"Please don't think me harsh. As I said, this is so very painful for me, also. I hope you have a good life, John. I do care for you, and I shall never forget you.

"As ever, Anita."

He had tried to call again, to apologize, to excuse himself, to beg her to reconsider. He really didn't know exactly what he would say to her. But no matter, she was never available, and never returned his calls. He went to the Finnish dance in Chassell hoping to find her, but she wasn't there. He felt it was hopeless to go to Houghton and try to see her; he wouldn't be allowed past the front door.
After three weeks he gave up altogether and a great bitterness about the matter rose within him. He decided that he cared nothing for dances or women, but then, wasn't it really the fault of those red niggers in the green pickup? He told himself "If they hadn't been where they were at that time, none of this would ever have happened." He thought they had been responsible for so much grief in his life, from his very birth. This was just another example of their loathsomeness; and he tucked the bitterness down deep in his gut where it rode in silence.

The gravel along Skanee Road had turned into the pavement of L'Anse and Kohler paced the streets, up and down through the town, walking off the anger, walking off the darkness. Dusk had come, and night, and still he walked, brooding about Anita, and all that had transpired since that summer. It had been what, twenty-seven, twenty-eight years?

He sighed and finally stopped his pacing, drew a package of Rolaids from his shirt pocket and popped two in his mouth. He drew both palms across his face, as though he was trying to wipe away an obstruction from his eyes, and suddenly he felt very weary. Pulling an old black pocket watch from his jeans, he saw that it was well past 10:00. He had been wandering around in a daze for hours.

All he really wanted to do was to go home to bed. He was so tired, more exhausted than after a hard day in the woods or shop. Kohler turned toward the restaurant and shortly arrived at his truck. He glanced at the door of the establishment with a mixture of embarrassment and anger. Surely there were no customers there who had witnessed his earlier lack of self-control. But Paul was here. He desired to apologize to the man for creating a scene in his restaurant, and yet, Jarve should know better than to allow the Indians to eat there! The devil with the law, anyway. They shouldn't be allowed. But not everyone thought as Kohler did in the matter. And how many times in years past had Kohler vowed to live and let live? If others didn't mind the company of trash, let them be. Nevertheless, incidents of this sort had punctuated his life, and somehow the price had always been a relationship. Well, what could he do? *No use crying over spilt milk*, he thought.

He drew himself up straight in the truck seat and turned the ignition key. The engine caught and headlights cut a white swath from the darkness. He headed south on the highway toward Wolf Lodge and again resolved to keep his nose out of other people's business, especially with Rachel coming to spend the summer. She was on her own. Now he just desired to sleep, and was thankful when his own dwelling appeared from the blackness of the forest. He stopped the truck and entered the house, weary in soul and body. The bed would feel so good. But Kohler didn't sleep well.

CHAPTER THREE – BLOOD TIES

He was in his workshop in the late afternoon on June 6th, carefully planing the end of a piece of lumber, when he heard the unmistakable humming of a VW engine in his drive. *Rachel has arrived, then*, he thought. He put down the plane, shut off the lights in the shop and walked out to meet her.

The girl was pulling bags from the front of the car. She seemed thinner than the last time Kohler had seen her, but that was last summer, when he had gone for a short visit to Saginaw. And he really hadn't spent much time with her then, since she had a summer job in the daytime, and was usually gallivanting at night. *But she's turned out to be a pretty girl*, he thought.

"Good grief," he said, "where in tarnation did you find such an ugly vehicle?" The Volkswagen was a bright lime green, nearly florescent. It reminded him of some insects he had seen near St. Ignace one summer.

She turned from her preoccupation with the luggage. "Uncle John! Hello!" She came and hugged him tightly. "I'm so excited about this summer. Thanks for letting me stay here." She took a deep breath. "The air smells so good and fresh from the pine. I never get to smell that in Saginaw."

"Yeah, you city slickers have it rough, all right. You hungry?"

"Starved. I stopped for lunch about noon, but I've had nothing since then."

He picked up two of her bags. "Good. I put a pot roast on. It should be ready." Rachel took two bulging book bags from her car, grunting with the strain. "Well, let's go eat," she gasped.

"What'd you do, bring the entire Saginaw Public Library?"

"These are my research books and notebooks."

"Well, better let me take those; here, you carry your suitcases."

They exchanged burdens and walked into the house.

During supper Kohler said, "I suppose you'll be running off directly to do whatever it is you're going to do up here."

"Well, if it's all right with you, I thought for the first few days we could hang around together in the evening and talk. I have so many questions to ask you. I remember when I was a little girl you'd tell me stories for hours. It's been a long time since we've done that."

"Yes, young miss, but that's because you became one of these know-it-all teenagers and your Uncle John bored you."

"No!"

"Yes!"

"No, not really!"

He looked at her and cocked his eyebrows reprovingly.

"Well, maybe," she acquiesced. "But we can make up for it now, can't we?"

Kohler smiled. The doubts that he had about his niece staying with him suddenly seemed silly. *I've been living alone too long*, he thought to himself, *and I've forgotten how nice it is to have some family around.*

"Well," he said, "I suppose we could hash things over a bit."

After they finished the meal Rachel was quick to begin the dishes. Another change, reflected Kohler. As a kid she was never eager to do chores; always wanted to go out and play or read. He dried while she washed. It took little time to finish up.

"You'd better take those bags into your room and settle in. You want to go into L'Anse or anything later?"

"No, unless you want to. It's so peaceful out here, no traffic or noise. Do you have some pictures of the family that we could look at? I think that would be nice."

"Well, I have one old photo I know you'd like to see. It's a real gem. Merle saved all of my Dad's stuff for me; my father built a wooden chest when he was a boy, and he kept all his important papers and souvenirs and the like there. Merle turned it over to me some years before he passed on. This picture was in amongst the family history things; it's one of my great-grandfather back when he was a lumberjack in Saginaw. Must have been taken somewhere around 1855 or 1860. Its in pretty good shape for its age."

Kohler went into his bedroom and retrieved a simple, varnished pine box. After placing the chest carefully on the floor near the couch, he removed the small padlock from its hasp and opened the lid.

"There, look at this. See any family resemblance in any of these characters?" he handed an old daguerreotype to his niece.

"Wow, this is great!" Rachel studied the picture, which showed a group of about twenty lumberjacks standing in the snow outside a rough-hewn board building. Most of the men were dressed in greatcoats, some wore caps. Four brandished axes and the two on each end of the front row held the handle of a long crosscut saw. "I'm sorry I can't recognize anything in any of these men. But after all, my great-great-grandfather! Fat chance I should be able to pick him out of this group."

"Well now, look on the back of the picture. It tells which one he is."

She turned the picture over. The writing was in dark ink, with a flowing script. "Wilhelm Kohler, Saginaw. Third from right, back row. Pipe and watch fob," she read aloud. She flipped the photograph over again. "So this is Great-great-Grandpa Wilhelm." She studied the man identified as her forebear and Kohler looked over her shoulder. He never tired of seeing the picture. Wilhelm appeared to have been a tall man, perhaps six feet. He had a short, well-kept black beard, and a neatly trimmed mustache on his finely sculpted, Germanic face. A long pipe was clenched in the right corner of his mouth. He wore a billed cap on his head, but no coat. Light colored suspenders were accented against the dark shirt and trousers. High laced up boots completed his apparel. A watch fob hung connected from the middle of his chest and led down into a loop and back into his left breast pocket. He was the only lumberjack in the picture with such an adornment.

"Quite a legacy, eh?" Real pioneer stock, we Kohlers ."

"Do you have the entire family history?"

"I've been able to piece most of it together. Aunt Eva had a few things, and Uncle Mike kept some records of family dealings in Saginaw, old business records and such. But my father had all of this stuff in his chest here since he was a young boy. Must have had a bit of the historian in him; that'd be where you get your itch to dig around in old records and stuff."

Rachel seemed to be carrying on her own line of thought. "If the family started out in Saginaw, and most of us are still there, why did Grandpa Wilhelm come up to the U.P.?"

"What causes most folks to move around? Work. My Dad came up to work in the iron mines. Here, let me show you this, so you can get the overall picture." He carefully lifted another stack of papers from the pine chest and sorted through them, withdrawing a crude sketch of a family tree.

"Now, your great-great-Grandfather Wilhelm Kohler immigrated to America in 1851..."

"Wait!" Rachel rummaged in one of the book bags until she found a small tape recorder and a pack of cassette tapes.

"What in tarnation is this paraphernalia?"

"I'd like to get some of this information on tape. I'm just as interested in my own roots as I am in my studies. Actually, Grandpa's leanings aside, it's been my interest in anthropology that has given me a desire to know about my own history. Look. Here I am in the U.P. studying other cultures and trying to preserve their history," (Kohler winced slightly when she mentioned other cultures) "and I don't even know much about my own. I guess I've realized that every person's experience is unique, and somehow it's a shame that anything is lost. You can teach me so much, Uncle John, and to me that's what anthropology is all about; learning people's personal lifestyles and cultural influences and gaining the wisdom from that experience. Do you know what I mean?"

"I don't suppose I ever thought about it in that exact way, but I guess I see what you're getting at." Kohler was developing a respect for his niece. Indians or no Indians, she seemed to care about things that were important.

"Will this tape recorder bother you?"

"Nah, I'll get used to it. Where do you want me to start?"

"At the beginning, where I so rudely interrupted you."

"Let's see. Four score and seven years ago…"

"Uncle John."

Kohler grinned. "All right." He held up the family tree so she could follow it. "Wilhelm Kohler, fella in the picture. My great-grandfather. He was born in 1829 in Hamburg, Germany and immigrated to the United States in 1851. I don't know anything about Germany or his parents and such. I do know that he came to America to find work as a logger. The country was growing fast by that time, and it was built of timber, first from Maine. But they'd got all the good stuff from there by mid-century, so the logging companies started packing up and moving west, through Pennsylvania and into Michigan. Where you live, my dear, used to be nothing by pineries, vast stretches of forest."

Kohler stopped and stared at the corner of the room, not seeing it, but seeing something else. "Bean fields," he said sadly. "Now it's just bean fields and cities. But when your great-great-grandpa arrived in Saginaw it was a timber town. I've read some stories about goings-on there that would make your blood run ice cold! Not too respectable, Saginaw. In those days whorehouses were a dime a dozen. 'Course, most lumberjacks weren't made for church meetings. They were a rowdy lot. I suppose your great-great-grandfather held his own, but he couldn't have been a real dyed-in-the-wool pine man, because when the pine ran out of the area he didn't keep moving north with the trees.

"Wilhelm stayed in Saginaw, got a job in a lumber mill as a sawyer. Sometime around there he met Beulah Campbell; they married in 1862. I don't know a whole lot about her, except that she was born in Saginaw in 1835 or thereabouts, and she came from Scotch-Irish extraction. I suspect that she may have something to do with Wilhelm not following the pine.

"Now, they had three children, Hilda in 1863, Thomas in 1867, and Emile in 1870. Emile was my grandfather. He grew up in Saginaw, owned a store there. But then, you should know a little about this stuff."

"A little bit. Mom has a couple of things Aunt Eva gave to her. There's a picture of the dry-goods store with great-grandfather out front, and a wedding picture of him and Great-grandma Elizabeth. I don't think Aunt Eva cared much about it, really."

"I have a picture of the store, too." He carefully lifted a few more papers from the box and drew out a yellowed print of an unsmiling man standing in front of a store with a sign that announced "Kohler's".

"Sure don't look very friendly, does he?" Kohler remarked.

"It might just be because he had to hold still for the picture. I look at a lot of old photos in my studies, and I can count on one hand the number of times I've seen someone smiling."

"I suppose so. Well, Grandpa Emile married Elizabeth Morrison in 1890. Now we're getting close to my territory. They had four kids; Robert in 1893, Michael in 1894, Eva in 1898, and my father William in 1904. Everybody stayed in Saginaw but my Dad. I got the idea that Dad didn't care for the soft life below, least that's how Merle made it sound. The U.P. was still a rough and ready boom area back in the 20's, even though the pine had been cut out of here around the turn of the century. They were still logging plenty of hardwoods up until the fifties, and there were the copper and iron mines. So he came on up here and got a job in the Glover Number Two mine over in the eastern end of the county. He met my mother in L'Anse a couple of years later. Let's see, he came up in

1924, and they married in 1928." Kohler took another stack of pictures from the left side of the chest and chose one.

"This was my folks' wedding picture." William had been a handsome young man, with dark hair and eyes, and a seriousness that showed through his smile. Kohler's mother Rachel, his niece's namesake, had finely-chiseled features with full lips, soft dark eyes, and dark brown hair.

"Your mother was born after four years of marriage, and then I came along in 1935. And that's about it."

Rachel sat bent over the pictures, studying the faces intently. "What about Grandma Rachel? It seems like her family is never mentioned. Didn't she come from L'Anse ?"

"To tell the truth, I don't know much about my mother's family. Merle told me that my mother was an only child and that my grandparents moved to Minnesota soon after my folks were married. I do know their names. Grandfather was Paul Delatour, and Grandmother was Helen Keleva. French and Finnish. This area is made up of a high percentage of Scandinavians, mostly Finns, who came to work the mines. The Frenchies were the first white men in the U.P. Lot's of priests, fur traders, and that type. Most of them left when the English took control, but you'll still find a pretty heavy influence, especially in names. But as far as I know, both of my grand-folks passed away when I was a boy. I never got to meet them."

"O.K. So then what?"

"I've told you as much as I know. I guess you know what happened to your mother."

"But what happened to you?"

"I grew up and lived happily ever after. You don't want to hear anything about me, for Pete's sake! I should think you'd have had your fill when you were little."

"No, I have not had my fill. I know I've heard a lot of your stories about Oregon and stuff, but I was too young then to really appreciate them. I think you've lived such a fascinating life. You were always kind of a mythological character for me, Uncle John, and you're different from the average man. In Saginaw most men work for someone else, or they have commonplace jobs and live mediocre lives. You've always been such an adventurer; it's like having an uncle who's a cowboy, or something. And you're an artist in your own right. You use your own hands to make a living, and people from all over want your furniture. You could probably start a factory, but instead you live simply and maintain the high quality of your work. I think that's great, and I really respect you for it."

"Good gracious, girl! You do have your head in the clouds. Don't you know that old saying about flattery?"

"I'm not saying any of this to flatter you. I mean it."

"Well, all the same, it don't seem like other people think like you do about me. I'm not a hero, or a cowboy. I'm just a cantankerous man that likes the company of a trout more that that of a human being. Generally, that is."

"I don't believe it. You're a big faker, along with everything else. Will you tell me about your life, or will you send me back to Saginaw a desperate and broken-hearted person, never to become a real anthropologist because of the shame of not even being able to record her own uncle's history, doomed to obscurity, forced to get a job washing dishes in a greasy spoon restaurant....."

"Kohler moaned loudly. "You're absolutely right, you shouldn't be an anthropologist. You should be in the pictures 'cause you're a born tragedy actress. You've beat me into a corner. I give up!"

"Oh good. Maybe we can go an hour tonight, then pick it up again tomorrow, that is, if you don't have anything else planned."

"Nothing planned until the weekend. At least once a year I run up to Keweenaw County for a kind of pilgrimage, and I was thinking of going pretty soon. I'll just be gone for two or three days; it'll give you a chance to get started on whatever it is you're going to do."

"What's in the Keweenaw that's so special? I mean, I know it's nice up there, Copper Harbor, and the agate beaches and all."

"Well, one of the few groves of virgin white pine left in the state is up there, and I like to go up and look at the big trees. They came close to logging them out a few years back, but folks got together and created a preserve and saved them. I'm glad, too. We need to save what's left of them."

Rachel was thoughtful for a few moments. "But you were a lumberjack. You used to cut trees down for a living, and you still use them to make your living, even if you don't cut them yourself."

"That's true, but I'm not using wood from the old trees like the virgin stands. And I'll tell you something else, you'll never see me waste a piece of lumber. Trees are useful, but they're also...." He paused "........beautiful. Now, I don't want to stop cutting them altogether, so we can just stare at them, or something. When I was out in Oregon, though,

I saw all those old growth forests being taken down. Trees and plants that had been surviving there for hundreds of years. At first it didn't bother me much. I was like the loggers have always been, thinking that there was so much timber we'd never cut it all. That's what they thought about Michigan, you know. They hit Saginaw, and they said, 'This will last forever.' But it didn't, and in a few years they moved up here and they saw those pineries around Seney and west, and they were sure that they'd never cut through it all. But by 1900 the white pine in this state was all but gone.

"And there I was, out there in Oregon, cutting out these big trees that we'd never see the likes of again, and as time went on, I realized that they wouldn't last either. It'd be another Michigan, or Maine, and all we'd have left is a couple of outdoor museums where somebody thought we'd better keep a few just to look at, to remind us of what we'd destroyed. And it started souring on me, cutting all those trees. That was one reason I worked on the Tillamook Burn Reforestation Project.

"Now, I feel like we got to manage those trees, all trees. It's o.k. to use lumber. And you're right, I've made my living off of trees. Sure couldn't eat off the trout flies I tie and sell! But we can harvest second growth forests carefully, so's we don't waste anything. Far as I'm concerned, we shouldn't be cutting anymore of that old stuff, the redwoods, or the old growth in the Northwest. I'm just against it."

"You sound like a regular environmentalist, Uncle John."

He snorted. "Well, I'm not. I just have some sense, and I appreciate the woods."

"Tell me why you were a lumberjack to start with. But do it right, for the sake of my tape. Start with your birth."

"I still feel a bit silly. You've heard all this before, but here goes.

"I was born February 12, 1935." Kohler paused and scowled at the tape machine. He felt like he was on trial. "Born a few miles west of Nestoria. My folks lived there because it was close to the iron mine where my dad worked. My mother died having me, because there was a midwife instead of it being a hospital birth. Merle told me it was the midwife's fault because she didn't know what she was doing, and that's why my mother didn't make it." Kohler thought it best not to bring up the fact that the midwife was an Indian. *No sense in interfering with Rachel's business*, he reminded himself. "My dad, your mother and me lived in the same house until I was four. That's when dad was killed in an explosion that went cockeyed at the Glover. Of course, the mine shut down two years after that, anyway. So I guess all this made me an orphan at an early age. But a lot of folks have had a much rougher life," he hastened to add. "I was lucky because my dad had good friends, like Merle Nyberg. Merle took me in, since he was my godfather, and he treated me like his own kid. Of course, Aunt Eva took your mom. I'm glad I got the opportunity to stay here in the north, rather than be raised down in Saginaw."

"And Merle lived in L'Anse?"

"That's right." Kohler told his niece about the big old Finnish farmhouse located west of town, where he had been raised. It was built by Merle's parents with money they saved from working the copper mines in the Keweenaw after they settled in the United States. After the mine work the Nybergs had gone into dairying. The one thing he always remembered about that house, he told Rachel, was the windows. They stretched from the ceiling to the floor, so that as a very young child he could easily sit on the floor in front of the window and watch the first snow of the winter as it fell against the backdrop of young pines at the side of the yard.

Merle had a sauna in back of the house. It had been built as the first building on the farm. The Saturday night sauna was nearly a religion for the Finnish population, and Merle had continued frequenting the building for the ritual. He and one or two of the other local Finnish men would enter the small building in which a fire had been roaring for many hours in the old style stove, which was constructed of igneous rock and metal. The temperature in the two rooms would soar to around one hundred and seventy-five degrees.

After disposing of their clothing in the outer room, they would enter the inner chamber and sit on the bench that ran along the wall. First they took dry saunas, with the sweat running in rivulets down their nude bodies until they turned bright red. Then, after the proper cooling period, dippers of water were thrown onto the stones of the stove to create great clouds of steam.

John was cajoled to come into the steam room and sit in the heat while the men talked in low tones of fishing and hunting, but after a few minutes the boy would invariably feel faint and ask to be excused. Merle would laugh and say something in Finnish to the other men, and they would laugh too, and chide the boy for not having enough Finnish blood to be able to appreciate such a luxury as the sauna, curer of all ills, and creator of general good health. Abashed, young Kohler would hurry to don his clothes and retreat to the house.

John spent much of his time after school and in the evenings at Merle's restaurant. "It was probably those hours at the Iron Pine that got me to thinking about being a lumberjack." Kohler told Rachel. "When I was still quite young, about eight or nine, two old timers used to sit in there for hours and talk about the good old days of lumber-jacking. They'd sit up against the back wall, just a few feet from the corner table where I would be trying to learn my arithmetic and spelling. Matt and Lew were their names. Both in their seventies, and they had seen the real McCoy in the U.P. They knew about Seney, they'd been there. They personally had seen Silver Jack, who was a legendary lumberjack hereabouts. He was your Paul Bunyan type; could chop any tree faster, harder, better, than any other lumberjack in the north woods, and could handle a two-man crosscut saw by himself. He could take down a five-foot thick white pine in a few minutes, could drink more whiskey faster than anybody, and pound the living daylights out of a whole raft of tough lumberjacks with one hand tied behind his back, or so the legend went. Silver Jack died right up there in L'Anse, and I used to dream about his ghost. Old Matt and Lew, they'd tell Silver Jack stories for hours, each one bigger than the last, and I'd sit there with my mouth hung open and my eyes as big as saucers, not getting too much homework done. Matt and Lew followed the trees from Michigan into Wisconsin, then to Oregon, in their day, but they came back to the U.P. to retire, so to speak. I was fed that steady diet of romantic, exciting information about logging for most of the war years.

"Seems funny to me, now, a big war going on with Japan and Germany, and all those two old geezers wanted to talk about was the good old days in the north woods. Then a couple of years after the war was over, the Paul Bunyan stories came out, and I just about inhaled those. I suppose that they helped seal my desire to be another Silver Jack, only maybe not quite that rough. Look here", he said, as he delved to the bottom of the pine chest. "I still have this. Merle bought it for me; I guess I must have driven him to distraction for this book." Kohler held up a tattered old cloth-bound edition of *Paul*

Bunyan of the Great Lakes by Stanley D. Newton. Its cover was so shiny from wear that one was just barely able to make out the figure of a giant lumberjack striding across the woodlands with the trunk of a mammoth pine thrown casually across his left shoulder, and an enormous double-bitted ax in his right hand.

Kohler grinned, feeling a bit sheepish. "I suppose you think your uncle's a little touched, huh?"

"No, on the contrary, I think it's great. I find people all the time who throw away things from their childhood that were important contributors to what made them the way they are today. And I usually find that they regret it. Paul Bunyan is a part of who you are, Uncle John. There's nothing to be ashamed of in that. Besides, that book is a collectors' item by now!" She carefully picked up the volume and opened the pages, examining a few of the illustrations before she put it down.

"What were your school days like, anyway? Were the schools large or small?"

Kohler thought a while. "There isn't anything of much importance, you know. Just school, same as any kid's school. Not big, not one room, either. I went to L'Anse Township when I was in elementary, then L'Anse High School.

"When I was in fourth grade I think we had the first ethnic festival in these parts, thanks to Miss Goodreau. It was just for our class, but she got us all enthused about it. We all tried to find costumes to suit our bloodlines, and for a lot of the kids it was easy. A good fifty-percent of the class was Finnish, and those people are a close-knit bunch that carry on all their customs into the umpteenth generation. Just like Merle, born here, but still used to that sauna. It's how come you'll hear plenty of young kids up here sound like they were born in Finland or Sweden and imported to the U.S.A. Yah, you maht say that aboot them, now," Kohler mimicked in a Finnish accent. "The French Canadians were pretty heavily represented, too, and the Swedes, like I said, and a sprinkling of Irish, Welsh, Germans, Poles, and so forth.

"I wanted to come as a mutt, 'cause I got a little of this and a smidgen of that, but Miss Goodreau folded her pretty arms and said, 'Now John, we don't have a mutt classification. You must choose a particular group. Kohler is a German name. Perhaps you could accept that as your heritage.' I wondered how my godfather, a full-blooded Finnish bachelor, was going to fix me up with a German costume. I was mighty sure that neither of us knew what one looked like! And he didn't strike me as being the sewing sort.

"Well, I ended up not taking part in the festival anyway, as punishment for fighting. I beat the stuffing out of Hans Sunukjian. Miss Goodreau asked if anyone in the class had Indian blood in them, which was highly unlikely, since in those days most of the Indian kids went to their own schools. But Hans piped up and said, 'I think John Kohler could be an Indian. He has black hair and brown eyes.'" Kohler stopped for a moment, then continued in a low tone. "I beat him until he couldn't stand up, and it took Miss Goodreau and four of the big boys to pull me off that little sap."

He heard Rachel catch her breath at the suddenly malicious temper of his voice, and the obvious satisfaction he still experienced at remembering the beating of Hans Sunukjian. Kohler felt as though the room had grown more shadowed, and he mechanically reached over to switch on the lamp by the couch. It was already on, and he stared at it dumbly for a few seconds.

"I gotta tie some Blue Duns for Harry Presslein and Rich Behrendsen," he said, rising abruptly.

"Can we talk again tomorrow night?"

"Fine." Kohler stalked off toward the kitchen. He also reached into his pocket for the antacid tablets.

The following morning he awoke at the first sleepy sound of a warbler outside his window. He got out of bed, dressed quietly in the darkness, then slipped out the front door into the chilly air. Kohler stood for some time, feeling a certain heaviness inside. Dawn crept into the horizon, turning it a deep turquoise. Plum-colored tatters of clouds fled before a boisterous breeze, and raced past spires of spruce trees silhouetted in black against the sky. He watched the morning's entrance silently, and something Merle used to say edged its way into his mind. "Whenever you feel out of sorts inside, the best remedy is work."

Kohler turned and went into the house, walking through the living room, to the kitchen. He flipped on the light and got the coffee out of the cupboard, measured it carefully into a filter, poured in the water and turned the machine to the ON position. While the coffee was dripping, he went through the breezeway into his workshop and hit the switch that turned on the long florescent lights along the ceiling. Work was what was needed. He had been lacking concentration lately, and was behind on several projects. He must have this order ready by the end of the week so it could be shipped down to Green Bay. He was glad that he was hiring someone to take it down for him. He didn't want to drive to the city right now, not when he was planning his trip to the Keweenaw for this weekend.

The coffee was ready, and he went back into the kitchen and poured himself a cup of the strong black brew, opened the cupboard where he kept the cereal, and then thought better of it. No, the coffee was good enough right now. He needed to get to work.

In the shop he began hand-sawing a piece of lumber so that the noise of power tools wouldn't awaken Rachel. Last evening's incident popped into his mind, and he winced. Why had he been so short with the girl? Surely she had recognized the hatred that he harbored in his heart for the Indians. *I must keep my feelings to myself*, he thought. *I mustn't interfere with her, or discourage her in any way*. Her image bore itself before him, sitting with her tape recorder, holding a picture from the pine chest. She was so attentive, so interested, he thought affectionately. It had been a very long time since anyone had shown Kohler that much attention, and a longer time since he had felt much sincere interest in another human being. Mostly he didn't think about such things. He took care of his business, fished, lived his own life. Sometimes he trout fished with one or two of the local men, but generally he was alone. *And I prefer it that way*, he thought. *Keeps a person out of trouble and entanglements*. Time had just brought it all about like that, and it was fine. But Rachel, she was a young girl, and a good girl. A serious girl, with a future, and he must be careful not to discourage her. And it was kind of nice to have her around.

He was startled when the door to the workshop opened.

"Good morning, Uncle John." Rachel was dressed and looked fresh and rested, but Kohler detected a slight caution in her greeting to him.

"You're up a lot earlier than I expected." He glanced at the window and saw that the sun was gilding the leaves of the maple in his yard a rich yellow.

"I hate to sleep in. I just wanted to know if you'd like me to fix you some breakfast?"

"No thanks, my dear. I'm going to work on this stuff until I get really hungry, and then I'll take a break. Do you have plans today?"

"I thought I'd just be a little lazy and go and look at waterfalls. I have a guidebook I picked up in L'Anse that lists all of them for Baraga County."

"You won't have to go too far. Ogemaw Falls is just down the road here a piece."

"And Canyon Falls, and Falls River, none of them are very far. I should probably start my research, but I still want to take some time off so I can feel like I had a real vacation."

"Well, have a good time. Pack yourself something to eat. We've got sandwich meat and junk food, or fruit, if you'd rather have that." He paused. "I'm really looking forward to our talk tonight. I'm going to tell you about Oregon, as if you hadn't already heard it a dozen times."

Rachel's face brightened, he thought. "Oh good. I never get tired of hearing about it, and besides, now I'm taping it for the sake of posterity."

When the girl left Kohler returned to his work with renewed enthusiasm, and soon found himself whistling a country tune he had heard on the radio. The hunger pangs began later in the morning, but he ignored them, and was surprised when he finally looked up at the clock on the south wall of the workshop and found that it was after noon. He had nearly caught up on the work that had refused to be done in the past week or so. During a short break in the kitchen he fixed himself a sandwich and sat for a moment at the table to eat. He didn't feel tired, though he had labored hard all morning. He smiled to himself. Not bad production, not bad at all. Presently he rose from his seat, grabbed a bottle of cola from the refrigerator, and went back to the shop, where he pursued his task with relish into the late afternoon. By 5:00 he was hungry again, and lay down his tools with considerable satisfaction. Several items were ready for shipment and he felt that the craftsmanship was excellent. But evening would soon be here, and Rachel would be coming in. He needed to think of something for supper.

Walking through the breezeway, he became aware of the odor of cooking food coming from the kitchen, and he found Rachel in the midst of frying chicken.

"Good night!" I didn't hear you come back," he said.

"I got here about 3:00. I knew you were working, and I didn't see the need to disturb you."

Kohler went to wash up, after Rachel insisted that she needed no help with the meal. He sat reading the L'Anse Chronicle until she called him to come to the table. Kohler had learned to cook from years of living alone, but he rarely fixed himself such a meal as was now set before him. The girl had prepared mashed potatoes and gravy, fried chicken, a salad, and biscuits. Something that smelled delicious was still in the oven.

"What's that baking?"

"Apple cobbler. You like it, don't you?"

"Like it? Yes, but we didn't have any apples around here, nor most of the other stuff you need for it."

"I stopped at the grocery store in town. Remember, I said that I was going to pull my fair share of the load, and it's the least I can do in repayment for being able to stay here." Rachel removed the cobbler from the oven and sat down at the table, which was set with a cloth and napkins, things that Kohler never used.

"Well, eat up," she said.

Kohler stabbed at this, and spooned out that, and ladled something else, ravenous after his day of hard work. But suddenly he stopped and stared at the pool of light brown chicken gravy that sat in the midst of his mashed potatoes, and he felt a strange constriction in his throat. It wasn't caused by the anger that often welled up in him, but by something else, by feelings that had been ignored or buried for so long they had nearly ceased to exist for him. He found himself trying to restrain the tears that were stinging his eyes. The tears brought disgust, confusion, frustration, all in a row, until he was a whirl of emotions and wondering why on earth he was becoming such a sissy and so sentimental. He told himself to stop this foolishness, and so he stopped. The constriction eased and he regained control, sheepishly peering up from his potatoes to see if his niece had detected his inward struggle. Thankfully she was busy with her salad, and seemed not to have noticed anything.

"Well", he said a bit gruffly, "this is real nice. Haven't had such a nice meal in ages, since I was down in Saginaw last, I guess. Looks like some young tough is gonna have it made marrying you."

"Oh, thank you. But I probably won't be getting married for a long time. I intend to go on and get my Master's Degree, or even my Doctorate, and I don't think I'll have much time for marriage for a few years."

"Humph," he grunted. "Women sure are different than when I was your age. All of them wanted to get married, then, and a man had to watch his foot or find it caught in some woman's snare."

Rachel laughed. "Times have changed. I want to eventually get married, really, but I want to make sure that I have the opportunity to do the other things in my life that are important to me, too."

The meal continued amid small talk of Rachel's day and Kohler's work on pending orders, and afterwards Rachel did the dishes and her uncle relaxed in the living room.

Presently his niece entered and took the tape recorder from a table in the corner of the room. "Well," she said, "are you ready to run your mouth some more?"

Kohler grinned. "Sure. Nothing I'd rather do than beat my gums. Get comfortable, now!"

When Rachel had taken her place on the couch, with Kohler settled opposite her in his easy chair, he motioned that she could switch on the tape recorder.

He began to tell her about high school, recounting dances and ice skating parties on the frozen bay in deep winter and about the small woodworking class with Mr. Bowman. It was there that he had discovered his propensity for working with wood, and had learned the use of the tools. Bowman had urged him toward continuing his work after high school. "Boy," he said, "you're more than a simple craftsman, you're an artist. You could take what you know right now and go out there and make yourself a nice living in this trade." Kohler had thought seriously about it, but there was the strong pull implanted in him as a young boy to go west, to be a lumberjack. After graduation those old dreams won out. He worked at the Iron Pine that summer for his godfather to earn sufficient traveling funds, and in the fall set out for Oregon and the great trees.

He arrived in the forests west of the Cascade Mountains and marveled at the Douglas Fir that grew in such numbers, and so close together, that the branches became entangled and made the forests nearly impregnable. The forest floor was soggy, since no sunlight could reach through the mass of growth above. Kohler preferred the areas that had more spruce and cedar, and where the floor of the woods was covered with salmonberry, fern and huckleberry.

On the eastern side of the Cascades the climate and timberland was very different. This was the country of the lodgepole and ponderosa pine, where the forests resembled spacious cathedrals, and the trees rose like pillars into the sky. Clearings were numerous, and the sunlight came driving through the branches like a lance, striking the soft, thick carpet of needles. In the summer heat these woods were pungent with the fragrance of the trees, making Kohler nearly drunk with the perfume.

The lumber camps were a disappointment to him, though, and the men, also. Gone were the days of the rip-snorting, plug-chewing, mean-mouthed lumberjack. The loggers of the new era were a different breed. They had families, smoked cigarettes, and played such citified games as golf and tennis. Most did not live in the camps, but drove to the work area from town. Few could handle an ax, and they hardly recognized a peavey. The camps that were open out in the woods didn't resemble those that Matt and Lew had known and talked about, the low-ceilinged, crowded, smoky, dark bunkhouses that smelled more like barns than human habitations. Now they were clean and neat, sleeping only a half dozen men or so. They had windows, fluorescent lights, and cots with mattresses, sheets and warm blankets. The cookhouses were large and clean, with nice dining rooms, and there were recreation areas for the men. No, the days of Paul Bunyan and Silver Jack were over, and lumber-jacking lost its enchantment for Kohler. He was forced to grow away from his childhood fantasy world.

"So my bubble was busted," he told Rachel. "But I stayed on, moving around for a couple of years. Then I ran into some people who were working on the Tillamook Burn Reforestation Project and I signed on for that. There was a lot of lore about how the Tillamook got set afire. I remember Matt and Lew talking about that, as they were in Oregon or those parts at the time it happened. They'd argue for hours about who was responsible for that blaze. Lost miles of rich timberland in that forest fire. I guess it was about the worst ever. Old Matt, he insisted that it was a fella name of Lyda, a logger working in the area at the time. The woods had gotten too dry during the day to keep working, and sparks from the machinery would catch the pine on fire like nobody's business. Matt said that Lyda was so greedy for the money he could make that he kept his crew working past the safe stage, and the worst happened. Traditionally, he's the one that took blame for the fire. But Lew, he'd come back and say that he'd talked to one of Lyda's boys, and he said they'd found a flashlight lens right near where the fire started. So I don't really know who started the thing. But somebody decided in the late 1940's to replant the area, and that's how I got involved.

"I remember the view like it was yesterday, and a darn sad one for someone who loves the forest. If you can try to picture it, you're standing on a hillside, and looking out over an area that stretches for miles. In the background are big, rounded hills, with a saddleback right in the middle. And there ain't nothin' on these hills but gaunt, dark snags rising up into the air. Just those skeletons of pine, like fingers pointing, charcoal black, and some lying on the ground, quiet and still. The only living things are patches of long, whipish-looking grass and some brush about eight or ten feet tall. That's how it looked. And we planted little trees for all we were worth, because that scene, a burned-up, dead forest, makes a man want to plant as many trees as he can, and get it looking like it used to again. Well, I did my share of the work, acres of it. Left a long time before it was finished, though. It took until 1973 to finish replanting that area.

"I got out in '60. I guess I was properly disillusioned with being a lumberjack, wanted to settle down some. Merle had once told me to look to my roots, that they were deep in Michigan soil, and to turn back to them in trouble or confusion. I just wanted to come home, so I did. Got a job at Kellen's – pretty mild work after the woods of Oregon – but I had this idea to follow old Bowman's advice, and I needed money for tools and such. And I needed to find a place of my own. It took me a while to get enough together to finish up buying the stuff I needed and start looking for a house that I could work out of.

"I heard about a house here in Wolf Lodge and it kind of appealed to me. Out here in the middle of the woods, an old logging ghost town, near a good trout stream. And this place. When I first saw it, I knew why it was so cheap. It was a mess! But it had a good basic structure, something I could work with, and it would be a challenge, nearly like building my own place. So I was able to pay quite a bit of the full price, and it didn't take me long to meet the rest of the debt. My furniture was starting to sell real good, and soon I had folks locally asking me to tie flies for them, and I even got to do a small business that way with Fournier's Tackle Shop. So," he concluded, "here I am. Not rich, but I do all right. I fish as often as I want and I'm my own boss. Guess that's about it."

Rachel was looking around the room, examining the walls of pine paneling, which glowed in the light of the lamp.

"You're really something, Uncle John. To see this place now, it's hard to believe it was ever run-down. But," she asked, "wasn't there ever anyone in your life? I mean, here you are, out here in the woods all alone. You've carved out a life for yourself, rebuilt this house, but you seem, so alone. Just an island unto yourself."

Kohler was silent for a moment. "Well, there was someone once, but it was a long time ago. I met her after I came back from Oregon, and we went around together for a while. Nothing ever came of it."

"What happened?"

"Oh, I guess we just had a difference of opinion on certain things. That's all."

"And there has never been anyone else, ever?"

Kohler got up. "Nope. Don't need anyone, anyway. I do fine here by myself. Now, I got some things to finish up before I take that trip up to the Keweenaw." He abruptly turned and went toward his shop.

CHAPTER FOUR – THE KEWEENAW PENINSULA

Kohler arranged for the shipment of the furniture to the city, and at the end of the week was ready for the pilgrimage to the tip of the Keweenaw Peninsula. He left early Saturday morning, after telling Rachel goodbye and giving her instructions on what to do in an emergency.

Driving north on 41, he followed Keweenaw Bay on his right for nearly thirty miles. Just past the Klingville turnoff the highway cut slightly inland before reaching Portage Lake and the official beginning of Copper Country. Then it was Houghton, Hancock, and the innumerable small villages that were once copper mining towns; Boston, Laurium, Kearsage and Ahmeek. Calumet had been the great granddaddy of them all, with one hundred thousand people at its peak years, but now the population was reduced to a mere three thousand. Mine shafts in varying stages of disrepair rose along the side of the road, and some were hidden back among the cliffs that rose on his right: The Quincy, the Delaware, the Phoenix.

Soon Kohler began to travel through thick hardwood forest, with the maple trees over-arching the road and creating a living green tunnel. The road to Lac La Belle passed on his right, and presently there was the sign for Mandan. He pulled in and spent time walking around the now deserted mining town. Kohler felt relaxed and somewhat removed from reality here in the Keweenaw. If a person believed in ghosts, surely this would be a good place for them. The beauty of the area was superimposed over the history and, in his mind, produced a sort of time warp.

He breathed deeply and walked back to his truck. It was a short drive to Copper

Harbor, and he was eager to see open water, without the confines of the bay. He headed north again, passed Lake Medora, with its haunting wilderness quality, and drove the curving road through the thick hardwood forest. The Keweenaw Mountain Lodge appeared on his right and suddenly, at the bottom of a hill, he entered Copper Harbor, and behind the town was Lake Superior, shining like a vast sheet of molten silver. Kohler proceeded through the village, which had survived the demise of the mines by becoming a tourist center. Where once there stood rows of miner's houses and saloons, there were now motels, museums, and craft and mineral shops.

His destination still lay beyond the village, two miles east, at the end of the highway. He arrived at Fort Wilkins State Park and asked for his favorite campsite, number fifty-six. The park was ideally located, he thought. On one side was Lake Fanny Hooe, long and narrow, and sparkling like a liquid sapphire in the midst of the north woods. Behind Fanny Hooe, to the south, and beyond Fort Wilkins to the east, lay the tip of the Keweenaw and wilderness. Three miles into the woods you could find the Estivant Pines. On the opposite side of the camping area, through a small stretch of woods and across the tail end of the highway, was Lake Superior.

Kohler set up his green, four-man nylon tent and watched out of the corner of his eye as several hungry chipmunks converged from holes hidden among the roots of the maples and white pines that surrounded his site. They examined his activities with curiosity, sitting on their haunches in silence.

"You fellas think you're going to wrangle something to eat? I'm not one of your soft city campers, you know."

As if in response to his words, one of the small beasts began to go about gathering the seeds that had dropped from the maple trees.

Kohler fixed himself some lunch and washed the dishes in a pan of water that he heated over the camp stove. After the chores were completed he settled down to simply enjoy the peace.

But as he gazed across the campgrounds at Lake Fanny Hooe, he felt his insides begin to expand; like everything inside was trying to move out and enlarge, and take up the space between the tall pines and maples, and continue across the waters of the small lake, then swell in the other direction and encompass the space over the great lake, until all the northern Michigan wilderness became part of him, and he of it. He breathed deeply, again, again, and felt himself continuing to expand in the sharp air. He took himself, expanded as he was, and crammed himself into the cab of his pickup, opened the windows to relieve the crampedness and drove out of the campground back toward Copper Harbor. He passed through the village, went by the Route 41` turnoff, and continued on as he began to climb steeply, rounding a curve, still climbing, climbing around curves for a quarter mile, until the road leveled off at a turnout and Kohler could see that he was already high above Copper Harbor. The coastline of Lake Superior was running away to the west of the town, to the point where the Copper Harbor Lighthouse flashed a weak daytime beam out into the blue-green expanse of the lake. And Kohler was still expanding, so he kept driving, now along a ridge that rose and fell, but still climbed toward the top of Brockway Mountain.

He could look back a little over his left shoulder and see the town, set among the pine forests, and the broad strip of woods, and Lake Fanny Hooe stretched out and running long between the small hills and the big lake. His pickup followed the ridge farther along until the sides of the mountain road to his left began to drop away in rust red cliffs, and the forests below became a great expanse of dark green spires of spruce and white pine projecting up sharply among the lighter hardwoods. He rounded another set of curves and Lake Fanny Hooe disappeared, and there was only the forest rolling away for miles over the hills of the Keweenaw, and a valley below with a cedar swamp in the very bottom, lying a quiet green and blue with snags of dead cedar trees along its rim. Kohler was still expanding, and he hurried along the mountain road, following the ridge for another mile until suddenly the horizon reappeared and Lake Superior emerged behind him far below, stretched like the top of a blue drum and fastened onto the horizon where the sky met it with a fainter blue. After another dip in the road, and another short climb, he saw the top of Brockway Mountain, with its small gift shop perched there. In a moment he was at the pinnacle of the peninsula, and he hurried out of the truck and felt himself released into the space on the mountaintop, and the crampedness disappeared.

The summit was a flat meadow that ended in a bluff overlooking the country toward the west, where the coast of Lake Superior jagged its way in the direction of Eagle Harbor. The gift shop and parking lot took up a little area, but Kohler walked away from these and into the grass near the edge of the cliff. He could turn from this vantage point and see the broad panorama of the lake on his right, lying a deep blue with lighter currents threading through it, in front of him the western coastline and Eagle Harbor, then high bluffs that hid old copper diggings miles back in the woods. To his left the forest lay in multi-shades of green, dotted with lakes and running away forever across the peninsula, and just below, over the cliff, the valley of forest and cedar swamps.

He settled down in the green and golden grasses of the meadow, and fed on the view and the space. The wind played through the wild flowers, which were scattered in a crazy quilt of color across the top of the bluff. Orange hawkweed, ox-eye daisy, buttercups, scarlet wood lilies, delicate pink wild rose, and violet-blue American vetch nodded all about him.

Kohler sat very still, very straight, with his legs crossed and his hands loose in his lap. He listened. He could hear the laboring of a semi-truck far below as it climbed a hill on 41, shifting its gears in the ascent. He blocked out the sound. The wind. It lifted the collar of his blue work shirt just briefly, and stirred the bright flowers of the northern meadow, bending them, releasing them. The wind had a faint, whispering voice, almost a whistle as it passed through the grass. Birds. A warbler lustily sang its complicated canzonet from below the edge of the cliff. Another piped a mediocre strain on his left. Kohler imagined he could hear the wind through the forests below, rustling in the maple and oak leaves, sighing through the needles of pine and spruce. The waves lapped steadily against the rocky shore, many hundreds of feet beneath the crest of the bluff on his right and he could not discern if his physical ear detected their rhythm, or if it was in his mind.

As though in a trance he sat in the meadow as the sun wended its way toward the lake. Once he withdrew a small packet of raisins from his left breast pocket and ate some, mechanically. Finally, when the afternoon shadows began to deepen in the forest below, and the mountain cast a darkness into the valley on his left, he rose to go. He was not thinking, only absorbing the sensations available to him for the past few hours. His body and mind were full of bright sunshine, nodding flowers, the shifting patterns of light and shadow across the forest and hills, and the subtle blending of scents produced by the heat upon the blossoms and grass and trees. And there was the perception of the wind through his being, as though it had swept through his insides the entire while, whirling about his organs, cleansing the putrid places, purifying the stagnant pools in his mind and heart, scouring each dark area, and leaving the windows open with the brightness glaring in and the curtains blowing in the fresh zephyr.

He felt less a man for the moment, but rather wholly absorbed in the wind, the earth and the sun, and yet, he was a man. Separate because he could feel the elements, he mused later. He could still distinguish the boundary between himself and the elements. And so it had begun. The mysterious experience of the Keweenaw, that drew him always to this point of peninsula, year after year, as though he were performing some ancient rite, his blood insistent, wooing, a magnetism irresistible. The first summer was 1961; he had been back in Michigan for one year. Then it became an annual migration.

Kohler came to himself entirely as he slammed the door on his truck and turned the ignition. He drove down the mountain slowly, savoring the last of the high places and craggy cliffs, then, too soon, was back in Copper Harbor. At the general store he purchased a steak and some beans and bread, and fixed them when he arrived at his campsite. He ate solemnly, in pensive silence.

The evening was still young when he finished. The northwestern exposure and close proximity to the lake held the light in the sky until nearly 10:30, so he cleaned his site and walked leisurely across the campground. Outside the restroom-laundry area he purchased a Milwaukee paper from the metal box and strolled on toward the edge of the campground, across a deserted picnic area, and into the confines of old Fort Wilkins. Built in the mid 1800's to guard the copper miners against possible Indian attacks, it was abandoned some time later and fell into disrepair. But some historically-minded citizens insisted it be preserved for the sake of posterity, and the state had taken it over and renovated it. Now it stood in the slanting golden light of the evening, nearly empty of humanity, silent, ghost-like. Surrounded by a wooden stockade, the fort was set up in a rectangle. Long barracks, painted a clean, bright white with kelly green trim, lined one side, and across the yard was a long mess hall, identical in construction. At one end of the area stood the officers' quarters, the building not as long, but of the same appearance as the others. In the back corner stood the squat, heavily built fortress of the armory. The opposite end of the compound opened onto the shores of Lake Fanny Hooe.

A young couple leisurely walked a Labrador Retriever around the covered sidewalks of the buildings. They held hands as they strolled, and Kohler watched them nonchalantly. He mused that they looked as though they belonged in an advertisement, not in the deserted old fort.

He shrugged his shoulders, turned his back on the compound, and walked toward the shores of Lake Fanny Hooe. Near the edge of the water was the fort's flagpole, a tall thin spar of pine, placed upon a hexagonal platform that served as the base. Around the bottom of the platform was a bench with one side facing the water. Kohler sat down beneath the flag, which was snapping smartly in the breeze, and opened the newspaper. He spent the next hour reading about accidents, killings, kidnappings and robberies, sales and awards, in a world far removed from the Keweenaw. Curious. Milwaukee could have been Mars; it would have made no difference. Sometimes he would glance up and stare out across the blue waters of the lake and watch the golden evening light inflame the white pines that lined the opposite shore. The rest of the world was far removed from this northern wilderness.

When the wind finally began to raise goose flesh beneath the sleeves of his shirt, he folded the newspaper and walked back to his campsite. Though it was still light, he crawled into his sleeping bag and fell immediately to slumber.

Kohler awakened sometime in the night. It was pitch black. He could hear the moaning of the foghorn out at the Copper Harbor Light, about a half-mile away, and could distinguish the lapping of the waves as they gently rolled against the stony beach of Lake Superior. Must be really foggy for sound to be carrying so well, he thought; then he fell back into a deep sleep.

The following morning he was awakened just after dawn by the vociferous scolding of a chipmunk which sat a few feet from his tent. Kohler slid from his bed and went about his camp dispensing of morning chores and breakfast, then showered. There was still a heavy, patchy fog. The pale full moon, not yet setting, was framed between the branches of the tall pines above the campsite. He decided that this day would be perfect for the bush roads.

After his shower he set out in the pickup along the paved highway in the opposite direction from Copper Harbor. Presently the pavement came to an abrupt end, and a rough lane trailed off into the forest before him. He put the truck into low gear and drove on carefully. The bush road followed the contours of the land, which was part of the granite Canadian Shield. The farther he proceeded, the rougher was the road, and the foggier the weather became. No longer in dense patches, it was a solid blanket over the woods. He drove slower, trying to avoid the outcroppings of magma that lay in ambush for his vehicle. Then, through the fog ahead, he could see something in the road. It wasn't a rock, or a pothole. He slowed to a halting crawl and strained to see through the mist. *It can't be*! He thought to himself, and stopped the truck. In his path stood a bald eagle, the fog swirling about it and giving it the unearthly appearance of a bird of omen, some sort of esoteric messenger.

Kohler cut the engine on the Ford, carefully got out and stood by the truck. The raptor followed his cautious movements with a slow, but fearless, turn of its snowy head. It remained otherwise motionless in the middle of the road. The bird's eyes were clear and animated, and it stared at Kohler fixedly. He felt himself holding his breath, immobilized by the steady gaze of the eagle. Minutes passed, how long? Finally, as if on some silent cue, the bird lifted itself gracefully on its mighty wings and drifted off into the fog, south, toward Bear Bluff. Kohler heard its high-pitched, wild cry a few moments later.

Shaken by the strange encounter with the creature, he slowly got back into the pickup and sat several minutes in silence. The only sound now was the condensing fog dripping in staccato rhythm from the leaves of the trees.

He was still sitting when the fog lifted, like a curtain raised on a stage production. In response, the warblers began a lusty singing in the tops of the aspen and paper birch. Kohler started the engine and drove on.

After about a mile he turned to the left and proceeded down a bush road that was in worse disrepair than the one he left. It rolled up and down in a crazy roller coaster pattern, with deep, water-filled holes at the bottom grades. The outcroppings of granite were even larger and more malicious in their pointed, volcanic fury, but the land became more pristine the farther that Kohler proceeded, with only the sorry path to show that man ever ventured this way. The forest all about him was entirely the green-yellow of aspen and white of paper birch that stood in innumerable small pillars. Eventually he could proceed no further along this path, and stopped the truck. He walked through the forest in the general direction of Lake Superior and was careful to look around him and admire the land. Blueberry heaths abounded, with clearly marked trails in their midst that were made by bears. Tucked demurely away beneath sheltering trees grew tiny orchids; the delicate calypso, and the pale yellow Hooker's orchid. The treetops rang with the songs of vireos and warblers.

Presently the woods opened onto the shore of the great lake and a deserted pebble beach, which curved around like a horseshoe to create a quiet harbor. At the far end the area was protected by enormous outcroppings of volcanic rock which heaved up thirty or forty feet above the water level and created a barrier that looked like giant sawteeth. The air was now entirely clear, with no sign of the fog, and the lake water glowed a deep blue. For some time Kohler meandered along the beach, examining the fragile purple blossoms of the butterworts where they grew from a seeping mass of rock, and bending now and then to inspect a stone for agate qualities. Eventually he gained the giant sawteeth at the opposite end of the harbor and climbed up the side of one by using the natural toeholds in the vertical side of the rock.

On top, he settled down to enjoy the scenery. He could view the entire harbor from his vantage point, the great expanse of the lake, and the coast running back to the west. He stayed on the rock, just watching the water, the rest of the morning and into the early afternoon. The only sign of human life was an occasional lake freighter plying its way past the harbor, far out in the water. He could hear the deep bass rhythm of their engines as they traveled toward Duluth. One ran very close to the shore, within a quarter mile of his rock, riding very high in the water, obviously empty. *Sightseeing,* Kohler thought. The captain spotted Kohler on the rock and blew three short blasts on his horn in greeting. Kohler took a red bandana from around his neck and waved back, and the boat blew another short blast to acknowledge his signal. He felt his throat tighten with the same reaction that he had experienced that night at the dinner table with Rachel, and he felt himself coloring in embarrassment at the thought that this greeting from the unknown captain of a lake freighter could elicit such an emotion. *I must be getting old and senile,* he thought, and rose from his resting-place on the top of the rock.

He walked west along the ridge of magma, away from the harbor, until he came to a friction break about four feet wide, which he bridged carefully. From there he turned inland and climbed down the side of the rock to a sheltered area behind it, which ran like a narrow corridor between the sawteeth and the forest. As he passed through the brush he came upon a grove of Balm of Gilead. He broke a leaf off and took a deep breath of the aromatic plant, then crumbled the rest onto his collar and into his left breast pocket. He continued on toward the harbor, stopping again to pick some wild strawberries, which grew in profusion in the sand.

When he reached the pebble-strewn beach the sun was very hot. Kohler felt euphoric from the pungent odor of the Balm of Gilead, the gentle lake breeze and the seclusion and tranquility of the place. He walked to the edge of the water, hunched over and stared in. The bottom was perfectly visible for many yards out, and he could see a bone white vein of calcite running through the rock-ribbed lake bottom, on and on, toward Canada. It shimmered and glittered like a rod of jewels beneath the calm surface.

He bent closer and became absorbed in the shadows and patterns in the depth; how strange they were, how unique! Then he reverently dipped his cupped hands into the icy draught, raised them to his mouth and drank. The cold bit his lips and numbed his tongue, and he could feel the course of the water as it passed into his innermost being, cooling him. He drank again, and once more, then sat back at the edge of the shining seawater satisfied and suddenly sleepy. Settling back against the pebbles, he slept.

Kohler was awakened by the loud, dull throbbing of another freighter running close to the coast. The wind had changed direction and increased, and now blew straight from the lake. He found himself chilled and hungry. The afternoon was gone and the sun cast long shadows from the saw-toothed rocks that spurred him to pick up the trail leading from the beach and hurry to his pickup. He jolted along the bush roads back to Copper Harbor, ate supper in the Tamarack Inn then spent the rest of the time until darkness in the deserted fort beneath the flag pole.

That night the wind moaned through the pines above his tent and brought rain, the drops falling with a subdued staccato rhythm on the nylon rain fly. It was 5:00 a.m. before the shower ceased, and by the time Kohler unzipped the tent door at 6:15 the ground had absorbed the water. The trees still dripped, and the bracken fern glistened with moisture, but the clouds were moving away and the sun was shining brightly in the east.

Kohler was glad that the storm had passed. For this was to be his last day in the Keweenaw, and the pinnacle of his trip, in a sense, what he really came for. Today he would go to the Estivant Pines Preserve to see the big trees.

After a breakfast of eggs, sausage, and rolls, he drove the two miles to town and parked the pickup near the Isle Royale National Park visitor center, on the road that led

into the hills toward Manganese Falls. Outfitted with a small daypack he began walking

south on the blacktop, past the Fanny Hooe Resort, then past the town dump, where the

tourists parked around the stinking perimeters in the evening to watch the bears. *It looked*

like a drive-in movie, he mused, the vehicles of all varieties and sizes, from Saabs to

motor homes, lined up facing the garbage. How anyone could bring popcorn and soft

drinks into that stench and eat without vomiting was more than he could imagine. But

they did. He had gone one evening to watch the tourists, some years before.

The road rose gently and led past the sound of water falling into a deep gorge. A

small sign identified Manganese Falls on his left. Presently, after about another mile, he

turned onto a dirt road leading into the forest. It ran wide for about a half mile, then

began to narrow. A sign pointed the way to the old Clark mine, and a mile further he

passed a cedar swamp full of snags, their images reflecting down into the still water as in

a mirror. There he turned to the right on a rutted logging road edged on either side by

thick hardwood forest. In another twenty minutes Kohler arrived at the preserve

boundary, which was announced by amateurish signs made by the local residents who

had saved this section from the chain saws. One such signboard warned NO MOTOR

VEHICLES PAST THIS POINT, but he saw ATV tracks leading into the preserve, as if

in purposeful defiance of the command.

The edge of the area was taken up by virgin cedar, a tangle of rough trunks,

windfall, and snags that even the animals would have found difficult to navigate. The trail

led up a rise to the beginnings of the white pine, which was initially mixed with brushy

hardwoods. The deeper Kohler progressed, however, the more the pine increased and began to dominate. The trees continually increased in girth and height until finally all around him Kohler found nothing but white pine, trees with diameters of three to five feet and rising one hundred and fifty feet into the air. He slowed his pace to a leisurely stroll, approached one of the giants and looked up toward the crown. The trunk stretched up and up, without a knot, until the branches began about seventy-five feet from the ground. He could not see the top of the tree, only the mass of needled branches tangled together with three other giants that stretched upward nearby. They met above him and formed a peaked roof reminiscent of a cathedral ceiling of green and brown.

He pushed on deeper into the center of the shrine, walking quietly, reverently, on the soft trail, then finally pressing into the forest off the path to his right. He halted beneath a tree with a girth of nearly ten feet and dropped his small daypack from his back. The spot he had chosen was located a few feet from a deep ravine that ran parallel to the trail. In addition to the huge tree, which he now stood beneath, there were five other of the ancient pines in close proximity, spaced about twelve to fifteen feet apart. Each magnificent trunk rose shot-straight into the keen blue sky, its crown creating a feathery canopy against the bright sunlight. At the base of these king trees were a few juvenile white pine, and a profuse display of bracken fern that stood thigh high. Kohler withdrew a buck knife from its black sheath on his belt and began to cut some of the largest of these ferns and stack them beneath his tree. He was careful not to strip any one area of all of its ground cover, but picked and chose until he judged his pile was sufficient. He re-sheathed the knife, arranged the plants bottom-side down upon the carpet of needles, and sat down carefully to test the effect. He sighed and smiled. A better cushion could not be found anywhere, and the sweet smell of the bruised ferns rose up around him like a subtle cologne.

The forest was devoid of any man-made noise. A stream gurgled faintly from the bottom of the ravine, and the breeze stirred through the needles of the pines with an indistinct sighing. A chickadee whistled its lilting tune among the young trees, and a fox squirrel scolded from high on the trunk of a pine near the trail behind him.

Kohler leaned back against the tree and pressed his cheek against the rough bark. He tilted his head so that his eyes followed the straight trunk up into the branches. He thought about Jack and the Beanstalk and felt dwarfed. The other trees nearby seemed to incline toward the crown of his tree, the massive trunks like leaning pillars topped by wild-fine strands of hair, and from the ground it appeared that the pillars and the lowest branches went on forever into the crown, and there was never, never, any end to the tree. He stayed pressed against the bark for a long while, until he developed vertigo from the seeing.

Finally he brought his gaze back to eye level and turned and leaned his back against the tree. The sun rode high in the sky, now, and it sent spears of light through the needles and branches and fell upon the bracken fern in a dapple of light and dark. Kohler sat very, very still and studied the effects, yet not with his mind, but with another part of him, as though it were his blood, or soul; not thinking, yet cognizant of the changes in the forest that were brought about by the movement of the sun across the sky and the presence of a vireo on a nearby young pine. The bird fixed its red eye on him curiously, without fear, and even ventured a song. When a cloud passed over the face of the sun, all changed again, each moment unique from the next, the breeze and the wildlife and the sky constantly recreating a new, living portrait of the forest. He sat entranced, and heard his own heart beating in the very midst of the woods, not foreign, but as a part of it, as belonging. And again he lifted his eyes to the crowns, fascinated by their appearance against the bright sky.

Some time later a movement among the bracken fern stirred him from his apparent stupor. A shy cottontail nosed its way into a bit of clearing about eight feet to his right. It crouched, watching him with its large dark eyes, and their enormous pupils. Man and animal observed each other in silence for several minutes until the rabbit turned and hopped back into the brake.

Kohler reached into his daypack and brought out an army canteen of water and a sandwich on a long roll. He ate and drank meditatively, then watched the forest again, absorbing its peace, its strength.

Some hours later the rays of the sun were slanting through the trees from the west. Kohler still sat motionless, but was again stirred from his silence by a noise among the bracken fern. It was the unmistakable sound of the chase, and he saw the ferns waving wildly in a zigzag pattern and, a second later, to move more violently as something larger followed along the pattern. Then, nearly at the clearing, a high-pitched squeal, a thrashing of the ferns, and a wild waving; then quiet, and a final shake. Kohler remained frozen against the trunk of the pine and a coyote emerged from the edge of the ferns with a rabbit clutched firmly in his jaws. The cottontail hung limply, its great soft eyes flat and blank and lifeless. The coyote saw Kohler in an instant and half crouched, ready to flee, and even to drop his prey, but the man didn't move. The canine, muscles tensed, eyed him warily then loped away through the ferns, casting a backward glance before he disappeared.

Inside Kohler a sore spot developed. The peace had been broken and his thoughts returned to swirl through his mind. Paradise lost. He had lived in the woods his entire life, and had seen the dichotomy all those years, yet it always presented a confusion to him. The beauty and apparent cruelty of nature. The perfection and distortion. The peace and violence. He knew that the coyote very likely had a den full of cubs and he felt no hatred for it doing what was natural and necessary. His mind kept trying to reason out the facts of the matter, explaining the law of survival. But his heart was unsettled, and the spell of the trees was broken. The forest presented a contradiction to him, one that he could not understand. He picked up his pack, rose from the ferns, and moved back toward the trail quickly. He hiked through the preserve with hardly another look at the trees. He could not bear it.

During the walk back to Copper Harbor Kohler was much distracted. His mind and heart continued to do battle, and he chided himself for being disturbed over a fact of life he had witnessed a hundred times, and accepted for himself. Wasn't it so that he also lived by gun and rod? Then why should this prey upon his mind? Bah! That was the true forest. Benign and smiling and innocent, then strip back the veneer to reveal a skull. Life. It was life. Death was intrinsic to it. Yet the soreness continued and he wondered why it should be so. Let there be peace. But, no.

He reached his pickup past dinnertime and debated with himself about going to Johnson's Café to eat, but in truth, he was not hungry. Instead he drove to the Brockway Mountain Road and began the four-mile ascent to the top. Perhaps the space and high places would remove the constriction from his gut; he wished to throw it off like a winter coat in the warm spring.

He hurried up the road, faster than most dared to drive, and arrived quickly at the gift shop. The sun was low toward the horizon and the water of Lake Superior to the north stretched like an endless sheet of pewter, solid and still, until a darker line, ruler straight, was drawn across it and the sky took over, flint blue, cloudless and hard. He felt his gut relax just a little, ever so little, and he struggled again with the feelings that he knew were silly. He exited the truck and turned to go into the gift shop, a small building of rough-cut lumber painted a light grey. The young woman behind the counter smiled at him when he entered. She had long brown hair and a pleasant face, and wore a sixties style dress with a light shawl thrown over her shoulders.

Kohler thought he would pick something up for Rachel, and he began to examine the items for sale in the shop. He passed by the stationery, the Keweenaw key chains and the plastic place mats that displayed pictures of Lake Superior and the surrounding area. One table held handmade Keweenaw soaps wrapped in simple white paper and labeled with a pen. He picked up one that said "lavender" and smelled it. He tried another that was lemon, and thought that perhaps his niece would appreciate such womanly stuff, so he took a bar of each. At the other end of the shop hung agate wind chimes and copper jewelry around shelves of books about the Upper Peninsula. There was a reprint of Paul Bunyan by Newton, and several books on the old logging and mining days. To the right of the books hung necklaces, mostly agates and amethyst, or a nugget of copper or copper-silver mix. The amethyst caught his eye, with the delicate purple and crystal, and he removed one from the rack and held it up to the evening light in the window. It was nice, so he put it with the soap. Taking the items to the longhaired girl, he made the purchases and walked back to the pickup.

Kohler felt better, but still there was a heaviness that was difficult to shake. He gazed at the lake for a while longer, watching as the metal color of the water darkened with the sinking of the sun, then finally climbed into the truck for the drive down to Copper Harbor.

At the end of the mountain road he sat for a minute, trying to decide on a course of action. In a few minutes he had a hamburger and root beer safely on the seat beside him, and was on his way down 41 to the inland lake. Medora was large, with a crooked shoreline full of inlets and coves that made for good fishing. There were several trucks and boat trailers in the state access at the east end of the lake when he arrived. Parking his Ford head-in toward the water and, taking his meal from its bag, he watched as two newcomers unloaded their rowboat and fishing gear from the back of their pickup. From their appearance and conversation he gathered that they were father and son, setting out for an evening of fishing, and Kohler felt a twinge of something in his chest. But he could not admit to loneliness, or less, to jealousy at the scene.

The blazing tangerine sun rode atop a small cloudbank above the water, then slowly disappeared behind it. The sky gleamed orange all around the clouds for ten minutes, until the glowing orb reappeared above the hills at the far end of the lake, suspended just to the right of a small island covered with spruce. The water became molten, flaming glass. The father and son were far out in their rowboat, riding the shining trail of light from the setting sun. In a few minutes the glory was gone, the lake and hills and the fishermen melded together in varying shades of gray. Kohler wadded the A&W bags, pitched them in a nearby trash barrel, and drove back to Copper Harbor.

It rained again that night, and the pines still dripped steadily as he extricated himself from his goose down bag the next morning. He quickly packed his wet tent into garbage bags. He didn't even stop at the Tamarack Inn for breakfast, but drove down route 26 along Lake Superior's foggy coast until it jagged inland to join 41. He reached L'Anse in two hours.

CHAPTER FIVE – SHADOWS

It was only about ten o'clock when Kohler reached home. He had mixed feelings at the sight of his small house and shop. This had been a very different trip to the Keweenaw, and he felt a dissonance in returning this time. In a way it had been a disappointment, but he told himself how stupid that was. What was to disappoint? The weather had been good. He had rested. He tried to go back over the past three days hour by hour. The eagle. Now that was something. The time atop Brockway Mountain. It was the same Keweenaw, as beautiful and desolate and nourishing as it had ever been. And the big trees were there, and they were safe from ignorant men who couldn't see their value but in board feet. The business with the rabbit? It was just unexpected, and that's why it shook him up so badly. Just unexpected and out of the ordinary for his experience up there. No big deal. But he still felt strange, not quite right, not satisfied, somehow. He tried to ignore it.

Rachel met him at the door and hugged him. "Hi! How was your trip?"

"Fine, fine. I have something for you." Kohler retraced his steps to the pickup, reached beneath the seat and retrieved the package from the gift shop, and handed it to his niece.

"You didn't need to get me anything!" she opened the bag and withdrew the plastic container holding the amethyst necklace. "How nice," she said.

"It's native up there, you know. Kind of caught my eye."

She was holding the small bars of soap to her nose and breathing deeply, with her eyes shut. Kohler was very satisfied with the expression on her face.

"Do you like them?"

"You're a smart guy, Uncle John. I love stuff like this. I can put these in my dresser and they'll make my clothes smell so good!"

Kohler thought about how much Rachel resembled her mother at this moment with her hazel eyes and brown hair. *Yes*, he had to admit to himself, *it is nice to have her staying with me.*

"So what did you do while I was away?" he asked.

"Mostly went exploring. I think I spent at least four hours at the tourist information center in L'Anse. The man who is there in the morning is quite the historian. I should do my paper on him!"

"Harry Swensson. Yeah, he's a regular natural resource around here. When we have our historical festivals and the like he's got a finger in every pie."

Kohler walked to the back of his truck, opened the tarp and took out the two large plastic bags containing the wet tent. "Rain here much last night?"

"A little. I read until about eleven o'clock and I heard it start. I bet Mom wishes it was raining down there. She called while you were gone, and is despairing about her garden. It's far too dry for this early in the summer."

"We'll send some down to her. Right now I'd better get this tent on the line so it can dry out."

They walked around the yard to the back of the house, where Kohler had strung two clotheslines.

"Mr. Swensson really was helpful, though," Rachel continued the previous line of thought. "I enjoyed listening to him. I think he has a good perspective on what history is all about, too. He gave me some good ideas about where to go to find information that he couldn't give me, and got me started on some projects. First I'd like to get a sort of overview of the forces that have affected this area, a frame to fit my particular studies in, I guess."

"Sounds important." Kohler smiled at his niece's enthusiasm. She was so serious about what she was doing, as though she would make some enormous difference in the world, cure cancer, or something. He could understand her fascination with history, all right. He liked to muddle through some of the old facts himself, and to look at the old daguerreotypes. But for him it was a pleasant pastime, not a life's work. In fact, he couldn't really understand how anyone could make such an activity his vocation. He needed to feel his hands creating, shaping things, building something solid and useful and beautiful; something that could bring pleasure to both body and soul. So his niece was a curiosity to him, though he respected her for her zeal. Besides, if this is what she liked, running after things that were dead and gone, and trying to fit them into some sensible pattern, and studying people who weren't worth the study, well, if she could make a living off it, and she was happy, who could complain? It was still pleasant to have her around.

He finished draping the sopping nylon tent over the lines and they returned to the house. When he entered the door Kohler was taken aback by how confining the walls seemed after sleeping for a few nights in a tent with the flaps open. This strange reaction took place each time he camped for a few days. But he knew that the sensation would pass, and the house would regain its familiarity.

"So what's up for today?" he asked Rachel.

"I'm going over to the Sand Point archaeological digs to look around. Mr. Swensson sold me an old Baraga County historical book from 1973 that has an entire article on the WMU excavations. I really want to check them out."

"They're not still digging over there? Good lord, it was fifteen years ago people were stirred up over that. It's just a bunch of old hills of dirt anyway."

"But they were created by a special culture! That's so important for those of us interested in archaeology. It means that an influence of a group of people that no one thought ever got farther north than maybe the middle of the lower peninsula made it all the way up here. It gives me chills just to think about it! To imagine those Indians creating the mounds and burying their dead, to have had their rituals on that very site."

`Kohler snorted. "Which proves that they were just a bunch of savages. Weird, spooky rituals." He began to feel very peeved and unpleasant that Rachel was talking like this.

"Well, Uncle John, from an anthropological viewpoint, they weren't any weirder than we are as a culture. We have our rituals, too, like funerals with flowers, spreading the ashes of somebody cremated, or even giving out cigars when a baby is born. No human can live without rituals to help give his or her life meaning and structure. We're all the same."

Kohler felt the blood creep up into his face, and he concentrated on fixing himself a cup of coffee. He could taste blood in his mouth where he was biting his lip. He was angry at himself for the reaction, but it was involuntary, and rose from deep within him like something from the bottom of the sea, uncontrollable and willful. He had determined not to meddle with Rachel's beliefs or studies, yet words found themselves on his tongue before he could think rationally. All alike indeed! Nevertheless, he resolved to let this go, for the sake of his niece, and for the sake of their mutual peace.

"Well, you enjoy yourself over there, anyway," he said, dismissing the conversation. But he was too short with her wasn't he? He turned toward her. "What time you think you'll be back? I'm not a bad cook myself; I'll make us something special for supper if you'd like." He did his best to smile as he pressed his tongue against the raw place on the inside of his lower lip.

"I could be back by five o'clock. Would that be o.k.?"

"That would be fine. All I'm going to do this afternoon is some consarned paperwork for the business and a little planning for my next projects."

"Can I bring anything back?"

Kohler checked inside the refrigerator and freezer. "No, I don't think so. Thanks anyway." He felt the anger and disgust ebbing. "Be on time, then."

His niece left and he went into the shop and concentrated on bills and invoices until two o'clock, then spent another hour on a cabinet design for a man in Marquette.

In mid-afternoon he went into the kitchen and poked at the package of stew meat he had left thawing on the counter. Satisfied with its condition, he took a large black cast-iron Dutch oven from a cabinet next to the stove and placed the meat in it. While it was browning over a low flame he fixed the dry ingredients for corn bread, washed tiny red potatoes, carrots, celery, and onions. When he had arranged the entire concoction suitably, he left things to cook and spent most of his time before five o'clock catching up on the L'Anse Chronicle. He began to feel quite mellow and forgot about the flare-up at Rachel's plans for the day. He looked forward to her arrival and wondered if she would be home for the evening. Rachel appeared just as Kohler determined that the meal was done.

"Mmm. If the taste equals the smell, I may just hire you to do all the cooking," she teased as she tossed her book bag in the corner chair.

"Well, sit down, it's ready." Kohler placed a pan of steaming yellow corn bread on one end of the table, and lifted the large iron kettle onto a trivet in the center. He had picked some ox-eye daisies and buttercups from the back of his lot and put them in a glass of water. He felt entirely pleased with himself as he removed the lid from the main course and handed Rachel a ladle.

The girl filled her plate with stew and cut a slice of corn bread. She tasted the creation.

"This is really good beef stew, Uncle John, but it has such a ... different taste. What spice did you use in this, anyway?"

Kohler grinned. "Do you like it, or is it too strong?"

"No, I do like it, it just has such a unique flavor. I mean, let's face it, beef stew can be kind of humdrum. But this is very good."

"Well, that spice you taste is pine bark." He watched Rachel's face for her reaction.

"Come on, don't tell me this is a Euell Gibbons dish."

"Nah. The pine bark is right in the meat. It's venison stew. Ain't you never had venison before, girl?"

"This is the first time I've had it. Daddy isn't much of a hunter, as you know. But I really do like this."

"Well, if you'd had venison from the Lower Peninsula, you wouldn't be able to tell it from beef, anyway. All the deer down there are as corn fed as the cattle. Up here there aren't that many fields to snack from, and our animals have a much wilder taste. That's your spice. Now venison steak, that's something else again. There's a special method of cooking that to reduce the wildness.

"First you get yourself a good slab of oak board a bit bigger that the steak, see. And then you nail that piece of meat right to the board and douse it with some marinade, and you let that sit for a couple of hours. Then you pour off the marinade and put the whole thing, board and all, in the oven at three hundred degrees and bake it for about four hours. When it's done you take it out of the oven, throw the steak out into the woods, and eat the board."

"Now stop this! I actually believed you right up until the end! You make me feel like a child, or something." But the girl was laughing, and Kohler, too was chuckling at the joke.

They spent the rest of the meal just talking. Rachel asked him to tell her about his trip to the tip of the Keweenaw, but when he related the incident with the bald eagle she gave him a reproving look. He had to assure her that it wasn't another of his tall tales.

"You can find just about any bird in the eastern part of the United States in the Keweenaw," he said. "I talked to a bonafide naturalist up there who told me it's because birds get lost in storms down below, sometimes even way down in the southern states. They lose their bearings and kind of get swept into Michigan, which of course, is surrounded by water. They stay with the land and keep flying north, and get funneled right into the Keweenaw Peninsula. They've even found some pelicans up there."

He described Horseshoe Harbor, the freighter that had greeted him from the lake, the meadow on top of Brockway Mountain, and the virgin trees in the preserve. He didn't tell her about the rabbit, but somehow having his niece to talk to gave perspective to the incident, and he was able to relive the good parts of the trip. The meal was long and enjoyable.

Afterwards Rachel washed the dishes, and chided her uncle for making a mess of the kitchen.

"Can't cook a meal right if you don't make a mess," he said. "What's your game plan for tonight? Are you off again?"

"No, I think I'll do some reading. Tomorrow I'm going to Houghton to the M.T.U. library. I'll be gone all day."

"All right. Do you think you'll have some time in the next few days for something special with your old uncle?"

"You're not old! And what special event is this?"

"I thought you might enjoy learning to fly fish."

"Oh, I'd love it! When can we go?"

"How about if we plan it for Friday evening? That will give me enough time to get a few things done around here, and you will know how to plan your time, too."
So the fishing expedition was arranged, and Kohler was as excited as a schoolboy. Teaching Rachel would be a real treat. He worried over which rod she should use, and what spot to try. He wanted to insure her chances of catching something.

Friday afternoon arrived and he stopped work earlier than usual. Rachel arrived from Houghton and they ate a cold supper of potato salad and sandwiches and were on their way as shadows began to grow long from the west. They drove a short distance to a spot on the Sturgeon River near Tibbets Falls.

Kohler showed his niece how to bring out the leader on the fishing rod and work it. He scrutinized the conditions on the river and decided which fly to use. Her first few tries at casting were near disasters. The fly whirled around and snagged twigs, fortunately low enough that it could be retrieved, and once very nearly caught Kohler.

"That would have been a big catch!" Rachel laughed. "We could have taken a picture and sent it to my mom."

"And she would wonder how this fits into all the studying you're supposed to be doing. I can hear her now. 'I sent that child up there to work on intellectual pursuits so she could be a famous anthropologist, and that brother of mine had her out playing in the stream.'"

"Oh, she would think it was nice that you're teaching me how to fly fish, or trying to teach me. She told me to have a good time along with all the studying. I think mom feels I'm too serious for my age, but I just call it mature beyond my years." Rachel stated the last phrase in a droll voice.

"You know, speaking of catching a whopper, I was fishing one time down in Ontonagon County and had to help out a couple of young fellas. Here," he interrupted himself, "just draw this leader out a little more and ease it a bit. O.k. Now aim for that place there behind that rock, see where I mean? Remember, a trout always has his head pointed into the current, and he isn't real fond of a lot of light, so you've got to use those things against him if you plan to catch him. Anyway," he continued, "I was fishing and there were quite a few other guys up and down the stream, working it, too, and here comes this big kid, in his early twenties, I'd say. Looked like a big Swede. Tall, gosh, he had to been six foot six if he was an inch, and blond, blond hair, blue eyes, and that white complexion with real red cheeks. Gangly guy. He was with a shorter fella that had German written all over him. Just his face and heavy mustache. I'll tell you, he reminded me a little of that picture of Great-grandpa Wilhelm.

"They came wading up the stream, real deliberate-like, and for the life of me I couldn't figure out what the big blond kid was eating. Until he got just about up to me, that is, and I saw that he had a dry fly caught through his lip. Well, I'm sorry, but I just laughed 'til I thought my gut would bust, and I know it wasn't funny. I mean, it had to be painful. A little dribble of blood was running down this poor kid's chin, but it was just the idea! And these two young guys walked up to me as serious as a heart attack, and the shorter, German-looking one says, 'Excuse me, sir, but do you have a pair of wire clippers on you? We have a little problem here.' I near busted out laughing again. But that fly was clean through that big kid's lower lip. Lucky I always carry a pair of needle nose pliers with me in my waders, so I took them out and clipped the tip of the hook, and they managed to draw the rest out. I asked them which one of them was responsible for that catch, and the big Swede admitted that he had done it to himself. I gave him some antiseptic and they went on back up the river, but I bet that everybody heard about it from the short guy once they got back home. From down below, I think they were, somewhere near the Ohio border."

Rachel finally mastered the basics of fly-fishing, and was able to place her fly near a good spot several times. Her toil was rewarded with a nice twelve-inch brown trout, which she hooked when it was so late that the water glistened a slate grey beneath the twilight sky. She let the fish go; she informed Kohler that she was unable to think of it in terms of supper or breakfast. It was pitch dark when they left the stream, and Kohler lit a Coleman lantern to guide them to his pickup.

The two of them laughed and joked all the way back to Wolf Lodge. Once inside the house, Kohler brought some strawberry ice cream from the freezer and they celebrated Rachel's fishing success with two large bowls of the desert.

They had just finished when Rachel said, "Uncle John, there is one more place I want to visit before I get down to the more current events and research here, and I wondered if you could give me good directions. Mr. Swensson told me about an old Chippewa cemetery north of L'Anse and I'd really like to find it and take some pictures."

Kohler's face and the back of his neck began to tingle, and he cleared his throat loudly. "You don't want to go over to that place," he said.

"Oh, but it's important that I do! I've never been in an Indian cemetery where any sort of traditional practices were still visible. It's really essential for my understanding of the culture that I get to see and hear everything possible."

"Hang your understanding, and hang the culture! Girl, don't you realize that an Indian bone-yard is no place for anybody to go; certainly not a defenseless young white girl. No, I won't allow it!"

Rachel's face revealed amazement and confusion. "Uncle John, I'm sure that it's quite safe. As I understand it, the Pinery Cemetery is a popular tourist spot. Mr. Swensson sends a lot of people over there."

"Well, I won't have you going alone. It's out of the question."

"Then go with me."

"Absolutely not! I stay away from places that can bring nothing but trouble and so should you."

Rachel set her jaw, and Kohler watched her nervously, his heart racing and the blood pounding in his ears.

"I want to go," she said quietly. "And I really don't understand why you're acting this way, as though it were a big deal. You've never said anything to me when I wanted to go sightseeing to waterfalls or drive up to Houghton. What is it about an old Indian cemetery that's so dangerous, for heaven's sake? Don't tell me you believe in ghosts?"

Kohler felt weak in the knees. "No." He realized that he was acting like a fool in front of his niece again. And he desperately wanted her respect. He drew himself up, took a deep breath, and forced a smile. "No, no ghosts. I've just heard things, living in this area for so long. Stuff about some crazy old Indian hanging around out there and I was concerned for your safety. If you're bound and determined to go, I think I should go with you." He wished she would change her mind.

"Wonderful!" maybe we could go out there first thing in the morning so that you wouldn't have to take too much time away from your work. Thanks, Uncle John, for your concern for me. No one mentioned crazy people frequenting the cemetery." She rose from her chair and kissed Kohler on the cheek, then took the empty ice cream bowls to the sink and washed them.

Kohler went to bed soon after, but lay staring up into the darkness, listening to a screech owl that was far back in the woods. It was nearly four o'clock when he dropped off into a fitful sleep.

Rachel was up at 6:30, rattling pots and pans. The odor of frying bacon wafted through the small house and lifted Kohler from his bed. He pulled on a pair of jeans and a flannel shirt and wandered into the kitchen.

"Do I have time for a quick shower?"

"Sure, this stuff won't be ready for a few minutes."

He went into the bathroom and viewed himself in the mirror. His brown eyes were bleary looking, and there were bags underneath from insufficient sleep. It seemed that the crow's feet and the lines in his forehead and around his mouth were more prominent. He realized that he was looking old. It was not something that he ever thought about. He could do a good day's work, and could still stand a good hike through the woods. *But what*, he asked himself, *do I have to measure time against, anyway?* The trout streams flowed as swiftly in his fifty-fifth year as in his twenty-fifth, the lake levels rose and fell in their cycles, and the trees grew at the same rate, or certainly not with perceptible changes. At times he remarked on the rising lumber prices, but it had never caused him to be especially cognizant of the passing of time in a personal sense. Yet now that Rachel was here, fresh, young, and full of energy, and especially with her plans for a future that stretched before her almost endlessly, his years seemed marked and measured behind and before him.

His stomach burned, and he opened the medicine cabinet and took a long swig of Maalox. Having her there had also stirred up old wounds, memories, and grudges, so that he often felt himself smoldering inside, as though a fire near-dead had felt a breath of air and begun to catch the dried bits of pine needles and birch bark near it, producing a small flame.

"Aaa," he said aloud, slamming the medicine cabinet door. He showered meditatively and went to breakfast in a pensive mood.

"Come on, Uncle John, this will perk you up." Rachel placed four strips of bacon on his plate and a bowl of scrambled eggs and some canned peaches on the table. Kohler still hoped that his niece had changed her plans for the day.

"I think we could get out of here by about eight o'clock and be back around ten or so. Then you'd still have most of the day to work. I promise I won't bother you anymore the rest of the summer. You still want to go with me, don't you?"

He forced a smile. "No problem. And I don't mind you bothering me," he added gruffly.

He felt livelier after his first cup of coffee, and chided himself for his apprehension. Following their meal Rachel cleared away the plates quickly, readied her camera and notebooks, and they left.

Kohler drove slower than usual up the highway into L'Anse, and his feelings of dread grew again when he turned from Skanee Road onto the Indian Cemetery Road, a few miles from town. He arrived at the burial ground sooner than he cared to. The area was located in the midst of a pine woods, shaded and sun dappled, with bare patches of red dirt alternating with unkempt tracts overgrown by weeds and bracken fern. Beneath the trees were a few diminutive houses, five or six feet in length, which covered the Indian graves. Complete with walls and roofs, they stood only about a foot off the ground. This was the traditional Ojibwe method of burying the dead. Elsewhere the graves were surrounded by fences, some straight and well kept, others leaning crazily, the wood gray with age and weather. These were the products of missionary influence upon the tribal people. The old traditional methods of burial involved a spiritual aspect unacceptable to the Catholic priests and Methodist ministers who had proselytized the Chippewas.

Rachel was out of the pickup in a moment, exclaiming over the grave houses and lamenting the many that were in sorry condition. She began taking pictures, but Kohler hung back by the truck. He felt strange, and weirdly out of place and time, as though the universe had mysteriously warped at the entrance to the cemetery. His blood was beginning to pound and rush, and a clammy fear gripped his spine. Still the girl walked bravely about the premises, bending somewhat reverently here and there, taking a picture in another place.

"Come here and see this grave house!" She was examining a structure, well weathered, that bore four chimneys, one on each corner of the roof.

Kohler was pressed against the side of the pickup, an invisible force pushing on his chest. His breath was coming in short, shallow gasps, and sweat beaded on his forehead. His eyes blurred, and he hardly saw his niece, for his mind was playing out a scene from the past.

It had been a hot July day. He was nine years old, and his chum, Roy Tollefssen, was ten. They had covertly planned an afternoon expedition along Skanee Road on their bicycles, and they knew that if Roy's parents or John's godfather found out, there would be a severe penalty to pay for them both. But they were filled with the bravado of Huckleberry Finn and Tom Sawyer, which they had been reading, and they were determined to have an adventure.

Much discussion had ensued in the days preceding about what course of action should be pursued. They had considered constructing a raft to be launched in Keweenaw

Bay and paddled to Houghton, but the idea sounded too much like work. They spoke about running away to the Huron Mountains to the north and prospecting for the gold that the old timers insisted could be found in the hills, but they didn't have enough funds to finance a prospector's pick. The war was raging in the Pacific, and money was difficult to come by. Roy was enamored with the specter of Injun Joe in the cave chasing Becky and Tom, and dearly wanted to have a spooky adventure. It was he that suggested an expedition to the Indian burial ground.

"Haven't you heard about the crazy ol' Chippewa chief that haunts that out there?" he asked John.

"Don't have nothing to do with red-skins."

"But maybe we could see him! Just think what an adventure it would be. Then somebody like old Mark Twain would write a book about us someday!"

The idea carried a certain amount of appeal for John, though he remained very apprehensive about setting foot in a specifically Indian cemetery.

"Why can't we just go to the old Finnish graveyard, anyway?"

"Ain't no ghost of a crazy anybody in with us Finns, and there wouldn't be any adventure to it. We ought to go where we know we have a chance to see a real ghost."

And so it was settled. They lied to the adults, stating that they were off to ride around L'Anse and eat a picnic lunch down by the bay, and they would probably be gone for a while. But as soon as they were safely away, they headed their bikes north on Skanee Road and into the reservation.

The boys had arrived near mid-morning at the cemetery, where neither had ever been before. They dismounted and left their bicycles leaning against the fence outside and cautiously entered the premises. It was very still with only the sound of a pine siskin singing in one of the trees to disturb the peace.

"Now watch out for yourself," Roy said. "That ghost could be anywhere around here."

The graveyard appeared benign, and somehow sad. Most of the graves were in very bad disrepair, with weeds growing up and choking the grave houses. Some could not even be identified above the foliage. The two boys walked silently between the burial sites for a while. John finally sighed. "I think we shoulda made the raft. This is no adventure."

"Now listen, don't give up. I bet if we just hang around here long enough we'll see something. Did you know there's dogs buried in here?"

"Thought you said it was red-skins."

"Yah it is, but my old man said they used to kill the brave's favorite dog when one of them passed on, so's the pooch could go with him to the happy hunting ground."

John snorted. "That's stupid. Ain't no dog goin' to anyplace with anybody dead. That just proves what Merle says. Indians are the stupidest things on earth. Waste the life of a good dog, too."

"Well, they did it, anyway. I think we ought to just sit and wait for old Pauguk to come around."

"Pauguk? Who the hang is that?"

"He's the one I been telling you about. Pauguk, Paugut, something like that. He's the spirit of the old medicine man that comes here. They say he wears a ragged buffalo robe and has a skull face. Comes around when somebody in the tribe dies."

John looked at his friend. Roy had carrot red hair and freckles, and blue eyes that glowed with excitement. John felt only disgust.

"Come on, let's go. This place is stupid. Ghosts don't come out in the daytime anyway. We'd done better with the Finns in town. At least we could have gone after dark, there." He began walking back toward the entrance of the cemetery, frustrated and disappointed. "Dumb Roy! Stinking savages!" he punctuated his words with a vicious kick at a rotting grave house roof. Half of the structure went flying off, revealing the bare, dank ground over the burial plot.

"Hey, don't do that! What if Pauguk gets mad at us or something?"

John whirled around. "There isn't any Pauguk, you knucklehead! There isn't anything out here but us and a bunch of dead Indians. I don't like being around here, around these scum. They stink when they're alive, and they stink worse when they're dead, and I'm goin' home!" To show his disdain, he aimed carefully and landed another kick on the rotting grave house, removing the other side of the roof.

Kohler never really knew what happened next. The boys hadn't been aware of any approaching thunderstorm, but suddenly the cemetery seemed particularly gloomy, as the sun disappeared behind a big black cumulonimbus cloud. Thunder rumbled ominously in the distance, and the forest beyond the burial ground grew dim and obscure. Back among the trees something made a loud crack, and the sound reverberated through the woods. The boys froze in their tracks as the wind rose, whirling the tops of the pine and spruce wildly, and moaning along the ground.

Roy stared at John with the eyes of a spooked horse. "Now you've done it!" he yelled. "Don't you know any better than to be disrespectful in a graveyard?"

"It's a thunderstorm!" John yelled back, though he felt a chill crawling along his spine.

"Yah, and funny it came up right now, when you're kickin' a grave to pieces! I'm getting' out of here."

The storm was approaching quickly, and a flash of lightning preceded a particularly threatening peal of thunder. Then, once again, came the loud crack back among the trees. Was that a shadow John saw back there, or what was it? The trees were waving wildly, now, but what was that back in the woods?

"What's the matter, Kohler? Why are you staring like that? Is it Pauguk? Oh, gawd, it prob'ly is!"

Another flash of lightning, blindingly close, struck something within a few hundred yards of them, and the roar of thunder was deafening as the storm broke. Rain fell in a deluge. Roy screamed and ran for the gate, but Kohler stood fast, nailed to the spot. He stared into the grey sheet of rain back into the forest. The water ran down over him in rivers, plastering his hair to his forehead, but he was paralyzed with terror. Was it a human shape he saw, covered with an old buffalo robe, and with the face of a skull? The apparition played with him, dancing in and out among the tree trunks, which were colored black with the pouring rain. He could not tell. He felt like a giant hand had encircled his body, around his chest, and was squeezing slowly, squeezing the breath from him. Terror froze his brain so that the thoughts moved as sluggishly as cold honey. He stood there waiting for Pauguk, and assured death, for what seemed to be an eternity, until finally Roy's hot words melted into his mind.

"John, come on!" Insistent, pressing. And his feet found themselves again and he whirled about and ran like the storm wind for his bicycle. He followed his friend, bearing down hard on the pedals, heading for Skanee Road.

"Uncle John?" Rachel still stood beside the grave house with four chimneys, calling out to him. "Are you all right?"

"Yeah, sure. Just a little acid indigestion." Kohler wiped his brow and reached into his breast pocket for the small package of Rolaids. "These'll fix me right up."

The girl walked toward him. Kohler's hands shook and the constriction still embraced his chest. It had been all those years, and still he felt this way. He chided himself for allowing a childhood experience to affect him. He had been a dumb kid with a great imagination, and the storm had aided the situation. In the broad daylight of his adult mind he knew he had seen nothing in the forest beyond the graveyard, and that the crack which Roy and he had heard was nothing but the creaking of the branches of the white pine in the rising wind. He knew it. He knew it. And yet his stomach insisted on knotting up on him, and his eyes perceived a gloom that the present sunny day did not endorse.

"You seem to need a lot of antacids. Have you ever seen a doctor about it?" Maybe you have an ulcer."

"It's nothing, really."

"Well, maybe we should go home if you're not feeling well."

"No, you go on and look around as much as you want. I think I'll just take it easy here by the truck."

"If you're sure. I'll just be a few more minutes. I want to get some pictures, and then I'll be ready." She stared hard at him again, then walked back into the cemetery and resumed taking photographs.

Kohler turned his back on the scene and studied the daises and orange hawkweed along the ditch on the opposite side of the road. He made himself look up into the sparkling blue of the summer sky, and at the tops of the white pine, with their asymmetrical form. He willed the day to take away the chill that clung to him.

Rachel finished her work and they rode back through L'Anse in silence, both deep in thought. Kohler was glad that his stomach had begun to relax, and he tried to think about the afternoon's work waiting to be done in his shop.

"Well, I feel as though I'm ready to change the tactics in my studies," Rachel said as they entered the house. "I think I'll spend the next few hours just sorting through what I have, and organizing it, then I'll decide how to proceed from there. But I'll fix supper. Anything in particular you want?"

"You don't have to feel like you're the chief cook and bottle washer around here all the time, Rachel. Good lord, it's like I've got a maid or something. This old bachelor isn't used to it."

The girl gave him a peck on the cheek. "I like doing it, and I'm getting my rent free. You don't want me to learn how to be a leech, do you? After all, we young people are so impressionable!"

Kohler laughed, "Well, I can't say I'm not enjoying it. You do as you please."

"O.K. Dinner at 5:30. And Uncle John, I wish you'd go to the doctor about your stomach."

"Humph. It's fine, I told you. Now, I've got to get to work."

He retired to his workshop, examined his list of orders and decided to start on some maple bookshelves for a couple in Green Bay. When they were completed he would have enough furniture to take a load to the city. He intended to drive the one hundred and fifty miles to deliver the stuff to a store that he had made a sales arrangement with. It wouldn't be worth it, except that the city people paid very well for his furniture, and he could make good money on the sale. Green Bay had become a major outlet for his work, and by far the most profitable. He would be able to run down there next week, almost a straight shot south.

He ate a sandwich he had taken into his workshop, selected the lumber he needed, and began working. His mind, however, kept bringing before him the Indian cemetery and the grave houses. He had noticed some new ones there, the lumber solid and barely weathered. It had surprised him, but he surmised that they were the burial plots of the traditionals, Chippewas who had clung silently to the old ways and old religion, or who had recently rediscovered them. He made a quick movement with his hand, involuntarily. The traditionals, with their rituals and ghosts and dances. And now he had nearly ruined a good piece of lumber thinking about them! They, more than any other Indians, disgusted him. A couple of them were loud and obnoxious, always blaming the whites for everything, and some believed that the white man would be driven from the land. They were the worst of the herds of red men and women, arrogant, filthy, savages! He thought of Thomas Crane, who always caused trouble, digging up old, moldy treaties, challenging them, taking away the rights white men had earned in this country, superseding laws made to protect the white inhabitants. And, if they found they could get away with it, breaking the laws. With impunity. With impunity! Kohler felt the rage building within him. Soon they'd take the country back to the 1800's with their savagery. Who knew, there could be another Indian war! Rachel certainly wouldn't become involved with the likes of Thomas Crane. No. She would stick to her books and study them, the way one studies animals. She would recognize savagery when she was confronted with it. The grave houses of the traditionals were only a curiosity for her, like the digs at Sand Point. Just a relatively harmless hobby. The pictures were nothing more than a butterfly collection.

He tried to work through the afternoon, but his concentration was poor. Stinking red bone-yard, anyway. *But why, why do I let it bother me so*? He asked himself. *Why do I continue to pay the price for their sins, the sin of the filthy midwife who killed my mother? They aren't worth the energy the thoughts take. And my work suffers.*

Rachel called him to supper at the appointed time, but he found his appetite lacking. He picked at his food and she asked him if his stomach still bothered him. He told her no, perhaps it was the heat.

Kohler sat after supper and opened the L'Anse Chronicle, but even then he was reminded of the tribe. The paper was too liberal for him. They were eager to cover Indian news, as though Indians were equal in importance to whites! He went to bed at 8:30, leaving Rachel to work with a legal pad of ideas and outlines at the kitchen table. He slept fitfully, with images of distorted grave houses wandering through his mind, and strange shadows flitting from tree to tree in the darkening forest. The forest. He was in the forest again, the trees towering above him, and the sound. That familiar, terrifying sound, always pursuing him, and the terror, and the sunlight falling like spears from above, and the dizziness and the terror. And again, the sunlit clearing, stumbling, groping his way toward it, rolling through the bracken fern, feet tripped by tree roots that seemed to suddenly reach up from underground and twine about his boots. But was the clearing closer? Was it? He couldn't tell, but the sound was growing louder, that pulsating, rushing, strange sound … something crashing through the undergrowth all around him, behind him, chasing him, getting closer. How can he avoid it…?

"Uncle John. Uncle John, wake up!" Rachel's voice seemed to be coming from far off to the right through the trees, and then closer. Oh no! It had his arm! It had caught him from behind … and Kohler shot upright in the bed as his niece's hand clutched his arm, shaking him awake from the dream.

The light from the living room shined into his bedroom and he knew that he was back in his own house in Wolf Lodge. He was safe, and it had been the hand of his niece, not the terror in the forest. He groaned and sank back upon the pillows, embarrassed to be caught in a nightmare, like a child who had consumed a tuna fish sandwich before bed. The girl turned on the small lamp beside his bed, and he could see the concern on her face. Kohler felt more and more embarrassed.

"You were really yelling in here," she said. "I don't think you've been well all day, ever since we were at the cemetery."

"You aren't my mother." He was insulted that this whip of a girl should come into his bedroom in the middle of the night, was it the middle of the night? Surely! But no, his alarm clock said only 10:38.

Rachel's concerned expression turned into one of hurt, and he was immediately sorry for his rudeness, yet he couldn't bring himself to apologize to her. She turned to leave.

"Good night, Uncle John," she said softly as she closed the bedroom door.

He lay with his light on for a long time, allowing his heart to slow its racing, and his stomach to settle. Conflicting emotions chased each other. He cared for his niece, but he resented her involvement with the savages, and her dragging him into it. Things were relatively peaceful before she came. He had his opinions, folks knew it, and everyone went on about their business with a minimum of problems. But now it seemed that things were being dragged to his very doorstep. He was going places that were nearly a sacrilege for him to visit, an old Indian bone-yard that he hadn't been to in over forty-five years, and most likely would never have seen again but for his niece. A blessing and a curse. Too close. She was getting too close, and no one had been that close for so long. He liked living alone and keeping to himself. He just wasn't used to all this company. And certainly not used to his own kin fascinated with the trash of the world. Damn, he wished he would have said he was too busy this summer, that she couldn't stay here. It was too late now. Too late. And too confusing. He didn't sleep for hours, and it was 3:00 before he finally dozed off again, his light still on.

When Kohler awoke the next morning he felt like his skin was filled with heavy, wet sand. He dragged to the kitchen; it was already past nine o'clock. He never slept this late, yet felt like he could have stayed in bed most of the day. There was a note on the table from Rachel.

"Uncle John, Going into L'Anse and then to the Tribal Center. Time to start my hands-on work. There is fresh orange juice in the fridge. I should be back around 4:30 or 5:00. Hope you are feeling o.k. Love, Rachel."

Kohler swore softly when he read that she was visiting the Keweenaw Bay Tribal Center. He was no longer able to distance himself from his niece's interests, and it was in vain that he tried to tell himself it didn't matter to him where she went, what she did, or with whom she associated. But he felt impotent to do anything about it. He slammed his palm onto the table and stood a few minutes with his head down, just leaning immobile against the tabletop. Finally he turned to fix some coffee, but he moved slowly, like a very old man.

As he sat drinking his coffee, he tried to decide what he would do for the day. He wanted to finish out the orders to go to Green Bay and hoped to be able to drive down within five or six days to make the delivery. His mind was not cooperating with him, however. The thoughts swirled around in a whirlpool that always degenerated into thinking about Rachel, the cemetery, and bits and pieces of flotsam from all of his past experiences with Indians. It was late morning when he went into his workshop to begin his labors. But even the wood seemed uncooperative, as though it too, had become his enemy. He gave up on an oak coffee table and decided to try and work with soft pine, which was being made into a bin for potatoes and onions. The bins were easy to construct, demanded relatively cheap materials, and sold surprisingly well. He had an order for five of them for Green Bay, and he had completed three except for the stain. The others were cut, awaiting assembly and sanding. His anger and frustration slowly mellowed as the wood finally yielded to his craftsmanship, and by mid-afternoon he had finished the two remaining bins, including the sanding. He began to stain the others.

The day was uncommonly warm and humid for northern Michigan, and even with all of the windows open in his workshop, the fumes from the stain began to bother Kohler. He finished the second piece, closed the can and set the rags out back on a rack to air. It was refreshing just to get out of doors, and he breathed deeply and meditatively for a moment. He still was not feeling his best, but rather weighed down physically and emotionally. He calculated what he had to accomplish for the Green Bay order, and decided he could take off and go trout fishing. And this time, he thought, he would not invite his niece. In fact, he would leave before she arrived home from her day's wanderings. The brookies would be running well in the Huron River up by Big Eric's Bridge.

He re-entered the house and retrieved some items from the refrigerator -a stick of butter, a lemon, two cans of cola – and placed them in a small cooler with some bread. After choosing his rod from the five he kept in the closet and clapping his fishing hat on his head, he was off. It was nearly 4:30 when he pulled out of the driveway, and he felt satisfied that he had avoided Rachel. He left her a note telling her to fix her own supper and not to be concerned with him, he was eating out.

The drive to Big Eric's Bridge took him through the reservation along the east side of Huron Bay, through Skanee, and onto a gravel road that threw up thick clouds of grey dust behind his truck. By the time he reached the state forest camp ground on the Huron River, the red paint of the vehicle was dulled to a rust color.

He set about fishing above the falls, but had little luck, so he wandered downstream past the bank where the campgrounds stood, out toward the mouth of the river. There, in two deep pools that had been scrubbed out of the sandstone riverbed by the swirling water and gravel, he caught three brook trout. It was suppertime when he splashed his way out of the water. The heat of the day was dissipating in the cool of the northern evening.

After returning to the deserted campground and spraying himself against the voracious hordes of mosquitoes, he tramped through the woods for a few minutes, picking up firewood. With the newspaper from the truck, and the wood, he had a pleasant fire burning in no time. He sat back on his haunches and allowed it to burn down to coals, then went back to the pickup and retrieved a camp grill and frying pan. Kohler quickly cleaned the trout, throwing the guts into the bushes, then melted butter in the pan and placed the fish carefully in a row in the bottom. He sat back again while they fried, turning them from time to time. When they were done he took the pan of fish to the picnic table, opened one of the colas and sat down to eat, foregoing plates or napkins. The fish tasted mellow and sweet and he settled into the meal, relieved and happy. The tenseness of the past two days flowed away into the woods. He could hear the rushing sounds of Big Eric's Falls below the campground, the scream of a Blue Jay high up in a big yellow birch, and the buzzing of the mosquitoes kept at bay by the repellent. This was more like it. Just the woods and river and the critters. No one to worry about, no one to argue with. Just sweet peace.

He finished the trout and tossed the leftovers into the bush with the guts, then wiped out the frying pan with a paper towel. Another few minutes among the trees produced more firewood, which he stacked near the small blaze and fed into the flames piece by piece. He sat by the fire, just staring, feeling sleepy, until the woods became quite dark. His mind played far from the incidents of recent days, but rather mused over some of the stories Matt and Lew had told in the Iron Pine, and tales Merle had told of the mines before the ore ran out. Kohler often amused himself this way when he was alone, just replaying old stories, old voices, and old days. He never tired of it.

The flames consumed the last stick of wood and he was sad, but he felt as though he could sleep for a year. It was time to head out. Too bad he had left his tent at home; it would have been so pleasant to set it up, crawl in, and be instantly unconscious. He kicked sand over the last glowing embers in the fire pit and climbed into the truck. The engine caught with a roar and he grimaced when the stillness of the forest was broken.

The house was dark when he arrived, but the VW was parked in the driveway so he assumed that Rachel had retired early. It was just as well. He felt ambivalent toward the girl, and really didn't want to see her. Somehow it would ruin his evening. He did not want to think about anything, be made to deal with anything. He simply wanted to go to bed and sleep the sleep of exhaustion and contentment, his belly still comfortable from the trout dinner. He didn't even turn on the lights, but made his way quietly to his bedroom, undressed, and fell into bed. He was asleep in a few minutes.

Kohler awoke at dawn, feeling rested and well. He immediately rose and went to the kitchen to fix coffee and some instant oatmeal, then proceeded to his workshop.

Later the door to the shop opened and Rachel stuck her head in. "Whew!" she said.

Kohler had been staining the last of the vegetable bins, and the room was stifling with the

strong odor. He looked up from his work and felt a coldness in the pit of his stomach.

I wonder what she has to say, he thought to himself, then steeled his mind against the

questions, the possible rebukes, the comments.

"You've been up for a while, huh?" she said.

"Yeah, I have a lot to do before I go to Green Bay in a few days." He waited for

her next remark.

"I know I've kept you busy lately; you haven't been able to do your own work.

My mother warned me about monopolizing your time so much that your job suffered.

She said she'd know what happened if she found out that you ended up on welfare; your

niece kept you from making a living!"

"I'm managing all right," he replied cautiously, relaxing a little.

"Well, I'm off, anyway. Have a nice day, hope you catch up on everything. I'll be

back in the afternoon sometime."

"O.K. Be careful."

"Always."

Kohler sighed in relief when she left, and chided himself for his anxiety. It was

like nothing had happened, and his rough thoughts about Rachel melted away. He kept

working and was surprised when it was noon and he was hungry again. After a quick

sandwich he returned to the shop and worked fervently through the afternoon. He enjoyed

the smell of the wood, dank and crisp and of the forest. He felt calm as the shavings curled from beneath his plane in delicate white featherings, lying like the wool of a shorn sheep on the floor of his shop. His creations rose from the drafting paper and became solid objects, and to him it was good.

When hunger drove him from his tools next, it was early evening. He was gratified to find a casserole of rice and chicken, and fresh rolls ready in the kitchen. He had not heard Rachel return.

During supper they did a delicate minuet around the subject of her studies, so the peace remained. Kohler told more Matt and Lew stories and Rachel talked about her family in Saginaw; she had received a letter from her mother that morning. After the meal Kohler turned on the radio to his favorite country and western station and sat at the kitchen table tying flies. Rachel retired to the living room and sat in the over-stuffed chair, busying herself with books and notes. He watched her furtively now and then, and wondered what it would have been like to be a father and have a child her age. Her mother and dad could be proud of her, he mused. She certainly wasn't lazy or spoiled, even for being the baby in the family. No, she was very responsible, though she did have some strange ideas. The evening passed without incident.

The day following, Kohler was up early again, and in the shop readying items for the Green Bay shipment. Rachel popped in briefly about nine o'clock to tell him hello and that she was on her way out. *She is a very considerate girl*, Kohler thought. He continued his work until after eleven o'clock, then stopped. It was Friday, and he needed to pay a visit to the bank, since he planned to go to Green Bay on Monday.

The day had turned cloudy by the time he started his pickup and headed toward L'Anse, and there was something autumnal in the sky, though the fourth of July wasn't until the following Thursday. But that was not uncommon in the North Country, when a frost was never really far away. Kohler could remember sometimes as a child when winter seemed to be near the entire year, and once a deadly frost hit the last of June. Gardens were decimated, and the old timers just nodded knowingly and talked about the storms off Gitche Gumee, and how no one ever quite knew for sure how the weather'd run up here. Kohler liked the unpredictability of the skies and wind just below the forty-seventh parallel. The adventure-craving young boy in him had never completely grown up.

By the time he pulled into the parking space near the Commercial National Bank, a few large raindrops were splattering down, making irregular dark splotches on the white sidewalk. As he walked toward the door of the building he noticed two people across the street, hurrying toward the L'Anse Café. Kohler immediately recognized his niece. Rachel was carrying her small rust-colored camera bag, a compact tape recorder, a notebook, and her purse. Beside her was Sam Whitefeather, with his hair combed back from his broad angular face, and dressed in his usual blue chambray work-shirt and jeans. Kohler flattened himself against the wall of the bank building and watched the pair enter the restaurant. As they reached the door it began to rain in earnest, but he hardly noticed. A shadow seemed to pass over his eyes, and the rain poured down harder, pelting him. But it could not cool his burning skin, nor wash away the sudden taste of bile in his throat.

He finally stumbled, dripping, into the bank, and stood blinking a few seconds, trying to refocus his eyes on the tellers. He became aware that the employees and a few customers were staring at him; and his thought processes began to function again, winding down from the pure hate reaction that had surged through him when he saw his niece in the company of one of the area's most prominent Indians. He knew that she must be interviewing him for her studies, and that was all, but hatred kept bubbling through his veins like molten lava. He mechanically walked toward the teller's window in front of him, simply to put some rational motion into his body, and he was surprised when he bumped into the shelf. The teller looked at him with her mouth agape.

Kohler stared at her, and finally found his tongue.

"Here." He pushed a check toward her.

She picked it up. "It isn't endorsed, sir. If you would kindly sign…"

"All right!" He snatched it back from her, and she colored. The teller was new, a young girl of about nineteen. Kohler knew most of them in the bank; his regular, Madeline Rayfield, was nowhere to be seen. He scribbled his name, nearly illegibly, and shoved the check back beneath the grate. She stared at the signature and looked up helplessly, then catching the assistant manager's eye, signaled for her to come over.

"What the devil is the matter?" Kohler asked, so loudly that the other customers stopped talking and looked at him again. "I've lived here nearly my whole life and I can't even get a check cashed?"

The assistant manager had arrived on the scene and patted the shoulder of the teller reassuringly.

"Good afternoon, Mr. Kohler." She turned to the girl again. "It's all right, Nancy. This gentleman is a regular customer. Forgive the delay, Mr. Kohler, she's just trying to do her job; she hasn't been with us too long."

"Well, hurry it up."

The manager gave Kohler a long look, as if she wanted to say something.

"Certainly," she finally answered curtly.

The business was transacted and Kohler stalked out of the bank into the rain. Glancing across the street at the L'Anse Café he gritted his teeth. On the way back to the truck he walked through the middle of a puddle and swore loudly. When he sped from the parking place and careened into the street, he barely missed colliding with a blue Dodge, but Kohler didn't even look back at the driver, who was angrily honking his horn. The sky was dark with blue-black clusters of clouds that were cruising like the members of an armada against the iron-grey backdrop. They rose from the horizon west over the Keweenaw Bay and stretched toward the Huron Mountains in the northeast. At the rear of the clouds was a sheet of hard, slate colored rain that pounded the earth briefly and then passed on, clinging to the edge of the storm. Stray fragments of clouds, the color of smoke from burning tires, rose here and there. Disengaged from the parent storms, they floated like dark ghosts behind. The weather was a mirror to Kohler's churning emotions. Everything seemed dark and strange and malevolent.

He was driving fast on 41 south, but didn't bother to turn at the dirt road leading to Wolf Lodge. He continued on east when the highway curved, and drove unconsciously until he reached Michigamme. He was shocked when he saw the shores of the large lake appear between the pines.

"Good grief, I'm halfway to Marquette," he mumbled to himself. He slowed the truck and pulled into the state rest area on the north shore, and parked facing the water. It began to rain again, converting the scene into a monochrome of grey. Kohler trembled with a sudden chill and realized that his hair was wet and plastered against his head, and his flannel shirt was soaked. He turned the heater on and watched the rain run in rivers down the windshield.

His anger subsided and a new and more difficult emotion usurped its place; a dull pain squeezed his chest as he thought of Rachel going into the café with Sam Whitefeather. An Indian! *No good could come from it,* he thought, *no good ever comes from associations with them. They've been the bane of Americans ever since the first white settler laid the sole of his foot on this soil. And now Rachel.* He had hardly believed that she would actually get personally involved with any of them. Archaeological digs and deserted cemeteries and stacks of books were one thing. Sitting down at the same table with a dirty tribal leader, especially in a public place, was quite another. Kohler moaned and put his head down against the steering wheel. The pressure in his chest increased and moved down into his stomach until he became quite uncomfortable. He sat up and fished through his pockets, then opened the glove compartment of the truck and brought out a half bottle of Rolaids. He popped three of them into his mouth. Thirty minutes later his head had cleared and the pain in his stomach subsided somewhat. He realized that he was wasting precious time sitting in the rain, feeling frustrated and angry.

"Buck up, boy," he said aloud. "Can't let some ignorant girl ruin my life or business. It's of no matter, anyway. Judas, she's old enough to make her own bed and lie in it. Summer ends, she'll be gone, and who cares?"

He drove back to Wolf Lodge, went directly to his shop, and spent the rest of the afternoon working. Rachel came home and made a pot of vegetable beef soup for their supper, but Kohler was withdrawn around her. Conversation lagged, and he noticed that she did not press it. He gave her credit for being perceptive enough to realize that he didn't feel like talking.

On Saturday the weather cleared, but the air was still cool from the storm. It was perfect for working, and Kohler was in his shop early and stayed the entire day. He saw his niece as little as possible. That evening he brusquely informed her that he was going out for supper, and drove into the Iron pine for a meal of fried lake perch. He wandered around L'Anse until nearly dark, then went back to his house and directly to bed. He heard Rachel come in at 1:15, but fell immediately back to sleep.

Sunday morning he was up at dawn again, putting the final touches on some of the pieces to be shipped the following day. Late in the morning he went into the house to place a telephone call to Rich Behredsen, his sometime fishing buddy, who often assisted him in loading furniture onto the pickup for trips to Wisconsin or Marquette. As he passed through the kitchen, his eye caught sight of a note on the table. "Uncle John," it read, "I went to church with friends up at Zeba. I was invited to their house for lunch afterward. I'll probably be home around 3:30. Love, Rachel."

Zeba! She was going to the Indian church! Zeba was the oldest Methodist mission in the state, and still had a strong Chippewa congregation. Her friends were obviously Indians, and she was going home with one of them to eat lunch! Kohler wadded the note into his clenched fist and hurled it at the wastebasket in the corner. He stamped into the living room and pivoted, not knowing where to turn or what to do to release the anger he felt. Rachel's course was like a speeding freight train, going faster and faster. He felt as helpless to stop her from sure ruin as he would standing on the tracks of the Marquette Northern and trying to stop the 2:43. It was impossible. He picked up a piece of driftwood from the end table and flung it forcefully against the opposite wall. It hit with a sharp crack, denting the pine paneling. He wanted to break things, and looked about him for something else to abuse. He visualized himself tearing the wall pictures from their moorings; but he didn't. Instead, he stomped outside, slamming the front door behind him, and walked quickly around the house into his small back yard and on toward the forest in the back of his lot. Within a few seconds he was on state land.

Kohler crashed through the underbrush at a fast walk. Brambles tore at his clothes, and bushes and thick ferns dragged at his feet, impeding his progress. He walked until the anger-energy began to subside, and finally stopped beneath a yellow birch. *Just one thing after another*, he thought.

He leaned his head against the rough gray bark of the tree and waited until his breathing returned to normal, then headed back toward the house. He was depressed, and the outburst of anger had drained him of much of his energy. But he still needed to prepare for the Green Bay trip, and he went to the telephone and wearily dialed Rich's number.

Behrendsen arrived forty-five minutes later. He was a stubby, balding man with a beer belly, a very round face, and light brown eyes beneath erratic eyebrows. He hadn't shaved lately, and his salt and pepper colored whiskers looked like weathered straw stubble.

"Hey there, John old man. Good morning, isn't it? Looks like we'll have clear weather for the next few days."

"Yeah, looks it."

"Where ya got your stuff to be loaded?

"By the door."

The two men began by taking off the snap-on tonneau cover from the bed of Kohler's pickup, and he removed some camping gear that he kept shoved up near the cab. They hauled the heaviest pieces of furniture out and placed them at the front of the bed, then worked in the bookshelves, and finally carried out the vegetable bins.

"These are nice little items, John. I bet Ida would like one for her kitchen. She's always complaining about not having enough space for onions and taters and such."

"I'll make her one. They're simple as all get out."

"How much you charge?"

"Nothin'. Partial payment for you helping me out. How's your fishing business coming anyway?"

The stubby man stopped what he was doing and spit a wad of saliva into a bush by the house. "Well, Kohler, you know that a self-respecting white man can't make nothin' on commercial fishing anymore. The Chippewas are out there scooping up every fish in the bay. They're even coming over from Wisconsin and fishing Keweenaw, now, and there's a regular tribal war goin' on about who gets to fish where. But we're the ones losing out."

"Yeah, I been seeing that in the papers. It's a real shame. Something ought to be done."

"Who's going to do anything? The government is so busy givin' the country back to the stinking redskins they won't even listen when an upstanding white man says he can't make a living no more due to them. Guess they want all of us in commercial fishing to get out and sell souvenirs or something, instead of working. I'll tell you, everybody's suffering. Even your sport fishing, now. You know damn well that them over-fishing the trout streams has caused a decrease, huh? You bet it has. You think back a few years ago before these Indians got it into their heads to conjure up this treaty rights business. You could go out here and see a hatch, cast your fly and that there trout'd be striking that fly a foot above the water every time. I don't listen to none of this acid rain garbage as to why we can't catch the trout like we used to. I know why, and so do you.

"Me and Harry was talking the other day sayin' we ought to do something ourselves, to slow the redskins down, at least. I mean, nobody's doin' anything. They're getting so proud, they don't think nothin' of going out here and over-fishing the DNR limits on the bay, even. And the DNR looks the other way instead of trying to catch them at it."

Kohler nodded. "Yup, but what cha gonna do? Government's for them, like you said."

"I told you, we'll go out and do something to slow them down some. Make them see that not every white man is afraid of being scalped in his bed if he protests the giveaways. I'll tell you who I'd really like to get my claws into, and that's Thomas Crane. That red boy is just cruisin' for a bruisin'. I swear to God, the way he talks about his people being here first and all that trash, just sets my blood to boiling. He hates whites so much he'd see all of us starve if he could. Well, I think his tanned hide would look real nice on my wall next to the moose."

"He's a bad one, all right. None of them are any good, though. Just bad, worse, and worst."

"Ain't it the truth."

"I wish there was some way to open the DNR's eyes, and those stupid fools down there in Lansing."

"I still say there is. In fact, Harry and I thought we'd have a little fireworks of our own come the fourth of July. A little present for the red boys, so they can remember that real Americans are white. Interested?"

"Depends."

"Listen, nobody gets hurt. We just slow down their production a little bit, a warning. Maybe if they see that they can't get away with messing up a white man's legitimate fishing rights and they're gonna get a fight, the cowards will back down."

"What you going to do, wreck their boats?"

"Naw, nothing that drastic. Not yet, anyway. I'm telling you, I don't think we've got to be drastic. Just a strong hint should do it. They'd be in a pretty fix without their nets now, wouldn't they?"

Kohler grunted and shoved the last vegetable bin into place on the truck bed.

"Well, continued Behrendsen, "we just might work on them for a while and see how they do with big old holes. How about it, you in?"

Kohler hesitated. Here was a perfect opportunity to teach his enemies a lesson. It appealed to him, but … But what? He felt uncomfortable.
"I'll think about it, Rich. Sounds good."

"You do that. Like I said, nobody really gets hurt. Say, I hear your sister's daughter is up here for the summer. She just here for vacation, or what?"

"She's studying up here."

"Oh yeah? What's she studying?"

"Uh, I guess she's just doing some historical research on the old lumbering and mining days and such."

"Boy, I bet you're in your glory, too. Tell her some of those yarns about Silver Jack that Matt and Lew used to spin?"

"Told her quite a bit. Here, could you help me with this tarp? I gotta get it down real tight."

The two men worked silently for several minutes, securing a black tarp to hooks Kohler had build into the sides of the truck bed. He made sure that every piece of furniture was covered against the possibility of moisture.

"Here, Rich, I've got something for you." Kohler led the way into the house and opened a drawer in an oak chest in the living room. He withdrew five trout flies. "Thanks for giving me a hand with my load," he said as he passed the brilliantly colored lures to Behrendsen.

"Now, you didn't have to do this! But I'll take them, anyway!" The short man laughed. "These sure are beauties. You tie the best flies in the U.P."

"Well, I'm glad you like them. Like I said, I appreciate the help."

"Yeah, just remember what I said about us helpin' ourselves out in other ways, too. These flies won't be worth two cents if we got no more trout to fish for. Savvy?"

"Sure thing. I'll be thinking about it."

"Give me a call, then."

Behrendsen left and Kohler returned to his shop to tidy up. He tried to avoid thinking about Rachel and where she was and what she was doing. The very idea nauseated him. He wished that he could drive to Green Bay that afternoon instead of waiting until the next morning. Maybe he could, why not? But then the thought of spending good money for a motel room, only to be kept awake all night by the parties and arguments and traffic, didn't appeal to him. And what of the furniture? It would probably be gone in the morning. No, it wouldn't work. He cast around for another possibility. Couldn't really take the truck anywhere loaded like it was but he did not want to see his niece when she returned. He was afraid that he would lose control of himself and say things that he would be sorry he uttered. But why this inner battle? The girl may indeed be his flesh and blood, but she was no Kohler in spirit. She was naïve and stupid, fooling with those savages. Why shouldn't he just kick her out? He wasn't obliged to give her shelter. No. Impossible. He would have no family at all, then. Grace would certainly never understand his actions, no more than she was aware of the great folly of her daughter's association with the Chippewas.

He finally grabbed a rucksack and went to the kitchen. Throwing a few items of food and drink therein, he hastily scribbled a note. Be polite, he thought. "Rachel, I have gone for a hike. I may not be back until late."

He struck out south on the dirt road through Wolf Lodge and then cut into the forest west, toward a small branch of Ogemaw Creek. It took him nearly an hour of beating through the brush and around deadfalls to reach the tiny tributary. He followed seven stepping stones into the water until he secured a large boulder in mid-stream, upon which he climbed and sat down. The configuration of the rock was such that he was provided with a back support, and he could position his legs comfortably. He settled into the afternoon sun and warmed himself like a turtle on a log, watching a small waterfall downstream as it gurgled around a shelf of shale. He brooded, and wished not to, and again turned to brooding. The entire afternoon was spent in this manner. He ate a supper of grapes, Swiss cheese and summer sausage around 6:30, and stayed on the rock until the forest became quite dark and he knew he must go. By the time he stumbled out of the woods onto the road to Wolf Lodge it was nearly pitch black beneath the trees.

When Kohler entered the house the girl was sitting by a lamp reading. She looked up with her brilliant smile.

"Hi!" I thought I'd never see you again. You're always off in the woods or working yourself to death in your shop."

"Well, yes I suppose so. If you don't mind, I've got to go to bed. I want to get an early start to Green Bay tomorrow morning." He said no more, but went to his room and retired for the night.

Kohler was up at four o'clock, had his breakfast and a shower, and pulled out of the driveway by 5:00. He took highway 41 and 141 south through patches of forest, northern dairy farms and small towns where people were just beginning to rise for the new work week. He felt relaxed in these pastoral settings, but a tension set in as he neared Green Bay some three and a half hours later. He hated the cities with their litter and congeston and their rude, harried people. Except for the fact that they were the consumers of goods produced by the people on the farms and in the forests, he could find very little good in them.

He drove to the shop where he had arranged to leave his furniture, did his business as quickly as possible, and was on the road again by late morning. As soon as he was free of the suburbs he breathed a sigh of relief. At midday he stopped for lunch at the tiny restaurant in the burgh of Beecher, Wisconsin, and lounged listening to some local men swap stories. He didn't hurry back to Wolf Lodge, and it was after three o'clock when he arrived.

Kohler drove slowly along the dirt road into the gathering of houses, passing by the old Post Office and coming into view of his own place. He saw Rachel's VW sitting in the driveway, and another car with which he was not familiar. "Now who in tarnation could that be?" he wondered aloud. "A customer, maybe?" He hoped not, because they didn't appear to have a great deal of money. The vehicle was an old Chevy Impala, early seventies vintage, and painted a sort of mauve over a lot of bondo. The rust, though, was obviously winning the war against the car's body.

Kohler pulled his truck along the road in front of the house and got out. Just then three people exited from the front door. Rachel was one, but the other two were dark skinned. A young man about Rachel's age was in the lead, tall with an olive complexion, dark brown hair and high cheek bones. A girl of about the same age chatted gaily with Kohler's niece. She was much darker, with black hair, and the somewhat round face common to Chippewa women.

"What the devil is this?" Kohler exploded. He glared at Rachel, who came to an abrupt halt at her uncle's outburst. "Don't you ever bring anyone here without my knowledge, and never bring the likes of this filthiness on my land!" he moved threateningly toward the young Indians. "Get off my property, you shitty assholes!"

The Indians moved away from the white man and toward their car, walking slowly, warily, as one would circle a rattlesnake.

"I said move!" Kohler screamed. He returned to the pickup and opened the door. Withdrawing a tire iron he waved it menacingly at the two, who were in their car and trying to get the tired starter to turn the engine over.

Kohler suddenly felt a hand and the weight of a body dragging on his arm.

"Uncle John, please!"

He whirled and saw Rachel's face, her eyes full of fright and confusion. She appeared to him through the veil of his mindless rage as one distorted, a monster, and he cast her off with one swing of his arm. She stumbled backwards and fell into the yard, and Kohler turned his attention to the youth in the Impala.

They had succeeded in starting the car, and the boy threw the vehicle into reverse and floored the gas pedal. A thick spray of gravel hit the rocker panels as they lurched backward into the street. When he dropped it into drive the gravel spurted behind, and Kohler went charging after the car, screaming wordlessly. He hurled the tire iron at the retreating vehicle and hit the right rear tail light, shattering the red plastic onto the road. He continued to run after them until he could see nothing but dust.

Kohler's lungs burned and his head pounded. He slowed, then stopped and stared around him. His house was a quarter mile away. He stood dazed a few moments, the anger and bitterness ebbing slowly in his veins, but his body aching like he had the flu. He shook his head, trying to clear the cobwebs, and a snapshot of Rachel presented itself to his mind's eye. She was sprawled upon the grass of the front yard, her legs flung out and her arms in a positon to break a fall. Her face was a mosaic of disbelief, anger and pain. The picture remained there, frozen in his brain.

He turned and began to hurry back toward Wolf Lodge. He found that his legs would not carry him very fast, but he did not really want to run, anyway. Thoughts were pouring through his head like a stream through a sluice gate. *Rachel had invited Indians into his house, where he worked and ate and slept. Filthy, foul Indians, into the sanctity of his home*. He was confused, torn between the desire to take back the violent motion that threw his niece to the ground, and the desire to thrash her further. Sweat poured down his face.

When he arrived at his driveway, Rachel was not in sight, though the VW was still parked there. He stood for a few moments, simply staring at the front door, then went in quietly. The door to the spare bedroom was closed, and no sound came from behind it. Kohler hesitated again, then turned and went into his wood shop, intending to work. *She'll get over it*, he thought, *and I have work to do*. But he sat staring at some lumber until 5:30.

He entered the house, finally, and began banging pots and pans around in an effort to fix some supper. Rachel left her room and came into the kitchen. Her expression caused Kohler to turn his head away from her.

"I presume you want me to move out, Uncle John. I can be gone in the morning," she said in a strained voice.

He didn't answer immediately. "No," he said slowly, "you don't have to go if you don't want to." He turned toward her.

"Well, after what happened this afternoon, I just don't know what to think. I have been wondering all this time why you seemed to act so strangely anytime I talked about my studies, but I just pushed it out of my mind. Now I find that you're a bigot!"

"Watch your mouth, young lady! You're still in my house, and you needn't call me names."

"I apologize if you think I've called you a name you don't deserve, but I just don't understand. I suppose I shouldn't have asked anyone here, no matter who they were, even for a few minutes, but I have the feeling you wouldn't have treated my white friends like you treated Jill and Rob."

"Damned right." Kohler made an exasperated sound. The two emotions were battling again in his chest. "You just don't realize, girl. Those are bad people you're getting involved with. I'm just trying to protect you from them, from getting yourself hurt."

"Oh come now. They're people just like all other people. There is good and bad in every race. You're just prejudiced and bitter, Uncle John, and I can't believe this is really you! I'm so disappointed in you."

Her last words stung him. "I'm trying to help you, I'm telling you! These aren't just like other people, they're not. Not for us, Rachel."

"What do you mean, 'not for us'?"

"I mean that our family wouldn't be like it is today if it wasn't for an Indian. You might even have a grandma who's still living, and maybe other aunts and uncles. And me and your mom would have had a mother instead of growing up without one."

"I still don't see what that has to do with Indians. You sound like Grandma was killed in an Indian raid or something."

"I don't think your mother ever believed it, so I suppose she never even suggested it to you. I tried to tell her, though. I sure did, but she said it was Merle's interpretation of what happened …"

"What are you talking about, Uncle John?"

Kohler was beginning to babble. "Your grandmother was killed by an Indian, girl. That's what I'm getting at."

"She died in childbirth with you."

"The midwife was a squaw! She was an ignorant, filthy bitch from the reservation that was practicing her voodoo stuff on your grandmother, and for all you know those two young nits you had here today were some relation to her! You go over there and consort with those, those, people, and you could be hotten-totten with the very blood that murdered your family! It's a mighty sad affair that justice was never done, and that it can't be done now! My God, Rachel, I can't believe you can even be in the same room with them and not have your blood tell you something's not right. You got to see, you got to!"

Rachel pulled a chair out from the table and slowly sat down. "So that's it," she said, and was silent for a moment.

Kohler, too waited, hoping, believing, that perhaps she now understood the truth of the situation and would alter her course.

"Listen," she began, "I don't know why you think that this midwife killed Grandma; I don't even know why there was a midwife there, but your father would have known if she really was responsible for what happened, that is, was negligent in some way. I just can't believe he would have let it slide. Be reasonable, Uncle John, or at least have enough faith in Grandpa to believe that he would have made things right. And you got all this from Merle. Maybe Merle was wrong. He wasn't there when you were born, was he?

"I'm not trying to disparage anyone. Maybe he was mistaken, that's all. And besides, even if somehow it were true, which I don't believe is the case, it was a long time ago, and it shouldn't reflect on an entire race of people. For heaven's sake, if the

Indians I've met blamed all white people for the Trail of Tears, or the many massacres of their tribes by whites, I suppose I would have been killed some time ago."

"What's the matter with you, anyway?" Kohler felt the blood rushing to his face. "You make it sound like it's the white race that's the savages. You don't know what you're talking about! You don't live around any of them, down there. Well, I was raised within spittin' distance of the red devils, and I know what they're really like. You don't know what they do to folks up in these parts – the rapes, the property destruction, the breaking of the law, the murders, too. You read all that sniveling stuff in your books that makes them sound so persecuted, so put upon; well, it's just so much hogwash! They oughta get rid of all of them!"

"Stop this! I always looked up to you as an intelligent man, and I'm hearing such ignorance! I can find a white person who has committed rape or murder just as easily, more easily! How can you justify yourself?"

Kohler was perspiring, and his stomach burned like he had swallowed molten iron. "Well, if this doesn't beat all!" he bellowed. "I take you into my house, do everything I can for you, for the sake of my only sister, and you got the gall to call me ignorant! I try to save you from God knows what might happen to you because of who you're associatin' with, and this is the thanks I get! I guess it's true what they say about this new generation of youngsters. You got no respect, no brains. For all I know you're on drugs, or something, too."

Rachel's face was very white, so that it accented the tiny freckles that were not normally noticeable, and anger made her eyes a deep green. "I'm sorry. I didn't mean to say that you're ignorant, but I just don't understand how you feel. And you didn't need to say those things about me, either. I don't do drugs, and I thought you took me in because you cared for me, too, not just my mother, or that you felt forced into it." Rachel's face seemed to get whiter and whiter, and the freckles glowed like they would simply leap from her skin. "I thought maybe we could resolve this thing, but it appears not. I"ll leave tomorrow. Now if you wish."

"No! you don't have to leave. You just go ahead and do what you want to do. Don't feel like you gotta go. Just don't talk to me about anything you're involved in, and if something happens, don't come crying to me. We're still blood." He paused, confused. "We're still blood, and I have respect for that, even if you don't."

The girl sat and just stared at Kohler for several seconds. "I'll see how it goes, Uncle John, but I don't know how this can work out, now that I realize how you feel about everything, and maybe how you feel about me." She got up and turned away, and a few minutes later drove off in her car.

Kohler's muscles were as tight as great clock springs, wound to the breaking point. He hurried to the bathroom as soon as Rachel was out of the door and took the Maalox from the medicine cabinet. Returning to the table he sat down, shook the bottle vigorously, and unscrewed the cap. He tipped the bottle into his mouth and swallowed the white, chalky liquid three times before he brought it back to the table top. After a few minutes his muscles began to relax, but he felt drained. He took another swig of the Maalox and then capped it. *Why did he tell her to stay?* He wondered to himself. *It won't be anything but trouble. How can such a smart girl be so foolish?* The thoughts swirled about, and the emotions rose and fell like November storm waves; anger, disbelief, concern, more anger, frustration. He played the day's scenes over and over again, trying to piece them together into something sensible, but not succeeding.

"Rot!" He slammed his palm down on the table and looked up a number in the telephone book that sat on a small stand nearby. He went to the phone and dialed.

"Howdy, Rich. This is Kohler. Say, you and Harry still want company Thursday?"

After the events of Monday, Kohler and Rachel again performed a subtle dance around each other, avoiding all but the most minimal contact. The man made sure he was up and in his shop before his niece rose, and Rachel packed a lunch to take with her on her daily excursions. She always left excruciatingly polite notes telling her uncle when she expected to return, but never detailing where she would be, or with whom. However, Wednesday she fixed sandwiches for Kohler and left them in the refrigerator for his lunch. "Thought you might like sandwiches for noon," she added at the bottom of her note. Suppers for two days were hurried affairs that Rachel cooked, with Kohler coming in from his shop when the meal was placed on the table, eating nearly silently, and then returning as soon as he was through. There was little to talk about; Rachel asked him what projects he was working on, and he responded with the briefest of descriptions. He resented her all the more for what he thought was surely a trumped-up attempt at politeness. *Little hypocrite*, he thought to himself.

Thursday arrived and Kohler rose at dawn and worked until mid-morning. When he stopped to clean up he was surprised to find Rachel still in the house.

"Thought you'd be out by this time," he said.

"Everyone seems pretty involved in the festivities today. I'm just going into L'Anse to watch the parade and go to the picnic.

Kohler bristled silently when he thought about Rachel at the picnic. He nearly asked her what she would be having to eat, barbecued dog? But he held his tongue. He congratulated himself on the clever idea, though, and made a mental note to tell Harry and Rich about it.

"Yeah, the fourth of July is big doin's in this county. I'm going to have some fun myself, so if you don't mind I'll be getting on."

He went into the bathroom, bathed, changed his clothes, and was out of the house by 10:15. When he got to the pickup he had a thought, and returned to his bedroom. He found his hunting knife and sheath, wrapped it in a towel, and carried it out and placed it behind the truck seat.

Kohler had agreed to meet Behrendsen and Presselein at the former's house near the L'Anse harbor docks. Harry was standing in the yard with Rich when Kohler pulled into the driveway. The three men greeted one another with handshakes.

"Sure glad you decided to spend the fourth with us, Kohler," said Presslein. Harry was a long man, with long yellow teeth that reminded Kohler of a beaver's. He opened his mouth wide when he talked, revealing a gap where the first molar next to his left eyetooth was gone.

"What's your Mrs.'s doing today, anyway?" Kohler asked.

"Oh, they'll be out directly, once they get their baked goods and whatnot. Mrs. Behrendsen asks if you'd be ornery enough to honor us with your presence at the picnic."

Kohler hadn't realized that the two wives would be part of the day's activities, and he hesitated. "I don't want to be a bother, now," he said. He wasn't used to picnicking with much of anyone these past few years, and felt uncomfortable with the new twist in the invitation.

"Baloney. I told her you was joining me and Harry for the celebration today, and she's glad to feed you. You don't want to miss her blueberry pie, now.'

"Well, that sounds good to me. All right, I guess I can force myself to accept your kind invite, and thank you."

The Fourth of July parade led off the day's scheduled events and was due to start from the corner of Route 41 and Main Street; the participants and floats would organize by the tourist information booth there. The procession would then travel down Main, turn right on Skanee, and go through the center of the business district. The three men and the wives decided to watch it from the Post Office, near the end of the route.

Rich took an extra lawn chair for Kohler and, after a short drive to the municipal parking lot, they set up the chairs on the sidewalk. The day was balmy, with a breeze blowing off Keweenaw Bay behind them. Kohler tipped his head back briefly and allowed the warm sun to bathe his face. The two women were talking about a new potato salad recipe Mrs. Behrendsen had found in the "Ladies' Home Journal" but was afraid to try on them at the picnic for fear it wouldn't come out as well as her old standby. Kohler thought about how rare it was for him to be in this situation, included in the activities of these two couples. His relationship with Behrendsen and Presslein was normally centered around trout and, occasionally, salmon, but here he was, practically like one of the family.

He thought about Rachel. Family. She would probably be with Chippewas today. The image of his hunting knife, the sharp ten inch blade and wound leather hasp, all wrapped like a baby in his old blue towel, burned its way into his mind's eye. He mentally took it out of its sheath and scrutinized the curve of the blade, the whet of the edge, and then carefully re-wrapped it. The Indians had separated him from his family and brought him together with these families. Common denominator. His eyes popped open.

"Hey there, John," said Presslein. "Where's that niece of your's today, anyway?" Rich told me she's stayin' with you, but nobody's ever seen her. Bessie here was hoping she'd come along with you for the picnic, at least."

Kohler remembered that he wanted to tell the men about the barbecued dog, and he opened his mouth, then shut it. "Uh, she's with friends. Somebody she met studying."

"Shame. Well, if she shows anywhere, you be sure to point her out to us."

"Sure, sure." *Not on your life*, Kohler thought. *Not on your life.*

The crowd had grown quite large, and stirred about like cattle before a thunderstorm. People craned their necks down toward the junction of Skanee and Main and murmured about parades never starting on time. But presently there could be heard the faint resonance of the bass drum, and then the whisper of trombones and tubas. Finally the first car full of dignitaries turned the corner onto Skanee. It was a red 1965 Buick LeSabre convertible, in mint condition. Kohler knew it was Roger Pagel's pride and joy. The mayor of L'Anse, William Lonenen, and the state representative of the district, Carl Pakkola, sat high upon the back seat, by the trunk.

"There comes trouble," said Behrendsen. "Pakkola ought to stop being so soft on Indian rights and start caring about the condition of the white commercial fishermen in these parts."

"Well, you know politics," said Harry. "He's climbin' the political ladder, and it don't matter what the little guy is going through, politicians got to stick to popular issues. They like the red boys in Lansing. Makes folks seem real big-hearted."

The first autos passed and the L'Anse High School Marching Band followed, then the floats. The Girl Scouts and the 4-H and Kelney's Insurance Company; just about every business and organization in town had something. The Keweenaw Bay Tribal Council sponsored the ninth float, and all of the members were atop the display. In the center was Harold Sharp, wearing a Sioux war bonnet.

"Whew! I thought I smelled something coming! Presslein held his nose and Behrendsen and Kohler smirked.

"Yeah, they're all farting from eating' barbecued dog," Kohler said.

The other two men laughed, and their wives glared at them. Presslein's long teeth gleamed in the sun. "Thought they wouldn't be eatin' that stuff 'till the picnic, now, John."

"That's true, but you know it's hard not to take a little nibble now and then while it's cookin'" he was pleased that he had been able to use the joke after all.

As the car carrying the tribal council passed, three men broke through the lines of spectators just a few feet to the right of where Kohler and his friends were placed.

"Red Uncle Toms!" they screamed at the Council.

"Apples! You betray the memories of our ancestors!" The men were dressed in blue jeans and scarlet, long-sleeved shirts. Each had long hair and wore a headband.

"We feel shame for you!" The leader had the longest hair, tied in a ponytail reaching to the small of his back. It was Thomas Crane.

"There's our boy," Behrendsen said with a snarl. "He's the one needs to be taught a lesson or two."

Crane and his companions walked out into the street and followed the Tribal Council. They continued to call "Shame!" and "Apple!" to the obvious discomfort of the people on the float. Finally Thomas Crane spit after the float, then turned on his heel and stalked away.

The crowd parted like the Red Sea and the three in scarlet shirts passed through and disappeared behind the Post Office, leaving the spectators murmuring and looking at one another and shaking their heads. Crane was not popular with the whites because of his vocal and unabashed racial hatred.

Kohler, now standing, glared after the departing Indians. "I sure would like to see him pickled in a jar," he said, his voice thick with hatred. The blood had rushed to his face and made it feel like it was aflame, and rivulets of perspiration were running from his armpits and down his sides.

"Don't worry, buddy. We'll back him down a bit," Presslein said in a low tone.

"Well, I think it's a stitch, if you ask me," said Behrendsen. "They can't even get along with each other, coming out here in front of the entire white public like that and making a show. Can you beat it?"

The parade straggled on, though the audience was obviously disrupted, and by the time the last few Boy Scouts marched past the crowds were dispersing quickly. Kohler and his friends folded the aluminum lawn chairs and toted them back toward Behrendsen's Dodge. The women stopped to chat with neighbors and the men chafed at the slowing of progress.

Finally Bessie and Ida arrived, chiding their husbands for their impatience, and Behrendsen and his wife took the front seat and Kohler slipped into the back with Presslein and his spouse.

The picnic grounds at Baraga State Park were already crowded with people from

L'Anse and the surrounding area when the five arrived.

"You see, Ida, I told you to get a move on instead of flapping your gums back there. Most of the good spaces are taken because you were dragging your feet," Behrendsen complained to his wife.

"You're just too much in a hurry to bite into the fried chicken, is all," she responded good-naturedly.

After locating a vacant picnic table the ladies laid out the chicken, baked beans, potato salad, relishes, and homemade breads and pies, and Kohler began to forget himself in the feast. He enjoyed the banter of the married couples, though he said little himself. Presslein had brought a cooler full of beer, and offered one to Kohler.

"No thanks, Harry. It doesn't agree with me too good."

"Come on. You can call a truce for the Fourth of July picnic, can't you?"

Kohler considered a moment, and decided to accept a can. If his stomach started up, he'd lay off.

"Good!" Presslein popped the top and handed the beverage to Kohler.

Kohler downed the cold beer, and stuffed himself with chicken and potato salad, then had another beer, and some more food. He was feeling physically uncomfortable, but jolly. The conversation of the couples never flagged. They left the picnic table and sprawled out on blankets and in the lawn chairs. Kohler selected a chaise lounge and settled himself into it.

"Hey, John, how about some of those old Matt and Lew stories of your's. Bessie, Ida, you'd love to hear these stories. He got 'em from a couple of old codgers when he was a kid."

"Oh, that sounds like something," responded Ida.

"Tell us some, John," Bessie said.

Kohler felt terribly agreeable and began to recount a Silver Jack tale. When that was through, he told another, then another. He lolled on the chaise lounge and had another beer, propping himself up on his elbow so he could gesticulate with his other hand. Suddenly he stopped cold.

"What's the matter with you, Kohler?" Behrendsen had brought his beer midway to his mouth and stopped. "You look like somebody just whacked you across the chops with a dead salmon."

Kohler watched some young people saunter past a few yards away. They were deep in conversation. There were three men in their early twenties, two with longish black hair, and one that had been at Kohler's house the day he went to Green Bay. With them were three young women. Two were Chippewas, and one was Rachel.

Kohler jumped from the lounge, a strange salivating reflex in his throat and mouth. He dashed away from the others, trying to find a restroom, but knowing he wouldn't make it to one. Stepping behind a clump of bushes, he began to retch violently, and vomited for what seemed like a long time. When he stopped and staggered out, wiping his mouth with a handkerchief, he was weak in the knees. He leaned against a nearby pine for a few minutes, then walked back toward the picnic table.

"Say, old buddy, you all right?" Behrendsen came close and stuck his round face close to Kohler's

He didn't answer, but just dropped his body heavily into the chaise lounge. His stomach was a white-hot kiln, and his limbs were made out of water. He lay his head back and spoke nothing for a few seconds.

"Just those beers," he finally said. "Guess my stomach couldn't take it after all."

"Is there anything I can get for you, John?" Mrs. Behrendsen bent near with a concerned expression. "I might have some Pepto Bismol or something here in the car. I always carry a nice little first aid kit with me."

"That would be fine, thank you."

Ida went to the Dodge and returned with the medicine and a large spoon. "Now open up," she said, as she poured some of the pink liquid into the utensil.

Kohler thought he would retch again at the sight of the color, but he managed to control the impulse and swallow the proffered medicine.

"Good Lord, woman, he ain't a child."

"That's all right, Rich. He isn't exactly feeling well right now, either. These bachelor boys need some sympathy once in a while."

Kohler was embarrassed and sat upright. "Thank you, Ida. I think I'll be fine, now."

Presslein looked at him. "Your sickness came on in an awful hurry, there, John. You have that happen often?"

"Just the beer, like I said. I got a bit of a tender stomach, I guess. I should never have had that brew. Sometimes even coffee'll do a number on me." He stopped talking because he suddenly perceived himself to sound like a hypochondriac.

The five people spent the rest of the afternoon at the park, gathering back around the picnic table for several hands of Euchre. Kohler felt better after the dose of Pepto Bismol, but he couldn't forget what had caused the sudden upset. He looked around warily, afraid that Rachel would return and see him. Her companions were obviously Indians. What could he say to Behrendsen and Presslein if she flounced up with her stupid little self and introduced her group? Especially considering what had been planned for the evening.

By six o'clock a cool breeze began to blow off Keweenaw Bay and the ladies announced that it was time to pack up and get for home. They had things to clean up before the fireworks. The friends all fit back into the Dodge and drove to Behrendsen's house. The men carried everything in and then lolled about on the porch while Ida and Bessie washed dishes and put leftovers in the refrigerator.

"We still on for later?" Behrendsen bent forward in the lawn chair in which he was seated. "What about it, John? You feel up to it?"

"I wouldn't miss it for the world," Kohler said.

"Well, we're going to have to come up with something to tell the ladies. They'll be wanting to go to the fireworks, from the way they was talking."

"Maybe we can say that we just want to go for a drive, check on some new fly equipment at John's place or something," Presslein said.

"Well, go feel them out, Harry. I guess that idea is as good as any."

Presslein went into the house and returned a moment later with a grin on his face. "Boys, we don't have to tell them nothing. They'd just as soon stay here. They're tired from all the cooking and cleaning up, so we can just go by our lonesomes."

The men waited until the sun hung in a blazing orange ball on the horizon, then stretched themselves and told the women they would be back after the show.

"I'll drive this time," Presslein offered, and they walked toward his Chevrolet.

Behrendsen transferred something wrapped in rags from his trunk to Presslein's.

"Hold on a minute," Kohler said. He strode quickly to his truck and withdrew the blue towel, then got into the back seat of the Chevy.

"What ya got there, John? We weren't planning on going for a swim, now." Kohler unwrapped the towel and took the knife from its brown leather sheath. He handed it to Behrendsen. Rich ran his thumb gingerly along the edge of the blade.

"Jimmeny, Kohler, this thing is whetted deadly sharp. It'll do some nice damage on those dang red boys' nets for sure. Harry and me brought some good hedge shears." He handed the blade back to Kohler.

"Well, just maybe I'll find some other use for that knife tonight."

Presslein leaned forward and looked over at Kohler. "Stop that joshin', John. We just want to slow these Indians down a little bit. We got no intention of hurtin' anybody bodily."

Kohler was silent for a moment and thoughtfully played with his knife, constantly stroking its edge, and using the tip to clean beneath his fingernails.

"I guess I'm ready to do more than that, if it comes to it," he said. "I been doing some thinking lately. More and more we all been pushed around by the redskins. We know that. You boys can't catch half the fish, a quarter of the fish, you used to catch, yet you have to watch while they go out and bring in just about whatever they want, whenever they want. Oh sure, they supposedly have their regulations, but you and I both know that it's only paper to them, and they're out there destroying your livelihood with their catches. They shoot deer whenever they feel like it, wherever they feel like it. They fish out of streams all year round, regardless of seasons. And I was thinkin' they've been doing things to me all my life, and if I ever did anything back at all it was in self-defense. "I remember years ago some old buck nearly run me off the road up here on 41. And what do we do? We take it and take it and let it go because we're good, law-abiding citizens. Well, I've decided enough is enough. I'm not willing to play defense anymore, boys. I'm going on the offensive. Search and destroy, as those Vietnam fellas used to say. And this little escapade is just the beginning."

"Well, Kohler, true enough they've done all those things you said, but you make it sound like your family's been wiped out by them, or something."

"Close enough." Kohler ticked off in his head; his mother, Anita, now Rachel. The Indians might as well have surrounded the wagon train and set it aflame, the losses were just about as heavy.

Presslein continued, "All I'm saying is that we have to use a little wisdom. I want things turned around, but I'm going to be mighty careful about how I go about doing it. I figure about everybody will be at the fireworks tonight. The tribal police and the sheriffs, too. That's why it's a good time to do what we're going to do. It's safe. But anything else? I don't think so. I don't care to get my butt put in jail."

The sun had sunk below the horizon and Presslein put his lights on in the dusk. There was little traffic on 41. A few stragglers to the fireworks were wending their way in the same direction as Presslein's Chevy, but they turned off down the short dirt road to Sand Beach. The Chevrolet continued on about a mile further, toward the tribal docks where the Chippewa commercial fishing boats were moored. Presslein slowed the car, cut the headlights and passed the entrance to the rutted road leading down to the bay. A few yards further was a small picnic area, set back into some pines and shielded from the road. The car glided in and Presslein shut off the engine, coasting to a stop beneath the trees. Though it was dark twilight on the highway, it was quite black beneath the pines. They exited the car very quietly.

"Shh." Behrendsen stood stock-still and whispered, "just listen for a minute."

The only sound was the faint murmur of voices carried over the waters of the bay from Sand Beach. After another moment Presslein quietly opened the trunk of the car and removed two pairs of hedge clippers, then carefully closed the lid.

When his eyes adjusted to the darkness, Kohler could make out a faint light scar on the ground that trailed off toward the bay. The three followed this path through the brush until it opened onto the road just above the boat docks. They stopped again in the shadow of the trees and surveyed the area. Nothing moved. There was no sound. Behrendsen motioned for them to continue and they stayed close to the trees until they reached the wide-open space in front of the docks. Three boats were moored in a row, fishing trawlers, with nets hung on large winches on the back of each craft. One final look around and they ran across the dim open area and leaped onto the first boat. Again they cowered and listened. Nothing.

Presslein spoke in a low voice. "Let's go right down the row. Be careful you don't trip over nothing."

They proceeded to the rear of the boat and began to hack and cut at the nets with shears and knife.

"That's Crane's boat next to us," Behrendsen said.

Kohler could just barely trace the word "Ki-wi-wai-non-ing" on the stern. It was the Indian word that had been corrupted to Keweenaw. He curled his upper lip in disgust.

The fireworks began with a bright flash high up in the night sky, and a spilling of red and white streamers of light. Several seconds later a hollow boom rippled out over the bay. The three men paused momentarily to watch as the explosives were mirrored like giant asters in the dark waters. Each new flash bathed their faces in light.

"Come on," Kohler said. "Let's go get Crane's nets." He felt an eagerness in the pit of his stomach, and reflected on how he especially hated everything that Thomas Crane stood for.

Harry took one more cut at the nets and the three vaulted over the side of the first boat onto the Ki-wi-wai-non-ing. They had no trouble seeing anything with the occasional explosions from the fireworks down the beach.

"Shh. What now?" Presslein ducked behind some gear on the deck of the trawler.

The flash of headlights and the crunching of gravel revealed a vehicle proceeding slowly down the rutted drive toward the docks. The beams of light bounced up and down as it hit each chuckhole. The three men crouched low and looked for cover.

"You know it's gotta be an Indian; no one else would be coming down here at this time of night," said Behrendsen. "Can you tell if it's the tribal cops?"

Kohler raised his head over a barrel and lowered it again quickly. "No, it's just a pickup."

"Our butts are in a sling, fellas, if this boy finds us."

The pickup drove up to the dock and stopped. Kohler could hear the hollow sound of footsteps on the dock approaching the boats, passing the first and continuing on toward the Ki-wi-wai-non-ing. Then the footsteps boarded her.

Behrendsen and Presslein were jammed beneath some gear as tightly as they could fit, but Kohler stood up slowly, against the wheelhouse wall, hardly daring to breathe. *It must be Crane on the opposite side of the boat*, he thought. Kohler pressed his body flat, flat against the wall, and his muscles were so taut he thought they would snap like an over-stretched guitar string. Beads of sweat broke out on his upper lip and he could taste the faint saltiness on his tongue when he ran it around the outside of his dry mouth.

The Indian checked something on the other side of the trawler, then walked toward the stern where the nets were hung. Would he make the round and come up this side? Kohler wondered. He became aware of the haft of his knife, gripped tightly in his right hand. And he knew if the Indian did come around, he would strike him, quickly, surely. He raised his arm just slightly, so that the blade was pointed out, at the ready. From the rear of the trawler he heard Crane mumble something unintelligible, perhaps in Chippewa, and move back along the opposite side of the boat to the spot where he had boarded. Then he slowly approached the bow in front of the wheelhouse, just feet from where Kohler was standing. The white man's muscles were screaming from the tension, and he longed to gasp hard for breath. *Come on, savage*, he thought.

Crane stopped and rested his arms on the railing. Kohler could just barely see him out of the corner of his eye. The Indian lit a cigarette, and the orange glow contrasted with the white of the fireworks reflected on the bay.

Kohler struggled inwardly and visualized the deed. All it would take, he thought, is one well-coordinated move. By the time he knew I was there, the knife would have reached its mark, but when he imagined the weapon striking the denim jacket, feeling the momentary resistance of cloth and skin, and then of rib. No. He nearly blacked out with the thought. And yet he desperately desired to strike out, to fight, to lash at ... at what? At what? Kohler blinked the perspiration from his eyes and stood frozen in his impotent hatred.

Thomas Crane leaned against the railing for a few more moments, filling the air with the cigarette smoke, a sweet smell when mixed with the scent of the bay. Kohler listened to his soft sucking and exhaling and the gentle slap of the waves against the side of the trawler until the Indian turned abruptly and climbed back down the side and into his pickup. The engine roared in the momentary stillness between two blasts of fireworks, and gravel and sand flew beneath the wheels as he drove away.

When the sound of the truck turned upon the highway , Behrendsen and Presslein slowly unfolded themselves from their positions.

"Jeeze, that was a close call." Behrendsen stood to his feet. "How the heck you got away with not being seen is more than I can know, Kohler. Guess that bull about Indians having a sixth sense isn't all that true after all."

As Kohler allowed his muscles to relax he was aware of being very cold. He reached to touch his flannel shirt and found it soaked thoroughly.

"Let's get out of here," said Presslein.

"No!" Kohler answered sharply. "We'll finish what we came to do." He stalked to the stern of the boat and began to slash viciously at the nets, harder and harder, ripping and cutting, like a man gone mad.

Presslein and Behrendsen said nothing more, but went to work with their hedge shears. When Crane's nets were in shreds, they boarded the last trawler and cut its nets, also.

The fireworks were ended by the time the men finished their destruction and they hurried back to Presslein's car and in seconds were on the highway. Harry turned on the lights when they passed the road to the docks.

"I thought you were going to kill Crane," Behrendsen said to Kohler. "He got so close to you, I thought you were gonna do it. I was prayin' to dear Jesus you wouldn't, but I was sure scared you was going to do it."

"I should have," Kohler answered. "I don't know why I didn't."

Somebody destroyed our nets last night. It must have been after I was there; I went over to the docks just as the fireworks were starting down at Sand Beach. Everything seemed pretty quiet, then.

As soon as Willie Barnett found the mess on his trawler this morning, he went straight to Dan Roche and they called an emergency meeting of the tribal council. They are putting up a reward for information about it, but I don't think too much of their solution. I figure it had to be whites; it had to be.

There's a lot of bad blood between the whites and Ojibwe, now. That's because some of us are finally standing up like men and honoring the memories of our ancestors. We are fighting for the rights that are inherently ours.

The white man has no business here. He came here as a thief and destroyer. He stripped our people of their livelihood and their humanity, and now he rages because we insist that he live by the treaties that were made between the government and the tribes. Everything that is wrong with this land is wrong because the white man came here in the first place. Before he set foot on this land the rivers and lakes teemed with whitefish and sturgeon, but no more. He has over-fished the waters and constructed the St. Lawrence Seaway so that the sea lamprey could come into the Great Lakes and destroy the whitefish. Then came the zebra mussel, and all the other invasive species. The whites' factories, farms, and mills dump poisons into the waters, and they must warn people against eating too much fish. And after all this, because we make the white man live up to the treaties and allow us to fish according to them, they complain and say that the Indian commercial fishing operations have ruined fishing in the Great Lakes.

So they did this to our nets. But we will replace them and go on fishing. I do admit, I do not always obey their laws. Why should I? They don't even obey their own laws. Maybe it would be better for the Anishinaabeg, our people, to over-fish the great waters and use all the fish, than for the whites to have any. Perhaps then they could begin to understand what it is to be subject to privation, to starvation. It would be good for their souls, if they have any. Nevertheless, I would not dishonor all our relations that way, and upset the balance that Creator placed on Mother Earth. The whites, now, they think nothing of balance or respect.

Yes, the tribal council will make an effort to find the ones who did this recent destruction, but what if they discover that it was a white man who did it? They will not exact a strict penalty. No, they will accommodate the whites, as they always do. I am tired of Native American people accommodating whites, like my father did. My given name from birth is really Thomas Laughing Crane, but my father just used Crane because he so much wanted to fit into the white way of living. He moved off the reservation into town and got a job in a factory. He became an apple, red on the outside, white on the inside. But he paid a price for trying to become something he wasn't, and he fell to drinking and died in a drunken stupor.

Our Ojibwe people are called Anishinaabeg, a word for original people. We came up out of this land, and we are part of this land, as are the rocks and the beaver and the deer and the trees. When an Indian is removed from the land and gets a job in a factory, or tills the earth in the white man's style of farming, he is emasculated. He is killed just as surely as if a knife were plunged into his heart. Let me hunt and fish for my livelihood, as did my forefathers, and I shall live. I also came into the traditional religion because it is in my blood. I am full-blooded Anishanaabeg; not a drop of white blood taints me. I am proud to be one of the original people.

Now, the whites have such silly beliefs about us. They have concocted a story that says that the Native peoples came from Siberia over a land bridge that has since been flooded with water. How is it that they think this? We believe that it was our people who were created first by the Great Spirit. We came up out of this land and some or our people traveled far to the north and west and crossed the Bering Straits and were the fathers of those tribes in Asia that resemble us so much. Why is this not possible in the white man's thinking? Because whites look at history from white eyes, and do not see that they may be wrong, that they are not the chosen people, and the earth has not come about as they willed.

A white poet wrote a great work that is based on Ojibwe legends. Everyone has heard it: "By the shores of Gitche Gumee, By the shining Big-Sea-Water." But Longfellow uses the name Hiawatha, which is not Ojibwe, but Iroquois, for his hero. And he distorted the character of that one, also. We know him as Manabozho, the trickster, and it was he that created the world as we know it now.

It all began many, many years ago, when Manabozho was coming across the ice on Lake Superior. He looked up and saw the wolf people, and joined them for the hunt. He called them his nephews.

These wolves fed him in ways that we do not understand today. One wolf said, "Our uncle is getting hungry. Feed him." And so another wolf threw a moccasin at Manabozho and told him to pull the sock from it. Manabozho thought that it was rude to throw this stinking moccasin at him, so he tossed it back to the wolf, who then pulled a tenderloin of deer from the sock. They cooked that tenderloin, and some bear fat, over the fire. Manabozho tried this trick himself, but it did not work.

The next day Manabozho went hunting with the wolves and more magic was done. He was accompanied by an old wolf, the father of the young ones in the pack, and this old wolf turned a pile of wolf dung into a good warm wolf skin. But Manabozho couldn't see things for what they really were, and so kept getting in trouble with the old wolf, who was trying to teach him about these things.

The young wolves had run ahead, and eventually the old one and Manabozho came upon blood, and then on the pack and their kill. The young wolves regurgitated a great deal of food and fed Manabozho well. He stayed with those wolves for a while and then, when they got ready to go, they left one young wolf with Manabozho, to keep him company and to hunt for him. Manabozho and the young wolf went on like this happily for some time until the manidog, some spirits, became angry and jealous. The manidog tricked the young wolf while he was hunting, and destroyed him. Well, Manabozho found out from a kingfisher what happened, and he was very mad that someone would harm his nephew. He decided that he would not allow this to go unpunished, and by and by he got to the place where the manidog sun themselves. He went up on a little knoll and turned himself into a stump.

The next morning was real nice, and the manidog sent turtles and sunfish close to the shore to spy out the situation. The manidog lived in the water, and the turtles and fish were their guards. Also, a red loon came up out of the water, and then a white loon. They both reported to the manidog that it was a nice day, so the head manido said, "Let's go up," and they did. It caused the entire lake to be riled up.

One manido was a big brown bear, and one was a white one, and then there was a big snake, and all sorts of other animals. One of these manidog took a hide out for the king manido to put his head on. Manabozho could see that it was the hide of his nephew the wolf, and he was very upset about that.

The manidog noticed the stump that was really Manabozho, and they were suspicious of it. So the king sent the snake to test the stump. He coiled around the stump and almost squeezed the heart out of Manabozho, but nothing happened. Then one of the bears scratched the stump until Manabozho thought he couldn't stand it, but he held on. Then the manidog stopped being suspicious of the stump and went and lay down in the sand, and Manabozho wished that they would go to sleep and they did.

When the manidog were asleep, Manabozho stopped being a stump. He got up and killed the king with an arrow, and shot more arrows into the ones next to him, too. Then he ran for all he was worth. A woodchuck hid him in her burrow and so he escaped the manidog that time.

Manabozho was wandering, and he ran across an old woman who was using basswood bark to cure the manido that he had shot and only wounded. At first the old woman thought that she might be talking to Manabozho, but he tricked her with words into believing that it was not he. Then she told him that, when the manidog killed his nephew the wolf, she had been the one who had eaten the nephew.

When Manabozho heard that he was very mad, and he hit that old woman over the head with his bow and killed her. Then he took her clothes off her and put them on himself and turned himself into one who looked like she did. Disguised in this way, he went to the house of the manido she was trying to nurse back to health with the basswood bark. They thought that Manabozho was really the old granny, so they let him in. Instead of helping the wounded manido, he finished him off, and then skinned the king, whose body was there. Other manidog were waiting outside of the lodge, and after a while they wondered why granny was taking so long, and they went inside. Manabozho had escaped already, but the other manidog saw what he had done. They were really mad, and they went right after him.

Manabozho was running as fast as he could, and as he ran, he felt the earth shake like an earthquake, and he could hear the roar of the water. He looked back and could see a great wall of water chasing him, turning over trees and rocks and everything. He ran like the wind for a big bluff that was in front of him. It had a tall pine tree right at the top. He got to that tree and said, "Brother, we are going to die," but the tree said, "No, just climb me to the top."

Manabozho still had the pack that contained the skin of the manidog king, and he wouldn't let go of it. He began to climb with that pack. He climbed to the top of the tree, and pretty soon the water came up to his feet. He asked the tree if it couldn't do something about that, so the tree began to stretch itself, and got away from the water for a while. But the water just kept rising, and the tree stretched, but after some time it couldn't do it anymore. The water got up to Manabozho's chin, and he had to stretch his neck. It finally stopped rising just below his nose. If it had gone two inches higher, he would have drowned.

He looked around him, and it was water everywhere, covering everything. In the water were all sorts of animals swimming, and he called out to them, "We can only be saved one way. If one of you can go down into the water deep enough to get a little earth, we might live."

The loon, who was a good diver, was the first to try and get the dirt. He dove down, but he couldn't hold his breath long enough and he drowned trying. Next an otter tried, but he died too. The beaver dove as far as he could, but he couldn't do it either. Finally Manabozho asked the muskrat to dive to get the earth. The muskrat dove all the way down and managed to get his paws into the mud at the bottom and start back up to the top. He passed out before he got to the surface, and Manabozho plucked him out of the water.

He felt bad that the muskrat had been so heroic and apparently not succeeded. But then he saw that something was clutched in the muskrat's paws, and he pried them open and got out a few grains of sand and some mud.

Manabozho took that earth and began to roll it around in his hands and it began to get bigger and bigger. He started to scatter pieces of it around him, and it became islands, and the animals were able to get out of the water. Soon there was enough land that Manabozho could get out, too. Then he summoned a big bird, the Gi-wanasi, to go around in a big circle, which made the island grow bigger as he flew. That bird flew for four days, and that wasn't long enough, so Manabozho sent the eagle out and he flew around a long time, until Manabozho was satisfied. When he was through, Manabozho said that this island would be where his relations would make their home.

And that is how the world began according to our legends. I heard this story from a grandfather named He Who Listens, a man who became my spiritual father, because my real father didn't follow the ways or our people, and didn't care. But I was destined to return to the old ways, and the old beliefs. The blood of our people runs hot in my veins. Some of the tribe scoff at those of us who believe in the old stories, and how we pass them on to our children. There are some of the Anishinaabeg who try to live in both worlds, the world of the white man, and the world of the red man. They believe the religions of the whites, and forget that there is no word for religion in the Ojibwe language. That is because our religion is who we are, our relationship with the earth, and with the water and the animals. This is the way I have chosen.

I have been called old fashioned and uneducated, even stupid, because I believe such things. But I am neither stupid nor uneducated. And my beliefs are no more foolish than any other belief. The Christians believe that a man in a great boat re-populated the world after the flood. Is that any less foolish than the Manabozho legend? I believe what I believe because I have chosen to believe it. For, don't we all choose to believe whatever it is that we hang the frame of our lives on? Yes. It is a matter of choice.

I have reason for my beliefs. Much more than some who believe based on the words of a moldy old book. I have the Earth. It sings and whispers. I have heard the trees muttering in the forest, I hear them speaking to me, for all things have spirits. I have heard the groaning of the rocks. I do not understand what they have to say, it is for holy men to know these things, but I know that I have heard them.

I think that too many Native Americans have accepted the white man's myths. They are ludicrous to me. Some believe, as do the Christians, that the Great Spirit sent his son to earth to teach us. That may have merit, but I don't think He would have sent him to the white people. I don't think it is true because of what the whites have done in the name of their son of God.

The most stupid belief the whites try to foist on us, though, is the one about how everything came into being; that some amino acids just happened to wash up on a beach millions and millions of years ago and were hit by lightening or something and then somehow became all things that we see and do not see; the amik, or beaver; or great makwa, the bear; or no-noskau-see, the hummingbird; and the Anishanaabeg! It makes me laugh to think about it.

I would like to be a member of the Midewiwin, the Grand Medicine Society. If it was not for He Who Listens I would probably be ignorant of these things, and still be nameless in the traditions of our people.

One day when I had turned twenty years old, I was in a pickup with an uncle, Ron Peske. We were traveling through the reservation on Skanee Road. Up ahead was a man walking slowly, and we could tell that he was an Ojibwe. Uncle decided to stop and pick this man up and give him a ride. When the man got into the pickup with us I was struck by something about him. He had long hair, in one single braid down his back, and it was streaked with grey. His face did not look old, really, though it was creased about the mouth and eyes. I could not tell what age the man was. He was dressed in jeans and a denim jacket over a bright green flannel shirt, and around his waist was a beaded belt of wonderful design, and hanging from the belt was a small beaver skin medicine bag decorated with porcupine quills.

Even though my father had tried to urge us away from the old traditions, I had heard of them. My mother said little to us, for she was afraid of my father, but another uncle, Daniel Laughing Crane, would tell some old stories to me sometimes when I was a child. But Daniel lived over in Minnesota on the White Earth Reservation, and I rarely saw him. Nevertheless, he had fed in me a desire to know more of these things, and when this man got into my uncle's pickup that fall day, I knew that I was sitting by a man of wisdom.

He did not say anything to us, really, and in his silence I was even more convinced of his knowledge. Before we let him off I asked him where he lived, and later in the week I sought him out.

"I knew you were coming," he said to me when he saw me at his door. "The mikinak, the turtle, revealed this to me in a dream last night. Come in, I've been waiting for you."

So that was how it started with me. He Who Listens was a medicine man and a member of the Midewiwin, a man of much wisdom. I spent many days at his house near the pineries, learning the traditions of our ancestors and participating in the sweat lodge. I felt like I had at last come home.

Then one night I had a dream that I was deep in the forest, a woods so thick with pine that the light was dulled as it came through the needles above me. I saw a strange lodge built of birch bark, and could hear the chanting of people, both men and women, from the inside. The drums and rattles accompanied them. It was the mikinak dancing around the outside of the lodge, and then I woke up. I went the next day to He Who Listens and asked him about the dream.

He just smiled and fixed me some tea. "You will join the Midewiwin," he said. "You have dreamed the dream of entrance." I have not reached that goal. It is said that a person must be purified to belong to the Medicine Society, and be of blameless heart, and let go of hatred and spite. I know I have not reached that place.

In the early days of our tribe it was customary that a young person not be named permanently until they were sent away into the wilderness to fast and learn who they were from Spirit. During this time they would have a vision or dream, and whatever they dreamed about would indicate what their name would be. If you dreamed about an animal, you would have the powers of that animal in your life. I, of course, had never done this. It is a practice not much adhered to today, even by tribe-members who care about our traditions. We have accepted the white way of the birth name, and usually it has little, or no, personal significance. I wanted to be one to follow all of the old ways, though, and I asked He Who Listens about going on the vision quest.

"You show your wisdom, Thomas. You should do as your desire dictates," he said.

"I am past the usual age," I replied.

"No matter, go anyway. You will receive the power of your ancestors through your commitment to this task."

I thought long and hard about where I would go and seek the vision. So much of the land is covered by white disease, and even though my people roamed this peninsula for many years before the priests and trappers came from France, I felt like there were few places where an Ojibwe could go and feel that he belonged. But as I thought, I was reviewing in my mind some of the lodge stories that He Who Listens had told me, about Manabozho and the windigoo, and I thought about where in this land there were spiritually significant places. The two that really came to my mind were Mackinac Island and the area that whites call Pictured Rocks. I had heard many stories about our father's pilgrimages to Mackinac Island, and how spirits dance there on certain nights. But that island has been entirely taken over by the whites. I could not go to accomplish my vision there.

Pictured Rocks and the Grande Sable Dunes, though, are not so cluttered with whites. Whites need cars, most of them, to get somewhere. Many of them are lazy, and will not go where transportation does not exist. Most of the Pictured Rocks can be seen only two ways, from a boat on Lake Superior, or by hiking the trails along the beaches and cliffs. There are a few roads, and a few people. The area is known in our lodge stories as the land where the great Manabozho walked. There was no question in my mind; I would go there for the vision quest.

My brother Jim drove me over there, about one hundred and thirty miles from the bay. One road stretches out to the cliffs into the national lakeshore area, and ends at a rock formation that the whites named Miner's Castle. Jim left me there and agreed to pick me up three days later, around noon or one o'clock. Before he left to drive back to L'Anse he tried to talk me out of my quest.

"You're crazy for doing this, you know," he said. "All this is old stuff, Tom, old meaningless myths and legends. They can't help us to live in the white man's world. Come back with me, and we'll just write this off as a nice drive."

What I couldn't seem to get through to him was that I didn't want to live in the white man's world, and somehow I believed that the Great Spirit would show a way of resistance, maybe of destruction, of the warped world that they had built. Finally Jim gave up.

"You're a fool, I think," he said, "but you're my brother. I'll be back on time. Don't let the bears get you."

"The bears are my brothers," I replied.

I sought my vision in the fall of the year. This is my favorite time, around the end of September and first of October when the leaves on the trees turn so many different colors. The birch and aspen shine like pure gold, and the sugar maples are butter yellow with pinto spots of scarlet. The pine and spruce look all the more regal in their dark green against all the bright shades. It is the time called Indian summer, which I always liked because of the name. The days are mild, and the nights cool, and the weather so clear you can see for miles across the waters of Lake Superior.

When Jim drove away I unpacked my lunch bag. I knew it would be the last food for a few days. I ate the Spam sandwiches and an apple slowly, and drank some water from the fountain that the park service had installed at the small picnic area at Miner's Castle. Then I struck out into the woods along the cliffs. My plan was to walk until I found a certain formation of cliff that contained a large indentation, big enough for a man to curl up in. I knew that such characteristics were common to the rocks along the lake. I had done a sweat two days before, and it would have to suffice as the prelude to the vision quest. For my quest I desired to be in touch with the earth and the wind and the spirits in the elements.

I walked for much of the afternoon, east, toward the Grand Sable Dunes, sometimes exploring a cliff, sometimes just gazing out over the water of the lake. It shines emerald green, as clear as a gem, off those high cliffs. All of the colors that day were so brilliant that they nearly blinded me, the water, the deep blue of the cloudless sky, the orange, red and gold of the trees. I felt overcome by the visual power of the scene.

It was late afternoon when I came to the cliff that was to be my resting-place. I knew it at once. It rose up like a ship from the sea of forest on one side, and jutted out over the lake in a series of ledges on the opposite side. I climbed around by the water and found a small cave several feet below the top. It was almost big enough for me to stand up in, and I am nearly six feet tall. It recessed into the sandstone about four or five feet, and was maybe five feet wide. A ledge in front reached out over the lake, seventy-five feet above the surface of the water. It was perfect. I was elated.

It was growing dark and I climbed back to the crest of the cliff where I had a view of the forests and the lake for many miles. I watched the night come and make kettles of blackness in the woods below; and the blackness spread like dark molasses and finally engulfed the trees.

By the light of the dying sun reflected from the great water I crept down into my small cave. When I leaned back against the rock inside, it was like leaning against the breast of my mother, warm from Grandfather Sun. The lake threw off sparks from the crest of the waves until there was no more light in the sky, and then it became a vast funnel of blackness.

After dark the air turned very cold, but the heat in the rock kept me warm for many hours. I could not sleep because my belly was gnawing at itself like a bear trying to claw grubs from a rotted stump. That's when I began to realize how soft I really was. There had always been something, somewhere, for me to eat, even when my father drank up everything we had. If there wasn't at least a can of beans, I could go to my uncles or aunts for a handout. But now there was no food purposely; I would have to become a man in the way my ancestors had for hundreds of years. What had at first seemed a very romantic and spiritual thing suddenly took on a physically painful aspect. That first night I also learned that there is only slight separation between the world of the spirit and the world of bodies. They are interwoven in ways we do not realize until we open ourselves up to that knowledge.

Before dawn my hunger pains subsided, but the rock had lost its warmth and I shivered violently against the north wind coming off the lake. I pulled my denim jacket about me as best I could and wondered if I really wanted to seek this medicine further. I trembled in the cold until the sky began to grow a charcoal grey color and lighten little by little. Then along the eastern horizon there was a streak of red and gold, and soon the sun came up. I climbed onto the cliff top to watch it rise.

After sunrise the air began to warm and my hunger came back, but I decided that this was something I must do, this fast, so I stayed there in the woods by the shore all day. I chanted some simple things that He Who Listens taught me, just messages to the spirits in the rocks and forest, and tried to remember as many lodge stories as I could, but I became bored. It was hard to concentrate on these things, hard to seek a sign from the Great Spirit.

My second night in the rock was worse than the first. I was colder, and I wish that I could have brought a blanket. But no, I wanted to leave myself open to the elements, to feel all that could be felt! I needed to do this quest the right way, without comforts. I was exhausted, and the hunger pangs would come and go. I fell asleep sometime before dawn. It was broad daylight when I awoke. I could not remember having any dreams, and when the hunger began again a new fear beset me. What if I didn't have any vision? What if the spirits failed to hear me, or speak to me, and I walked out of the woods in shame, with no medicine? What would He Who Listens think? It had never even crossed my mind that such a thing could happen. I was in a place of great medicine, of great significance in the legends of our people. Surely I would have a great vision or dream! That day I tried very hard to listen to the forest, and I prayed very hard. I did not wander too far from the cliff because I was becoming weak from lack of food. The thirst, though, was much worse, like a fire licking at my mouth, leaving it dry and crisp.

The night came again. I crawled into the small cave and thanked the sun that he had shined so brightly that day, for the rock was much warmer that the first night I stayed there. This was my last night, and I was very afraid that it would be light again and I would have to return home with no medicine. I was quite cozy in the rock; there was no wind, and I tried very hard to stay awake after the darkness fell, hoping that I would see or hear something. But I was feeling woozy from lack of food, especially since I am a lean person, with no fat to fall back on. My head and the inside of me was lighter than the outside, and felt like it wanted to float out of my body. The cave was warm and, try as I might to stay awake, I fell asleep soon after the light died from the sky.

I do not know what time it was when I awoke again. My first thought was that it was dawn because there was a light in the sky. Then I realized that it wasn't morning, but the northern lights that I was seeing. The faint green rays came in waves across the sky and looked like the blowing of a gauzy curtain against the backdrop of blackness. The vast stretch of water reflected the sky until the whole world seemed to be one great undulating flow of transparent green against deep black. I stared, unable to shut my eyes, and the hair on my head began to prickle and stand up straight. I fixed my eyes on the lights for a long time until I began to feel my being pulsate with them, my body and my spirit, ebbing and flowing with the lights in the sky and the great water around me.

It was later, I think that time had passed anyway, that I began to feel the prickling all over my body, and sensed a change in the atmosphere around me. I was still staring at the northern lights, but the sky began to change, also. I strained to see there, in front of me, what was happening. The lights were diminishing, breaking up, like someone was drawing them back to reveal the darkness beneath, and then it was darkness in just one area in front of me. In the center of the area I saw a swirling motion, like the vortex of a tornado, and it grew bigger and bigger until this section of sky before me was a swirling mass. Perhaps I realized at the time that my medicine was about to be revealed, but I remember sitting very still, experiencing a mixture of fear and awe.

Then, out of the very center of the great blackness, I saw the figure of a man, one who was colored blood red, all of him, even his hair. He looked very small, like he was a long way off, but I could tell he was coming closer, ever so slowly. Lightening flashed intermittently around his head. There was no sound for sometime, then I heard, very far off, the screaming of an eagle, such as it makes when it is circling high in the sky, hunting. Then I saw it, behind the red warrior, flying toward me. It was all black, with yellow eyes that blazed like the sun. The warrior and the eagle kept coming nearer to me, until I could see the man very well. The eagle began to circle around the warrior, always screaming. Its voice echoed off the rock around me. It circled slowly around the warrior four times, then flew very fast straight at me. It was coming, it kept coming, right at my head, so big I could tell that it easily had a six foot wingspan, and it was black as night. I raised my arms to shield my face just before it crashed into me, and that was the last thing I remember. All was darkness.

I awoke the next morning just as the sun was coming over the horizon. I felt strong, like I had eaten a good meal the night before. The thirst was gone, also. I climbed out of my cave and looked around, meditating on the vision I had, and wondering what it meant. I wished that I had a pipe to offer to the spirits, but all I had was a crushed pack of cigarettes in my jacket pocket. I took one out, tried to straighten it, then lit it and offered the smoke in each of the six directions.

I began to walk west to Miner's Castle, where Jim would pick me up. I got there before he did, and I sat watching the lake until he arrived.

"Well, how long have you been here? Chicken out?" he said.

"I just got here maybe an hour ago." I said nothing to him about the vision because I was afraid that he would laugh at me. I guess I was disappointed, too, that he didn't know that I'd seen it just by looking at me. I fancied that I had a different appearance. I knew I felt different.

"I brought you some grub. Here." He threw a bag at me with sandwiches and some cheese in it, and handed me a bottle of warm root beer. I ate before the drive back to the reservation.

I went straight to He Who Listens' house that evening, and when I got in the door he wore the expression I had expected Jim to wear. He knew that I had seen the vision.

"Tell me about it," he said, motioning me to sit down in a chair.

I told him all that had happened, from the first night until the time I met Jim back at Miner's Castle. He Who Listens smiled.

"Megasiawa," he said. "The Black Eagle. It is your medicine and it shall be your name."

"But what does the vision mean?"

My mentor seemed lost in thought for a few minutes. "I have heard of similar dreams and visions as I pow wow across the land. It is a prophetic dream, and you are a part of the prophecy."

"You called me Megasiawa. I am the eagle in the vision?"

"You are. You will go before the red warrior and tell people of his coming."

"And who is this red warrior? In my vision I felt that he had great power."

He Who Listens was quiet again for some time. "Since the early days many medicine men have believed that someone was coming to right the wrongs against the red man, to restore us to our land and our status as free men. You have heard of the ghost dancers. That idea never really died even after the whites put an end to the movement. Always there has been an undercurrent, here a prophecy, there a dream or vision. It is not widely known, and never spoken of to the whites. Most of our people do not believe, either," he said sadly. "But I believe that your vision is a part of this prophecy. You are Black Eagle, who helps pave the way for the warrior. It is a sacred mission. That is why you saw the megasiawa circle the warrior four times. Beyond this I can't tell you now."

I joined a secret society for those of us trying to resurrect the old ways soon after all this took place. It was one of the finest days of my life, listening to the Manabozho creation stories at the induction ceremonies, and planning how we would bring about the fulfillment of the vision and restoration of our rightful place on this land. Now I act as an emissary to our other red brothers all across the continent, and I tell them the vision of the red warrior and listen to their thoughts and re-countings of dreams. The movement is growing, and is perhaps the one good thing that has come out of the white man. Native

Americans of all tribes are banding together against the common enemy. I visited some Iroquois brothers recently and we shared stories, dances and songs. The sound of drums and rattles is common again, and it carries from sea to sea. It is strange to think that the Anishanaabeg and the tribes of the Iroquois nations were once sworn enemies. Their grandfathers drove ours westward through war and raids, but now we come together with one hope, that the red warrior will force the whites back into the seas that they crossed to come to our land.

Much of my knowledge of medicine has come from the tribes of the southwest. I travel to meet with Hopi and Navajo medicine men at least once a year, during the time that I cannot fish on the lake. The Hopi people have been most successful in resisting the white plague of Christianity and materialism. They have kept their medicine. I know that I have reached holy ground when I travel through those beautiful deserts with the rim-rock canyons glowing scarlet in the sunset of the day. The spirit world comes very close to you out there; you can hear the rocks speaking to one another in the night.

We have enemies beside the whites, though, that are even more dangerous. It is the Native American who has accepted the white world. The worst are those who have placed a price tag on reservation land, on the oil and coal beneath the surface, or on the trees growing up out of the soil. These so-called Indians are no real Indians, and I find that most of them are mixed. The white blood has tainted them and they are of less value than a full-blooded white. They know nothing of Indian ways or beliefs, but only of money and big cars. They have left the Earth, cut themselves off like miscarried babies, yet make much loud talk about how they are doing what is best for their people by allowing the whites to come in and rape the land and poison their tribes. These traitors will be dealt with someday more severely than the white offal.

There is also a group of medicine men who are allowing the whites into the most sacred ceremonies. They justify it by saying that many whites are seeking the spirits that are in the trees and all things, that they are seeking wisdom from our medicine men. I have seen these white people. They seek anything that seems spiritual to them because they are dried up from the cities and machines and the white way of life. Yes, certainly they are seeking, like thirsty dogs that do not discriminate between anything. The Midewiwin or the fortuneteller is all the same to them. They do not care where they get their spiritual experiences, just so they get them. These whites believe that our red warrior is the parallel of some god that they expect to come and bring in a new age of peace and love. Their religion is such a mishmash of ideas from Hinduism, Buddhism, ravings of wild men, and they wish to throw some of our Indian ways into their religious stew. These people talk peace and love and respect, but they are bad medicine. First because they are white, most of them, and second because they are confused. Whatever wind is blowing is what they sail on. They are stupid.

I have often had these religious scavengers come to me because someone tells them that I have medicine. They wish to learn from me, they say. With these I find that I have the greatest success in ridding myself of them when I tell them that I have only one vision, of the day when the Great Spirit will send the Deliverer to rid the earth of the white disease, and our land will be cleansed from this foul stench. Most run from me like a frightened rabbit. Sometimes I find one who will try to give me enlightenment. They go to great lengths to say that we are all a part of the Vital Force, and that the skin color is an illusion. We should all seek only to become one with the Force, they say, to become personless, sparks entering back into one great flame. I find my most successful method of making them leave me alone is to fetch my hunting knife and offer to send their spark back into the great flame immediately. I have had run-ins with the tribal police on two occasions due to these incidents, but they came to nothing.

Several days ago a white girl came to me with the most insulting request. Her name is Rachel, and she said she is an anthropology and archaeology student from a college down below.

"I'm studying traditional Indian beliefs," she said, "and I was told that you are a traditionalist. I was wondering if you could just tell me what you believe and what effect it has on the way you react to white laws. I know that you are also a leader in the fight for treaty rights, and I thought you could comment on the connection between your beliefs and the current treaty activism."

I was so angry that I couldn't speak for a few minutes. When I found my tongue I shouted at her.

"You stupid, ignorant white bitch! What do you think the Native people are, anyway? Frogs that you can put on a pan in science class and dissect? Go and study your own kind of strange creation! You whites are the one creature made by the Great Spirit that seems to have no reason for living but destruction. I'll answer none of your questions."

These whites are a constant source of amazement to me; they are so arrogant, they think that they are gods.

The fight continues against the treaty breakers. Bah! Their treaties were nothing but lies from the start anyway. More and more, though, I find myself living as my fathers lived on this land, taking the bounty of the Great Spirit, and thanking the spirits of the animals that give their lives up so I can live. Some of the tribal council have made great speeches about how we must conserve our resources and not over-fish and over-hunt, but I feel stronger every day that the red warrior's coming is close, and that when he comes and the white disease is scoured from the land, there will be plenty as there never was before. The Great Spirit will watch over his red people. He will cause the fish to multiply if necessary. These are the things that the wind seems to say to me when it blows through the white pine that stands behind my house. We will continue to fight until victory is reached.

Kohler slept poorly July Fourth night. In fact, his stomach woke him at 4:00 a.m. and he retched for a long time, trying to empty the organ of food that wasn't there. *The sick stomach at night is the worst*, he thought. When he was a child and had indigestion or a touch of the intestinal flu, he always dreamed horrible dreams before waking up to rush to the toilet. It was something he had never outgrown.

When he stopped vomiting and sat back weakly against the bathtub, the nightmare still lingered in his mind like the taste of some foul food. He couldn't even remember what it was about, it was such a hodge-podge of strange images. He had been trapped by some monster, yes, that was part of it, and he had been rocking back and forth, or the earth had been rocking, and it was the motion that had made him ill as much as the horror of the thing thrashing about in his brain.

After a few minutes Kohler began to feel chilled and he rose from the floor and rinsed his mouth out at the sink. He was sleepy again, so he shuffled back to his bed and turned his electric blanket on low. He drowsed and hung on the edge of full slumber, but something kept pulling him away from the warm darkness just as it was about to engulf him. His eyes slowly opened partway, and then the thought or feeling receded; he couldn't remember what it was, and he drifted toward the brink again, but the same thing happened. Finally his eyes opened fully, and he sat up and rearranged his pillows. The sensation of cigarette smoke and water bit at his nostrils, and he was surprised. He did not smoke. The sensation vanished, and left in its place the mental image of Thomas Crane, his back turned toward Kohler, and leaning over the side of the Ki-wi-wai-non-ing, sucking on a cigarette. Kohler rushed up behind the Indian and plunged the knife into his back, then the image vanished. He lay back on the pillows and sleep finally took him away.

He woke again past 9:00, rolled over and cursed when he saw the time. When he stood to his feet, he found himself to be a bit unsteady, and had to grasp the bedpost for a moment until the sensation passed. As he showered, he tried to think about the projects that he had to start that day. The L'Anse Craft Fair would be held at the end of the month, and Kohler intended to have his usual entries, primarily small stuff like end and coffee tables, but he would display a hutch and large bookcase, also. Most of the simple articles could be mass-produced by cutting many pieces and then fitting them together assembly line style. The hutch and bookcase would take more time. They would be his showpieces, complete with hand-carved motifs of the north woods. Pine, he thought. Boughs and cones. It would look nice.

Kohler received considerable business from the Craft Fair, since late July was prime tourist season, and young couples from Wisconsin and the Lower Peninsula would mob the grounds. They liked the simple style and obvious quality of his furniture, and many left the Fair with one of his coffee tables strapped precariously to the top of their car. And they all took his card, leading to sales later. *I should have been up early to get started*, he thought. Now it would be going on 10:00 by the time he got things organized. As he emerged from the bathroom, still toweling his hair dry, Rachel entered the front door.

"Where the hell have you been already this morning?" he asked.

"Actually, I'm just getting in. I tried several times to call you last evening to tell you that I was staying with some friends, but I couldn't reach you. Finally it was so late that I didn't want to keep trying for fear I'd wake everyone in the house."

Kohler's blood immediately began to rise in his face. "House," he said with a scoff. "Don't you mean lodge? Or maybe wickiup? What do those savages call their dirty little bark teepees, anyway?"

"Uncle John..." Rachel began, then just looked at him and shook her head. She went to move past him and he caught her arm roughly, swinging her around to face him. "I didn't say I was through with you, missy. Who'd you stay with last night, some young buck? I've seen those good-for-nothings you been running with."

Now Rachel's face reddened. "You have no right to make such accusations! I don't sleep around, and for your information, I stayed with an older couple, as old as you are, and their daughter. And yes, they are Chippewas. I certainly wouldn't want you to be entirely disappointed."

Kohler released the girl's arm and her daypack slid off her shoulder and fell to the floor. She stooped to pick it up.

"It really doesn't matter how old they are, girl. They're all filthy and entirely without any moral upbringing."

Rachel straightened. "Tell me about how moral white people are, Uncle John. One of the commercial fishermen from the tribe went down to his boat this morning and found the nets slashed to pieces on every one of the Indian trawlers. Now who do you suppose did that? With all the talk that I've heard, I'd be willing to bet that it was someone lily white who's responsible. It's probably some friends of yours!"

"Bullshit!" Kohler felt a tiny whirlwind of panic start in his stomach, and he moved a step toward the girl and clenched his fist menacingly. "You're starting to talk like a filthy red scum yourself! Listen to you, now. You got the judge, jury and hangman all ready to go before all the evidence is in. I can tell you who's responsible, as anybody with any sense can figure out. It's that stinking Thomas Crane. He's nothing but a troublemaker from the word go. Did you see him and his little band yesterday at the parade? He'd love it if this got blamed on the whites, now wouldn't he? He'd just feel all righteous and justified in breaking every fishing law on the books then, wouldn't he?" Kohler was grasping for breath, and stopped momentarily in his tirade.

Rachel started to walk toward her room, then turned toward her uncle again. "You know what's really funny, Uncle John? You hate Thomas Crane because you're mirror images of each other. You're both narrow-minded, racial bigots." She burst into tears.

Kohler nearly went blind with rage when she compared him with Crane, and he took steps toward her with the full intention of thrashing her, but her tears brought him up short. He stood for a few seconds, confused, not quite sure of what course of action to pursue.

"I'm moving out," Rachel said, regaining some control. Her eyes had swollen quickly from crying, and she stood wiping her face with the sleeve of her shirt. "I'm sorry this hasn't worked out. I love you, Uncle John, at least I thought it was you I loved."

"You do what you want to do," Kohler said with a growl. But he still stood staring at her.

"It's not what I want! I just have to. I can't live with the way you are, or the way you've become. I always remembered you as my favorite relative. I used to cry when I was little because my mom said it was too far to drive up here to see you. I thought you were the neatest person I knew and now, why, it's like I never knew you at all!" She started to cry again, and went into her room and closed the door firmly behind her.

Kohler was stung by her words. "That's o.k., missy!" he shouted at the door. "You just be that way. You go ahead and think you're better than anybody else, see if I care!"

He stamped back to his wood shop and slammed the door. A thought struck him, and he strode back into the house and stood before the girl's room.

"You'd better not tell any lies to your mother! She's my only sister, and I don't need any young whelp like you coming between us! She's not going to approve of you staying with some filthy savages, either, and don't you think for one second she will. She isn't a fool like you. You hear me?"

Kohler turned on his heel and went back to the shop, slamming the door again. He tried to think about what he had planned to do for the day, but his brain wouldn't cooperate. He walked around mumbling, looking at this and that piece of lumber. Nothing seemed to be in order. It was a good thing the girl was leaving. Ever since she had come it had been one trouble after another. But what would Grace say? What would Rachel tell her? Kohler turned the possible conversations over in his mind. No, if his sister heard it from the girl, she was sure to get the wrong impression. God knows what idea she might have! *Perhaps I should call her*, he thought, *get a jump on the whole thing.*

He put down the piece of maple he had in his hand, went to the door to the kitchen, and pressed his ear against it. She was probably gone, gone to live in some shack with her red buddies. Kohler's anger rose hot again at the thought of his blood kin with the Indians. He jumped back when a door slammed in the house, and a few seconds later he heard the buzz of the VW engine. It grew fainter and finally died away.

Kohler entered the house and went to the telephone. He picked up the receiver and began to dial the area code for Saginaw, then hesitated, unsure of what he would say when Grace answered.

"Hello, Grace?" he said aloud, as an experiment. "It's about Rachel. No, there's nothing wrong. Well, there is something wrong, but she's not sick or anything." He stopped, not knowing what he would say after that. "Your daughter's a fool? What's the matter with your kid, anyway?" Kohler placed the receiver back in the cradle and decided to wait until he had more time to think about it.

He returned to his shop and tried again to concentrate on the projects for the craft fair. He worked slowly, too slowly, he thought, but he kept interrupting himself by brooding over the morning's events and what he might say to his sister. When lunchtime came he wasn't hungry, even though, he had eaten no breakfast. At a break he went to a cabinet in the corner of the room and withdrew an object wrapped in newspaper. Undoing the covering, he took out a flat oval plaque of wood, about twenty inches long and twelve wide. It was made of maple, and varnished to a honey-gold color. On one side was an intricately carved image of a white pine. Kohler had worked many nights on this during the long darkness of the northern winter. Just touching the work reminded him of the wind howling around the corners of the house during the blizzard in the middle of January. The woodcarving was far more ambitious than anything he had ever created. He thought of it as art, and purely a thing of beauty rather than practicality, as were his other pieces with carvings on them. He sat in a chair and ran his fingers over the tree again and again, thoughtlessly and mechanically, and he derived some comfort from this. He intended to take it to the fair, but selling it was another thing altogether. He'd take nothing less than $500 for it, he thought, and maybe even then he wouldn't sell. Kohler sat cradling the carving like a baby, lost in thought. It was mid-afternoon before he began working again.

That evening he fixed himself a meager supper, opening a can of spaghetti and another of peaches. Twice he caught himself looking up toward the door, as though he expected someone to enter. The house was too quiet, and his eating utensils banged and clattered on the plate. He ate quickly, then returned to the shop and tried to work some more. After a while he gave up and went into the house and read the newspaper. Again the silence was oppressive, and he flipped on the television. He tried to concentrate on a game show, then a sitcom. He dozed and fell into a deep sleep.

The insistent jangling of the telephone woke him, and for a moment Kohler couldn't remember why the TV was on. He struggled against the inertia of slumber and finally stumbled to answer the phone.

"John? What's the matter? You took so long to answer."

"Hullo. Grace? No, I was asleep, I guess. What time is it, anyway?"

"Ten o'clock."

"Good night, I must have really been out like a light."

"John, Rachel called me a little while ago and told me that she's not staying with you anymore. She's with some family she met up there, and she seemed pretty upset. Now what is going on, anyway?"

"Oh." Kohler was wide-awake, now. It hadn't occurred to him that his sister might call him, and he struggled for words.

"Well, you know kids, Grace. They get ideas in their heads and off they go. I don't really know what kind of burr she got under her saddle, it happened kind of sudden."

"She told me that you were against her doing her studies, and that you'd had several arguments."

"I wouldn't call them arguments, necessarily, just misunderstandings, you know."

"Pretty serious ones, I'd say, for that child to move out. She always idolized you, and I'd like a better explanation than I'm getting from either of you."

"Well now, I'm not against her studying. I've just told her some things for her own good that she really didn't like to hear, is all."

"About the Indians."

"Yeah. She doesn't seem to understand that those people can be studied, and that's one thing, but you can't be friendly with them. God only knows what could happen to her, Grace, running around with that sort of scum. She doesn't believe her old uncle, but I know."

"Really, now, I think that's a bit silly, John. Or course she has to talk to them for what she's doing."

"But she doesn't have to like them!" Kohler's temper was beginning to flare. "They're dangerous, and not to be trusted, and she shouldn't be around them! You know yourself that it was one of the dirty beasts that killed mother. How you ever allowed your own daughter to get such an interest in those filthy vermin is more than I can know."

"Now wait a minute, dear brother. In the first place, that story about the midwife killing mother was always Merle's story. It wasn't even true. I think Merle made it up because of how he felt about mother, and he just had to blame somebody for her death. He couldn't hardly bring himself to blame you, you were just a baby."

"What in hell are you talking about, Merle's feelings for mother? And are you saying that I killed her?"

"Of course not, you just happened to be born then. She was weak, John. Apparently, she had been told not to try and have another baby after I came. She'd probably have died if she were in a hospital, too. And I can't believe you never heard anything about Merle and mother. All those years he raised you and he never mentioned it?"

"Mentioned what, for pete's sake?"

"Merle and Daddy were rivals for her hand at one time. Just so happened that Dad won. But I think Merle always loved her. He was just a real gentleman about losing."

"If that isn't the biggest bunch of hogwash I ever heard in my life…"

"No, it's true. Aunt Eva told me the whole thing, and she heard it from Dad."

"That old biddy was a liar from square one. The squaw killed Mother. Merle told it that way, and I believe it. You'd better remember that he raised me, Grace, and he was a fine, upstanding man. I never heard him tell a lie. And that settles that. As for your daughter, she's a little fool! I'm telling you the way I told her, those red devils are treacherous, and she's liable to be sorrier than she's ever been in her life. That family she's staying with is Indian, I suppose? And you're letting this go on?"

Grace sputtered into the telephone. "You are being completely ridiculous, John

Kohler! She said she had to leave your house, and I'm starting to see why. I never knew you could be so stupid, and I'm glad she's made other friends that are kind enough to take her in so her summer studies won't be completely ruined! You are truly a sightless bigot, like she said you were."

"I'm the one that's got to live up here with them! You live down there in Saginaw and haven't seen a real Indian in God only knows how long. You don't know a thing about it, Grace. I do! I listen to their garbage every day, and see their ways, and I'm telling you, they are the worst trash on the face of the earth. Now, I don't know what to do for you or Rachel to deliver you from what's surely going to happen."

"You talk like a fool, and I know the voice of hysteria when I hear it. I don't see any sense in carrying this conversation any further."

"That's just fine by me!" yelled Kohler. "My own family is made up of a bunch of scum-kissing idiots! Well, you'll be sorry!" He slammed the receiver into the cradle with such force that the entire telephone flew off the small table where it sat.

"My own flesh and blood!" he screamed as he walked aimlessly around the room, his arms flailing at the air. In his rage he tore a picture of autumn maples from the wall and flung it across the floor. The shattering of the glass startled him and he stopped dead still and stared. The television set still blathered some comedy and he quickly walked to it and shut it off. Now the house was so quiet, so empty, it was like a vacuum to him, as though what was there didn't exist anymore, and all things of value and life were being sucked into some sort of void. He looked around at his possessions and blinked, and wondered if any of those things were really things he had bought or made and set there for some purpose. His stomach was burning, and the pain reached through his confused thoughts and drove him to the bottle of antacid. He guzzled it, drinking down a third of the bottle before stopping. He then sat down, exhausted, on the edge of the tub.

"I don't understand," he mumbled to himself, and began to cry. The tears embarrassed him to himself, but he couldn't stop them, and they came faster and faster until his body was wracked with sobs and he slid to the floor. It was twenty minutes later when he rose, feeling drained, and stumbled into his bedroom.

At 3:30 a.m. Kohler shot upright in his bed, panting and clawing at the covers. He shook with cold and, wrapping himself in a heavy blanket, went into the living room. He turned on the lamp by the couch and sat there until dawn, half-drowsing, just waiting for the daylight.

Some days later Kohler was finishing up work in the shop. It had been a bad stretch, he thought. His hands were still all thumbs, and his arms refused to move quickly. He should have produced twice the number of pieces completed, but nothing was going right.

There was a crunch of gravel in the driveway and he hurried to put away the last saw and step into the house. Maybe it was Rachel. He hadn't heard from her since she left the night of their fight. His feelings had aged and mellowed. The anger had cooled in the nights when she wasn't there to fix supper or listen to his stories. Yet he wouldn't admit to himself that he missed her, much less that he was sorry for his treatment of her. Pulling back the curtain he peered out. Presslein and Behrendsen were closing the door on the Dodge and presently knocked at the front door.

Kohler opened to them. "Howdy, fellas. What do ya know?"

Presslein held a grocery sack in his hand. "Hello, John. Hadn't heard nothing of you since our Fourth of July festival of fun, so we thought we'd stop by and see what you was up to."

"Workin', that's all. I have a lot to put out before the craft fair. It always brings in new business, you know. What you got in the bag?"

The two men entered the house. "New product. Figured you might like it," Behrendsen said.

He withdrew a six pack of cans from the sack and placed them on the coffee table.

Kohler picked them up and broke off one.

"Pact Beer." He read the can, which showed a picture of a whitefish caught in a net. "What is this stuff, and where did you come up with it, anyway?"

"It's imported," said Presslein, "all the way from beautiful Wisconsin. I wish we would have thought up something like this ourselves."

"Yeah, it's great," said Behrendsen, picking up a can of the brew. "It's produced by a group of folks called Halt Indian Abuses, and every time you buy this here Pact Beer you're supporting the cause of stopping the redskins from getting away with all the treaty rights fishing and hunting they do."

"Right," Presslein said, folding his long frame onto the couch. "The red boys been getting all their cases won in court. Why? Because the white bleeding heart city slickers pay for fancy lawyers who concoct wild arguments, the stupid judges buy it, and right there you have it. The Indians get to run all over the country shootin' and snarin' and hookin' everything that moves."

"And the whites sit back and take it," added Behrendsen. "But we really aren't that stupid, just not so rich. So this organization over here in Wisconsin was got up by some of the local folks that are just as sick as we are of this whole thing. They're devoted to educating the public, you might say, about what a fiasco this treaty business is. First they're just going to raise a stink in the newspapers and such, get some airtime on TV and radio. Then maybe eventually whites can hire some fancy lawyers and put a stop to this; get the laws changed, elect our own representatives that will start standing up for Americans' rights instead of these damn Indians."

"And Pact Beer" said Presslein, "is the first link in the chain. It's gonna raise all the dough necessary to do what needs to be done."

Kohler was still busy reading the can, which explained what the two men had encapsulated.

"Well," he said, "sounds like a pretty good idea."

"Pop you one open" offered Behrendsen. "It doesn't have a bad taste."

"Ain't nobody in Wisconsin makes a bad brew," said Presslein.

"No thanks, fellas. You saw what happened to my stomach on the Fourth from that beer. You know I want to support the cause, but not this way."

"We want to see if we can't get a group together over here on this side of the border," Behrendsen said. "God knows we got the same problems as them in Wisconsin. 'Course, we did slow the buggers down with our little Fourth of July celebration, didn't we?"

Kohler felt slightly uncomfortable. "Anybody ever get wind of that, I mean that it was us?"

"Naw." Presslein popped open a Pact Beer and slurped some into his mouth. "They got no witnesses, no nothing. Sure the tribal police think it was whites, and

185

commercial fishermen are going to be the first they suspect, but they can't hardly arrest us on suspicion. The movement against the redskins is growing everywhere that people have to put up with their nonsense. Coulda been anybody. Coulda been kids."

"Say, Kohler, want to go and cast a few at some trout on the Sturgeon, that is, if the red boys ain't got 'em all? We got our fly paraphernalia in the car."

"I'd like to, boys, but I really have to get some work done on some flies I want to sell at the Fair. You act like you never work yourselves, runnin' over to Wisconsin to buy beer."

"We got to go out tomorrow morning and make up for today, that's for sure," said Behrendsen. "That is, if the redskins left us any fish in the lake."

The two visitors rose to leave. "Sure wish you'd put off those flies for a few hours, John. You can tell a good fishing spot a mile away."

"Got to make hay while the sun shines, as the farmers say. If I don't get the business during the summer at these fairs and such, winter can be mighty skimpy for me. Sorry."

"Well, here, keep a brew for a souvenir." Presslein tossed one to Kohler. "Can we let you know if we get together a meeting like the HIA? You sure were a stand-up guy on the net job."

"Sure, you bet."

Presselein and Behrendsen drove off south toward the Sturgeon and Kohler went to the kitchen to fix himself some supper. He opened the refrigerator, then the freezer. There were fish and steaks, and some blueberries that Rachel had left; she made blueberry muffins quite often. He felt a twinge of remorse, thinking about how much she used to slave over the meals. "Darn good little cook," he said to himself, "But a stupid, stupid little kid." He closed the freezer. He had taken nothing out to thaw earlier in the day, so he would have to open a can or a box. It had been that way since Rachel left, beans or soup or canned spaghetti every night. The cupboard yielded up some old chili beans from the darkest corner. Kohler couldn't even remember when he had bought them. He heated them and scrounged some saltines, which turned out to be crumbly and stale. The loaf of bread in the refrigerator had a blue-green mold around the crust. The chili tasted terrible, and he sat back on the rear legs of the chair and chewed in disgust. "This is ridiculous," he said. "I've got to get to the store and get some food. My life has gone to the dogs lately."

The two weeks until the Craft Fair passed quickly. Kohler found himself unable to concentrate on his work, and therefore forced to spend much more time on it. He rose at dawn and worked in the shop until evening, then pulled his fly-tying tools out and dominated the kitchen table with tiny vises and colorful feathers until 10:00 when he went to bed. Behrendsen called to tell him that two men representing the Halt Indian Abuses organization were coming to meet with interested parties in the Keweenaw area, but Kohler begged off because of the load of work. Behrendsen promised to come and help him load the truck the morning of the Craft Fair.

The Fair opened on Thursday and ran through Sunday. Participants were urged to ship their wares early on the first day in order to cut down traffic that might interfere with the tourists. The city erected a large circus tent down by the harbor area of town, with two smaller tents for overflow and refreshments.

Kohler was up before dawn on opening day, and he and Behrendsen had his two loads of furniture, the first containing the hutch and heavy bookshelf, and the second with the smaller, mass-produced pieces, in L'Anse and arranged by 9:00. Kohler set up a small folding table and placed upon it a notebook, ledger, receipt book, the oval carving of the white pine, and some of his trout flies. He made price stickers for all of the furniture, but hesitated when he came to the carving. He knew that, more than anything he had ever done in his life, it was a piece of art. And in a strange way, it was priceless to him.

Should I sell it? He wondered. He wanted to keep it for himself; it symbolized the North Country for him, but he also suspected that he could get an excellent price for it from the tourists, and money didn't always come easily. He decided to leave the price off and see what would happen.

The Craft Fair opened officially at ten o'clock, but many people were still setting up displays. Kohler decided to walk around for a few moments and look at the wares. After business picked up it would be impossible to wander far from his table. He removed the carving and flies and placed them beneath some rags in a box before he left. They were the only things that someone could make off with easily.

Baraga County was crowded with artists and craftspeople, it seemed. The largest tent was nearly overflowing with goods of every variety, and fine weather and lots of tourists would translate into sales and distribution opportunities for all. Next to Kohler's area was Marie Kelty, one of the local potters. She had two long display tables of her goods; hand-thrown pots glazed entirely in earth tones of brown, charcoal, dark greens and blues. She and her husband were making last minute adjustments to the small electric wheel she had brought with her. It was good that she was placed next to him, Kohler thought. She always attracted crowds of tourists who stopped to watch her work at the wheel, and the overflow would spill into his territory and take note of his work. It would definitely increase his business.

Kohler wandered on down the aisle. There were many women with small displays of dried flower arrangements, *too many*, he thought, and two basket weavers. One used local materials only, and had reeds in various stages of preparation. There was a glass blower, a ring maker who featured copper and amethyst from the Keweenaw Peninsula, a weaver with colorful rugs, a maker of dulcimers who was even now filling the tent with the instrument's strange sounds, several painters who emphasized shore scenes and wildlife, and as many photographers. There was only one other fellow who worked with wood, and his wares were all carvings. He looked to be perhaps twenty-two or three and a foreigner, which was Kohler's term for the young people who came to the U.P. from down below seeking to live and work, as they phrased it, in a more natural environment.

At the far end of the tent Kohler stopped, suddenly disgusted. "Trash," he said under his breath. A sign over a small table announced "George Elk – Native Art." Hanging on pegboard behind the table was a drum crafted from a hollow tree, with a real skin head, and sewed with sinews. There was a cradleboard, luxuriant with fox skin and woven with porcupine quills, a tomahawk and some birch bark boxes. Kohler had read about Elk in the L'Anse paper; he was the first person in the Baraga County tribe to return to crafting authentic Chippewa items using old tools and methods. The tourists ate it up, and paid an exorbitant price for the wares. Kohler knew that it was just a rip-off, no matter how long it took this old codger to make his filthy stuff. Elk was standing with his back to Kohler, fooling with something in a box. When he turned, Kohler spit very deliberately, then walked away.

They're invading everything, he thought. *And selling what? A few nasty old pieces of wood and stretched hide. Authentic savagery. That's all.*

He returned to his area, feeling cheated and betrayed. He had never considered the possibility of an Indian being allowed into the Craft Fair. It was sullied for him, tainted. *If it weren't for the money*, he thought, *I'd take my stuff and leave.*

The tourists had begun to arrive, and some of the local wives, through with their morning's occupations. Later in the day people would be driving in from Marquette or Houghton, college professors, who might be in the mood to buy a new hutch or bookcases. The customers began to stroll through slowly beneath the bare light bulbs hanging over the aisles of the tent, stopping here and there to examine an item and remark on its quality. Kohler figured that none of them would be very serious about purchasing anything until they had walked through and seen all of the displays. He settled back in a lawn chair and began to read the newspaper.

Business was slow for several hours, but in the middle of the afternoon a young couple stopped by and looked over his coffee and end tables rather intently.

"These are so nice, honey," the young woman said to her husband. She was dressed very fashionably in white slacks and a white knit top that had tiny green stripes. Every one of her auburn hairs was in place, and Kohler thought that she looked amazingly like a model that had stepped out of a woman's magazine. Her husband's clothing, as bright and crease-free as her own, was just as fashionable.

Unreal people, he thought to himself. *Stuck in an office somewhere all year, trying to claw their way to the top.* He viewed them critically, and played the guessing game he had made up for such occasions. Down below, certainly, he thought, and urban.

My guess is from around Detroit somewhere.

"You folks interested in anything, here?" he asked.

"I just love your coffee tables and end tables. They're really exquisite in their simplicity," said the woman. "How much are they? Not that it matters."

"Well, ma'am, that's solid maple, the wood I like to work with the most, so I charge $150.00 each for the end tables, and throw in the matching coffee table for another $200.00.

"That seems very reasonable, Kyle," she said, turning to her husband. "I'm so tired of our décor, and these would be the perfect start to a new living room suit."

Kyle looked thoughtfully at the furniture. "How would we get them home in the Beemer, though?"

"No problem" interjected Kohler quickly. "I have a shipper I use all the time. Can set it up easily to have them sent directly to your home address."

The couple excused themselves, stepped away and had a conversation in a low tone of voice. After a few minutes they returned and closed the deal.

"So," said Kohler, "where you folks from, seeing as I have to make this shipping slip out?"

"Livonia, a suburb of Detroit," replied Kyle.

Kohler smiled and felt satisfied with himself. *I'm such a good judge of people,* he thought. "What do you do for a living, anyway?"

"We both have positions in a large corporation," answered Kyle's wife. "I'm in advertising, and Kyle is in management. It's nice to get away from the rat race for a while, though, and come up and see nature."

"Well, we've got plenty of that," said Kohler.

He arranged to have the items shipped to them, to arrive after they had returned from their vacation. They seemed pleased with themselves. Kohler heard them mumble something about "helping boost the U.P. economy" as they sauntered away.

He sold another coffee table to a young couple later that afternoon, but they didn't seem so well to do and he only charged them $149.00 for it. A woman professor at Michigan Tech ordered two bookcases, and Kohler recorded the information in his notebook and charged her a deposit of $75.00. He promised to call her when they were ready.

At the end of the first day he took only the carving of the white pine home with him, since the city provided guards overnight in the tent to protect the wares of the merchants. Several people had commented on the beauty of the plaque, but when they asked what the price was, he told them $500.00. No one was willing to pay that much, and he was glad.

The following day he took an order for a hutch in the morning, sold a few smaller items around midday, and spent much of the rest of the time reading outdoor magazines. In the afternoon he was engrossed in a "Field and Stream" article about trout fishing in Montana when a voice in front of him said, "This is beautiful!"

Kohler looked up from his article, expecting to help a customer, but he immediately changed his attitude.

"Take your hands off that," he said menacingly.

Sam Whitefeather placed the white pine carving carefully back on the table. "I mean it," said the Indian. "This carving is one of the most beautiful pieces of art I've ever seen. How much do you want for it?" his expression was one of equanimity, and it infuriated Kohler.

"I wouldn't sell it to you if my life depended on it!" Kohler said loudly. Several people who were watching Marie Kelty throw pots looked over at him with alarmed expressions. "Get out of here," he said, lowering his tone of voice.

"I'll pay you whatever you want for it, John, whatever you're asking of the customers."

The tent was suddenly stifling. The air seemed stagnant and Kohler was acutely aware of the smell of canvas in the sun. He felt as though tiny spiders with red hot feet were climbing all over his skin, and sweat began to pour down his face. "You're going to ruin my business here, scum." He leaned toward the native to emphasize his words. "I want you out. Now."

Whitefeather sighed and continued to look at him. Kohler was baffled and angered by the Indian's expression. It was the sort that you'd have looking at a stray dog out in the middle of a sleet storm.

"I shouldn't have expected anything different, I suppose," said Whitefeather. "But I want you to know something before I go. Rachel is staying with Mary and I. She's quite well…"

"What?" Kohler yelled, causing the potter's crowd to look over again. He gripped the table until his knuckles turned white. "So that's where the little brat went."

"She's not a brat, John. She's one of the brightest young ladies I've ever met, and she's very hurt and confused about her uncle right now. She doesn't know I'm telling you any of this, but I think you should try to give her a call or something. Here's my number." He slid a piece of paper onto the table in front of the white man.

Kohler swept it onto the floor. "I wouldn't. And maybe you don't hear so well, or more likely you're just a good example of the stupidity of your breed, but I told you to get away from me."

Whitefeather nodded briefly and began to turn away. "By the way," he said, "I meant it about the carving. It's beautiful. You do great work."

Kohler felt as though he had been horsewhipped as he watched the proudly erect figure of Whitefeather disappear among the crowd. He sat down in his chair and broke open a new pack of Rolaids and ate two. The Indian had baffled him, showing no anger, and then complimenting him in the face of an insult. He hated him all the more for it. All the more, because Kohler felt humiliated before the entire world.

He opened the "Field and Stream" to the trout article, but the thought of Rachel living with the Whitefeathers kept intruding on his reading. He forced it out of his head. *It doesn't matter*, he told himself. *Why should I bother with that little fool? I can't believe she actually made herself to home with such trash. She's no niece of mine.* He rose from the chair, went to the front of the table and found the small slip of paper on the ground. He sat down again, lit a match, and held the slip to the flame and watched until the last digit of Whitefeather's number was consumed.

Just before suppertime Kohler looked up from his magazine to find a man of about thirty standing before his display examining the white pine carving. The fellow was well dressed in a grey business suit and a pearl-colored shirt that had tiny silver threads running through it.

"How much for this plaque?" he asked Kohler.

"$500.00" Kohler answered wearily.

"I'll take it," answered the man. "O.k. if I write a check?" he pulled a checkbook from the inside pocket of the suit jacket. "I'm representing the Governor's office, going around the state looking for art created by Michigan residents that best portrays various aspects of Michigan. This carving of the state tree will be excellent for the anteroom outside the Governor's office. It will go perfectly with the water color of the apple blossoms I picked up the other day."

"You'd really pay that kind of money for a piece of garbage like this?" Kohler asked the Governor's assistant.

"Sir, this work is certainly not garbage! I assure you, this is wonderful. I'd pay $800.00 for it!"

Kohler smiled bitterly. "Yeah, well I had an art critic come by earlier whose opinion I really respect. He made it out to be garbage. You go ahead and take it for the $500.00. And you're getting robbed blind at that."

CHAPTER TEN – SAM WHITEFEATHER

Sam Whitefeather walked out over the Kingston Plains. The reindeer moss beneath his feet crunched and crackled from the recent summer drought, and looked peculiarly like grey-green foam that had been cast upon the land by Lake Superior. For as far as the eye could see in each of the four directions there were stumps – three, four, five feet in diameter, standing silent and ghostly, like grave markers, an Arlington of the northern forest.

Sam's pickup was parked a half mile away, in the middle of the rutted and pot-holed track that served as a road between the small towns of Grand Marais and Melstrand. No one else would be coming along, he knew; it was a little-traveled route. He continued to walk toward a slight ridge on the horizon and, gaining it, sat down in the shade of a serviceberry bush. He braced his back against the stump of a venerable old giant, cut an hundred years before, and surveyed the area. The scene brought sadness to him, adding to the concerns he already bore.

"No-sa-non ish-pe-mig a-yah-yun gwa-tah-me-quan-da-gwuk ke-de-she-ne-kah-zo-win." He stopped and sighed. Somehow he had not the concentration to even repeat the Lord's Prayer. There was too much on his mind. Just in the past month the nets on the tribal fishing boats were destroyed, Rachel had encountered major problems with her uncle, and now Gerald Flambeau had asked to have a meeting with him in two days, and he had no idea what it was about. Not another difficulty, he hoped.

An eagle screamed, and Sam shaded his eyes and tipped his head back. The bird was high up, circling wide, in the bright blue sky.

It was Mary who had suggested that he take some time and stop somewhere on the way back from Sault Saint Marie. She had been up early the previous morning and fixed him a good breakfast.

"I'll stay the night with Claude and Eleanor," he told her. "No sense in trying to get to the Soo and back in one day. I'd be falling asleep at the wheel. Expect me early tomorrow afternoon."

Mary came and put her arms around his shoulders and stood behind him while he ate. He felt her kiss the top of his head.

"Why don't you take a few hours and stop off somewhere on your way back?"

"Too much to do. I should get right back."

"Dear husband." Her arms tightened around him and she laid her cheek against his neck. "You take too much on yourself sometimes, and you know it. Everyone needs to slow down and get some space."

He knew, of course, that she was right. The tribal business, church work, the hardware store, people's personal problems; he had a designated area for each situation, and sometimes found himself bouncing between them like a bearing in a pinball machine. "I suppose I should," he said. "I'll stop in the woods on the way back."

The eagle screamed again, but the call was fainter. His circling had taken him farther east.

"Brother Eagle!" Sam raised his arm in salute to the retreating bird. "Good hunting!"

The native sat for some time, as still as a stone, and watched the landscape. The old forest had never re-seeded here after being logged, and but for a few bushes and a small spruce or maple here or there, was now a prairie.

A sharp-tailed grouse scuffled through the grass and reindeer moss. It saw Sam and stopped short, scrutinizing him with its bright eyes. Sam did not move. After a few moments the grouse went on its way.

Whitefeather smiled. Wise wife, suggesting that he get away from things for a few hours. It was good to be out under the bright dome of the sky and to focus on the small miracles of creation. He meditated on the grouse and its intricately engineered eye. "Thank you, Great Spirit, that I don't live in the city! I can't imagine being trapped by the works of man alone, unable to see your glorious works! How insignificant all of my concerns become when I contemplate your artistry."

Having thus prayed, he rose and began to walk. He wandered about the plains for many hours, stopping and bending to examine a wintergreen plant growing out of a rotted stump here, or to catch sight of a scampering rabbit there. Yet the sun edged relentlessly toward the west, and he knew he must follow it back to the reservation. He hiked back to his pickup with far more peace of mind, feeling that all things had fallen into perspective, and he was able to once again deal with the problems with renewed vigor.

Sam kept his appointment with Gerald Flambeau. They met for breakfast at the Iron Pine.

"Hey, I just ran into a couple of white girls up town," Gerald said as they sat down at one of the red and white checkered tables. "They were trying to find a clothes store 'cause they about froze solid camping over at Au Train last night. I had to laugh. It's been awful hot up here this summer; I told them so, too." He grinned, his face breaking into scores of lines that lied about his age. "Thin-blooded people from down below."

A waitress walked up, a white girl with bleach blond hair and long false eyelashes.

"Take your order?"

"Give me some scrambled eggs, ham, toast and coffee," said Gerald.

"Same for me, please," said Sam.

As the girl flounced away, Gerald leaned toward Sam and whispered, "How can she see past those brushes on her eyelids, anyway?"

"Shh," Sam cautioned as she came back to pour the coffee.

Gerald added cream, three times, and three packs of sugar to his cup, then stirred exactly ten times, counting in a monotone.

"You make a cup of coffee look like science," commented Whitefeather.

"A good cup of java is a science." Gerald sat back in his chair and discarded his mischievous demeanor. "Listen. Going back to the tourists. I have a proposition for you which I think you might be interested in."

"What's that?"

"You know the stuff we're doing over at the Tribal Center for the tourists. They really eat up the craft displays and history exhibits. Well, we've decided to start something else the first of August, mainly a little talk, or lecture, if you want to call it that, on tribal legends and rituals - maybe the Mediwiwin - figured you'd be perfect for the job."

Sam ran his hand through his hair and looked at his friend. "Yeah, sure. I'm an elder in the Methodist Church, and you're asking me to do the talk on the Mediwiwin?

Why not ask one of the traditionals?"

"You know most of them would never talk about the Mediwiwin to the whites, and rightfully so. Then again, some one like Crane would probably scare the scalps off the tourists. It's one thing that he believes that Manabozho began the world with the mud that the muskrat brought up out of the floodwaters, but he is so full of hatred, too. 'Course, Crane would be the last one to talk to the whites. We feel you'd be best for the job. You understand the white world better than most, Sam, and you understand the white tourist. You have the authority of the Tribal Council, and you know traditions. It'll be two lectures in the afternoon on Tuesday and Thursday. How about it?"

"Is my hardware store supposed to run itself?"

"You could still be there in the morning. Can't Jim and Mary handle it in the afternoons? Come on, I know you'd like this, and it's only during the tourist season. There isn't that much of this summer left."

The conversation was interrupted by the arrival of the food. Whitefeather bowed his head briefly, then looked up at Gerald.

"Well, you're right. I'd love to do those talks. It's important for the whites to see us as a culture. All they know is what they've seen on TV. One group seems to think we're the noble savage, and the others see us as a bunch of drunks. Maybe if they understood that we have a tradition that has molded us, the same as their European ancestors had..." Sam's mind began to race with the idea. "Let's see. I could really build on that concept. Give some examples of traditions from Europe that influence white American culture, like Christmas and mistletoe, then tie in our oral traditions."

Gerald started laughing. "I knew you'd be perfect. But don't get too intellectual on us. We don't need a whole lecture on comparative culture, or whatever you call it. Mainly we just want to expose the lodge stories."

"Right, but I could spend just sixty seconds, or two minutes, drawing parallels. Just so they could see that though the differences appear to be great, we are all just human beings and are based on traditions."

"Do you think you can get something together quick enough? You only have a few days."

"No problem. I've been telling lodge stories to my kids for twenty years, and now to Rachel. I've got them memorized. The hardest part is deciding which ones to use."

"You know, speaking of Rachel, I can't believe that sweet girl is any relation to John Kohler. I got to meet her the other day at the Tribal Center. Her uncle is the biggest white jackass I ever saw in my life and I always thought that sort of thing ran in families."

"I don't think so, Gerald. And John Kohler is just a man, like any man."

"Oh, sure. You ever have him spit at you? I've never seen the sort of wild hatred in his eyes anywhere else. Even a lot of the good old boys are just prejudiced. Kohler, I don't know. He's something downright weird."

"Yeah, well, we've got our problems, too. I still wonder how much Thomas Crane's display on the Fourth had to do with the nets being destroyed that night."

"I don't know. Heard anything more on that? Any clues?"

"None. Everybody was busy with something else, fireworks and stuff. We'll probably never find who did it if they don't come forward themselves, and that seems unlikely."

The two men continued their discussion only as long as the food lasted. As Sam drove back toward the hardware store he thought about Gerald's comments regarding Rachel and her uncle. It was quite unbelievable that the girl was related to Kohler. They were night and day in their attitudes toward Native Americans.

Rachel had telephoned Sam one day in mid-June, identifying herself as an anthropology student from Central Michigan University. She explained that she was staying in the area for the summer and working on a paper for her senior year, and was interested in the current treaty rights turmoil in the Keweenaw Bay area. A girl at the tribal center had referred her to Sam. Whitefeather welcomed talking to the student, especially when he learned of her course of study. He had a keen interest in the same subjects, and did independent reading when he could.

They agreed to meet at the L'Anse Café for lunch. Whitefeather was shutting the door on his truck in the municipal parking lot when a green VW bug pulled in beside it. A girl in her early twenties got out caring a daypack and purse.

"Excuse me," she said when she saw him. "Are you Mr. Whitefeather?"

"That's right. You wouldn't happen to be Rachel Johnson?"

"Yes," she extended her hand to shake his, and he responded. "I recognized you from your picture at the tribal center."

"Oh, I always thought that was a bit pompous, having the photos of the Council on the wall. But I guess in this instance it worked out all right."

It was beginning to rain, so they hurried into the restaurant. Rachel set up the tape recorder even before the waitress was able to place two glasses of water before them.

"You don't mind if I tape our conversation, do you? It's a bad habit we anthropologists have. Thank God for modern technology, because I hate taking notes!"

"I hope I say something worth taping," Sam said with a laugh. "Tell me, why did you choose to come to Baraga County to do your research this summer" Most of the books I've read are based on research at the larger reservations in Minnesota or Wisconsin."

"It was a logical decision for me, really. My main interest lies in the tribes of Michigan, both from an historical perspective and a cultural one. I felt that the reservation here would be a good spot to explore the possible connections between the resurgence of traditional Indian religious beliefs and the treaty rights movement in Michigan. This area, because of its geographical situation, is much more prone to conflict in the area of treaty rights fishing and hunting, of course, than the Isabella reservation in the lower peninsula. I mean, it's almost all farmland, there. Plus I have an uncle who lives up here, and I'm staying with him, so that worked out really well."

"Oh, What's your uncle's name?"

"John Kohler. Do you know him?"

"Yes, well, no, not personally. I know who he is." Whitefeather immediately recalled the night at the Iron Pine a few weeks before, when Kohler had been so offensive. It was all Sam could do not to say something to him then. The man had insulted his wife, himself, and his people. He had controlled himself because he knew that words would only produce additional strife, then who could tell where things would stop?

And here was John Kohler's niece, studying the very people that Kohler hated with such passion. As Whitefeather talked to Rachel, though, he realized that she had not an inkling about her uncle's attitude. Anticipation and excitement were written all over her face, the sort of enthusiasm generated by a youth pursuing her love. She was very involved in her studies, and he decided she couldn't have a prejudiced bone in her body. She convinced him of her trustworthiness, even though she had questionable family associations.

She asked Whitefeather some personal questions while the food was being served; age, education and place of birth, which he answered without reticence.

"You seem atypical, if I may use that term, Mr. Whitefeather. Too few Native Americans have had any college at all."

"Unfortunately, that's very true. There is little motivation for our young people to go on to higher education, though that is beginning to change. There was even less when I was coming up. My father was a very important influence on me, and he urged me to go. I didn't make it the four years because my family fell on harder times than usual, and I had to return home to help out."

"I do hope that these facts change. The statistics in the textbooks seem unreal, sometimes. And it's so easy to reduce people to statistics, and it blunts reality. America has yet to wake up to the problems of your people, as they have to other minorities."

They continued talking on the subject for several minutes, discussing the efforts of the Tribal Council to enroll more Ojibwe in educational programs.

"Generally, the various churches have contributed greatly to efforts in educating the native peoples in this country," commented Sam.

"Yes, but the influence of Christian denominations seems to be waning among Indians, don't you agree? People are returning in droves to older belief systems. What about you, Mr. Whitefeather? Are you an adherent of traditional Indian religion?"

"First of all, please call me Sam. That is, if I may call you Rachel?"

"Sure."

"As for religion, no, I'm not a Traditionalist." He saw her face fall. "Have you tried talking to Thomas Crane, by any chance? I would say he's the most outspoken Traditional, and a leader in the treaty rights movement in this area."

"I've met him. He was, well, less than hospitable to me. Actually, he was rude."

"I'm sorry. I should have suspected that he wouldn't be very receptive to a white person studying the old ways. It's too bad, because he could be a wonderful source of information for you. But please don't get the impression that all of the Traditionals are rude. Crane is a man of strong and bitter beliefs. You would find him quite interesting."

"I received the impression from him that there is a great deal of tension between the whites and Indians in this area. Do you feel that this is true?"

"Not necessarily. You have to understand that Thomas Crane is probably as extreme a person as you'll meet around here, as far as my people are concerned. He is very distrustful of whites, and heavily involved in traditional beliefs, including a sect, if you will, that prophesies a coming messiah. This savior will free the red man and drive out the whites, returning the land to the way it was before your people came here. Crane's activity with treaty rights seems to spring from this belief.

"Then, also, there are some whites who are as violently opposed to the exercise of treaty rights as Crane is for them. It's inevitable that these two groups will clash. To an outsider, because both sides are very vocal, and because they are unable to compromise, it sounds like we're about to have another White-Indian war. But that isn't true. Stick around long enough, and you'll find that most whites and Ojibwe at least tolerate each other, and many attempt to work together. There are whites who completely support our right to hunt and fish under treaty provision. It's a mix."

"Well, let me be very bold, Sam, and ask you where you stand in all this. Certainly you've been much kinder to me than Mr. Crane, but how do you feel about whites? I hope this poses no difficulty for you."

"Not at all. I am one of the Tribal Council members who works closely with the white community." Whitefeather sat back a bit in his chair. "Please make no mistake about my loyalty to my people. I love the Anishinaabeg, and I am devoted to helping them advance and prosper, not necessarily in the white man's sense, but in the Native American sense." He leaned forward again, and became very serious, as he always did when he talked about the prospects of his people.

"The red man in America is the most abused and cheated of the minorities. There has been a systematic and concentrated effort by whites to destroy us from the word go. Indian religion was outlawed in this country in 1900, in a nation that prides itself on the Bill of Rights, which guarantees the right to practice your religion. But policymakers would not afford these rights to my people, who were considered for so long, of course, to be a vanquished enemy and prisoners of war. Prisoners of war in the very land that we roamed freely for hundreds of years!

"It seems that the general attitude of some whites is either to ignore us, or to put us on display as a tourist attraction, like Tahquamenon Falls or Lake of the Clouds. They do not treat us as a people, as a nation, with our own history and customs and unique way of seeing reality.

"But there is a movement, similar to the black pride movement of the 1960's, that is awakening my people to their heritage and promoting a new pride in who they are, and who their ancestors were. And I'm glad to see it!

"Of course, some people are so caught up that they have, I think, lost perspective. I don't believe that the Great Spirit is sending a messiah to drive the white man back across the Atlantic Ocean. We are not going to return to subsistence hunting and gathering. But we can still find our identity as a people, and that's my great hope."

Rachel was listening intently, and nodded her head. "This is great. I can see, Sam, that you'll be very helpful as I try to gain a proper perspective myself. But, going back to the practice of religion, I guess I'm a little surprised that you don't have at least Traditionalist leanings. I mean, you so obviously care about your heritage."

"Well, it's a little difficult to explain. I am not a Traditional, though maybe somewhat in leanings, I think. I feel that I can respect the cultural values of my people, appreciate them, and appreciate the importance of the old religion, without buying completely into the belief system. For example, I have a reputation for knowing and telling the lodge stories, so many of which have unfortunately been lost over the years. And I love them. It makes me feel good to tell them. I used to sit with my kids at night and tell those stories, the same way my ancestors did for centuries, and maybe the same way your mother read you a fairy tale from Grimms, or a Mother Goose rhyme. It gave me, and the kids and my wife, a sense of continuity with our past, a meaning of who we are as a people. But if you ask me if I believe that they are factual? Not really. I believe that our oral traditions were shadows of the truth, that there are indicators of the truth in them, but I don't adhere to them as religious truth. I support the practice of the

Mediwiwin, because I would hate to see the knowledge of that destroyed. It is a part of our heritage, and I wish to preserve it so that we know who we are as a people in relation to all other people. Does this make any sense to you?"

"Yes and no. In some respects it sounds like you are compromising, at least from the perspective of a real Traditional. How does someone like Thomas Crane, for instance, who believes he is a true follower, pure in his beliefs, respond to someone like you? Doesn't this cause divisions in the tribe?"

"Well, you have to understand that, again, there are varying opinions and positions within the ranks of my people who follow traditional beliefs. Some believe, as I do, that this is white America, and no matter what our religion, we must work within those boundaries. Some adhere to certain traditional beliefs, but not the messiah idea. Some belong to the Mediwiwin, but don't believe that the lodge stories are meant to be taken as literal history. We all get along o.k. because our major concern is the survival of our people in a hostile environment. That is our common ground, no matter where we stand on many other issues. There are limits, of course, to what I would do, or what many others would do. But with those few who are very extreme in their beliefs, the ones who refuse to work with the whites, who refuse to accept reality, there is very little communication. They are the ones who are living separated from the majority of the tribe, even though they may see themselves to be the saviors. That's where the conflict comes, surely. The extremists don't consider the rest of us to be, as you say, pure. They call us apples, though I certainly don't see myself that way. Their belief system says that whites are bad, all of them, all the time, and that Indians are a chosen people. And from a historical perspective it isn't impossible for an Indian to reach at least part of that conclusion about whites. The weight of evidence, you see.

"As for the chosen people, I suspect that the era before the white influx has been romanticized. The truth, of course, is that this land wasn't a Garden of Eden. Starvation was not uncommon for the northern tribes in a bad year, and war with the Iroquois was a fact of life for the Ojibwe. But, Crane for instance, believes that this red savior is going to appear and bring the Indian Eden back into existence. Given these ideas, he must respond to someone like me with hostility. He would betray his own philosophy if he saw it any other way. To him, I am a traitor to the people for being a friend to the whites, and a traitor to the truth."

They continued talking for another hour, diverging into various treaties between the government of the United States and the Ojibwe tribe. Whitefeather tried to give Rachel an accurate sense of how Indians viewed those treaties, now that tribal representatives were unearthing them and why there was such a conflict about them. At 2:30 she looked at her watch. "Oh, I can't believe that it's this late! I have another stop to make and still have to fix Uncle John supper." She rose. "Sam, I would like it very much if I could talk to you again. You've been so candid and helpful, so much better than a textbook! I can't tell you how much I've enjoyed this."

"How would you like to hear some lodge stories? I'm sure you've probably read them, but they lose something in the translation from oral to written"

"I'd love it!"

"I want you to meet my daughter Jill, too. She's about your age, our baby, and she still lives at home. You shouldn't be without friends your own age for the summer. How about if I talk to Mary and ask her when she could fix you dinner? Perhaps she'd make some traditional foods for you. Give me a call tomorrow, if you'd like, and we can set a date."

Whitefeather enjoyed talking to Rachel. He was convinced that she really cared about the treaties and traditions, and he found it easy to talk when assured of someone's interest. He realized that he had been very frank with her, and hoped that she wasn't offended by some of the things he had said about whites. If she was, she didn't express it.

Rachel came to dinner at the Whitefeather's small but comfortable house on the reservation the following Saturday. When she knocked at the door Sam greeted her in full ceremonial dress. He was proud of the authentic clothing and knew that he, indeed, looked like his forefathers had. There was a leather headband, dyed red and woven with black porcupine quills. On the right side of the headband, three wild turkey feathers hung upside down. His shirt was cream-colored and collarless, a plain affair, but over it he wore a long dark blue vest that reached nearly to his knees. On the vest were sewn large patches of the cream-colored cloth that resembled pockets, and on them were decorations of red, green, and yellow vines and leaves. Along the bottom hem of the vest were a number of tassels. His trousers were dyed the same dark blue, with patches of the vine design on his shins. White buckskin moccasins, fringed and decorated with dyed porcupine quills of red and blue graced his feet.

He twirled around like a model in a New York fashion show. "How do you like it?" he asked Rachel. "I have everything but the earrings."

"It's great!"

"Congratulate my wife, then. She is the marvelous designer and seamstress of all this."

Mary came into the room and Sam introduced her to Rachel.

"You'll have to excuse my husband," she said. "He thinks he's something special in his good clothes." She smiled.

Rachel examined the intricate stitching and weaving in Sam's clothes and asked Mary a dozen questions about how she made the regalia: "Where did you get the porcupine quills? How did you decide on the decorative pattern?"

Jill entered a few minutes later. Whitefeather thought she looked like her mother did when she was twenty; lithe, with high cheekbones and a beautiful dark skin. Her eyes were bright with intelligence and good humor.

The group sat down to dinner at the kitchen table.

"Sam asked me to cook you something traditional," Mary said to Rachel as she ladled a thin, pale gruel into a bowl in front of the girl. "Can you guess what this is?"

Rachel stirred the mixture with her spoon and smelled it. Let's see, we have blueberries, right?"

"Yes."

"And cornmeal, and some sort of beans, here, and some little pieces of meat. There's only one thing that this can be. My educated guess is sagamite."

"Right! You do know something, just like Sam said. I didn't make too much, just enough for a taste, really. Maybe my ancestors lived on this stuff, but I don't care for it much. I hope venison roast and squash sounds all right, because that will be our main course, with Fry bread. It's still traditional."

The dinner was a great success. Jill and Rachel seemed to hit it off immediately, and the student asked Mary many questions. After the meal, Sam told lodge stories until midnight, and an invitation was extended for Rachel to accompany them to church at Zeba the following morning. Rachel and Jill also made plans to see each other Monday afternoon, so that the white girl could meet some more of Jill's friends.

Monday was the beginning of all the trouble. When Jill had come home that evening and told her father about John Kohler throwing the young Ojibwe off his property, then running after their car like a mad man and flinging the tire iron, Sam was furious. His first thought was to drive to Kohler's and give him a piece of his mind.

"Daddy, I don't think that would be the best way to handle this. Neither Rob nor myself was hurt. Really, I'm more concerned about Rachel right now. I don't think she had any idea that her uncle could be like that."

"There's no telling what that crazy man might do to her," said Mary. "I can't believe he's kept his mouth shut this long, and her so involved with us."

"Maybe the very fact that he has kept his mouth shut is an indication of how much he really cares about Rachel," Sam said, "but if we don't hear from her soon, we're going to have to check into it. Better start thinking about a plan of action."

They were all relieved later when Rachel pulled up in her VW. She related the conversation with Kohler, and that she had offered to move out. Then she began to cry. Mary went and sat on the end of the couch beside the girl and put her arm around her. "Now listen, honey. If things get too rough with your uncle, and you need a place to stay, you can always come move in with us."

"Thank you," she answered. "I appreciate it so much, but I'm going to give Uncle John another chance. Maybe if I stay, I can influence him to give up these insane ideas he has. I still can't believe it, and I'm so sorry about him threatening Rob and Jill."

Whitefeather sat restlessly, his jaw set hard. He knew that he should not hate Kohler, but Sam felt such anger when someone innocent was hurt. And every time he envisioned the man running after Rob's car and throwing the tire iron – at his daughter! – he became angry all over again. Now, here was the fellow's own niece upset because he had said such horrible things to her.

"Well, I admire you for trying, Rachel, and I hope and pray that it works. But I agree with Mary. If you feel that things are getting too rough, you hightail it right over here. I still can't believe the way your uncle treated you!"

One of the family members saw Rachel every day after that, right up to July Fourth. She came into the store several times and had new questions for Sam, always recording his comments on tape. Jill invited her to spend the holiday with them, and they went to the parade together, and to the picnic at Baraga State Park. Whitefeather got the impression that Kohler and his niece had called an uneasy truce.

Instead of watching fireworks that evening, Jill asked Rachel to stay overnight, and they all returned to the house for popcorn and a game of Uno.

"I got the chance to talk to Charlie Lake a couple of days ago, Sam," said Rachel during the course of the game. "He seems to think that Crane has a point about a lot of the things he says. Charlie says that maybe Native Americans should just take what is theirs, by force, if necessary. It seems that Crane might be gaining followers from the moderates."

"I think chances are Charlie was exaggerating a little bit, Rachel. Probably for your benefit, too. Or maybe he was in the sort of mood that we all experience from time to time. You get mad, you get frustrated, things are moving too slowly. So you spout off and you feel better. I know Charlie, he's a pretty clear thinker, and I can't see him donning a red shirt and going out to purposely break the laws.

"Besides that, our people should recognize that Thomas Crane is basically wrong about how he approaches the problem. And I think that if he really considered with more logic what he was doing, he would stop some of his efforts, too. It has to do with what Charlie referred to as what is ours.

"You see, Crane overfishes, and calls it his right as an Anishinaabeg. There is some truth to that; the treaties give us certain fishing and hunting rights because that is how our people have survived for centuries. But is this truly anyone's right, Indian or white, just to fish non-stop, with no regard for the consequences? Crane lives, I'm afraid, in a fantasy world where the fish never run out. He wants to believe that the whitefish are still plentiful, but that isn't true. The truth is that the white man lives in this country, and he fishes, also. The lakes have been caught between the sea lamprey, industry, and fishing, and they are in danger of becoming lifeless pools of polluted water. And the more people Crane influences in this way of thinking, the worse it will be for the environment. The competition between him and the reactionary whites could go a long way to destroying our lakes completely."

"So, what's the solution? No one's satisfied right now."

"Personally I believe we must all alter the basic way in which we see the earth. The majority of the people have accepted the idea that land, the earth and all its creatures, are commodities, to be bought and sold, and used. Like furniture. Just purely utilitarian. That isn't the traditional Native way of viewing creation, of course. The red man, by and large, has viewed himself as an equal part along with all the other creatures. When a warrior killed an animal for food, it was customary that he thank that animal's spirit. He believed that the beast gave up its life to save the Ojibwe's. It was thought that it would then take another body and go on living.

"Also, there was no real concept of the ownership of land the way the whites have developed it. Owning the earth was an idea totally foreign to my people, and this undoubtedly had a great deal to do with why the white man was able to cheat the Native American so soundly. Title to Mother Earth was not something understood by my ancestors.

"Actually, some of what my people believed about land was consistent with a truly Christian view of the earth, which is what I personally hold to."

"Now wait a minute," said Rachel. "How can you say that you hold to a Christian view of the earth? Religious people have been the perpetrators of ownership of the earth, and they still believe that God gave them dominion over the earth to do with it as they please. You can't seriously say that Christians have an ecological view of anything! No offense Sam, I just think that if you care about the environment, you got it through your Indian heritage, not through going to church."

The night had turned cool and Sam got up from his chair and went over to the fireplace, where the newspaper and kindling wood were already laid out behind the andirons. Striking a match, he touched it to the right edge of the paper, then the center, then the left side, and sat back on his heels to watch the flames begin to lick around the kindling.

"It seems," he said as he got up and reached for a chunk of hardwood to place on the blaze, "that it depends on what your words mean. The people you refer to, Rachel, say dominion, but they mean tyranny. They perhaps have wrong motives, I don't know. It seems like we can act from mercy, or we can act from lust and greed. Christians should be ruled by mercy in relation to everything they do. Many who claim Christianity though, have allowed themselves to be molded by Western cultural ideas instead of Christianity, the way I see Christianity. Western cultures are usually highly advanced technologically, and I think the very technology has fostered an attitude of 'because we can do it, we should'. There is no mercy afforded the earth, or anyone who stands in the way of technology, and the fuel for modern technology is often greed."

"So what are you saying?" asked Rachel. "That these fundamentalists aren't true Christians because they don't have any mercy, or because they don't have a Christian view of nature? Boy, Sam, you'd better watch out, or you'll wind up being burned at the stake! Besides, how can any Native person want to call himself a Christian, considering all that Christians have inflicted on Native Americans? I can't understand why there is a church at Zeba, really. I think Christianity is one of the main reasons your people are in the mess they're in now, and your people that see the truth of that are turning back to the traditional beliefs.

"Talk about mercy. What kind of mercy did the nice white Christians ever show to your people?"

Whitefeather sighed and felt the old frustration returning. It seemed like he was forever defending what he perceived to be a misconception. And he did wonder how people that went to church each Sunday and read the same Bible he did could have done the horrible things to the red man that they did. He had a strong confidence in the faith he had chosen, but was sorely challenged by the record of history when he tried to present his reasons for believing to someone else, particularly someone who was hostile.

"Let me say, that if you do research into some of the early dealings with the tribes, you'll find that there were a few white churchmen who tried to be merciful and fair."

"Sam, they were a minority, hardly noticeable! History certainly doesn't show that they were very influential."

"That seems true enough. I can't defend the evil men in history who went by the title of Christian, nor can I defend those today who behave that way. But, for all that, I'm a Christian because I believe that Jesus Christ is who he said he was. To me that, and how I respond to his claims, is the basis for my belief system. I don't see Christianity as a white man's religion because it has been primarily the white man who has, up until now, been the main proponent, you see. All that matters is Jesus, and He transcends matters of race or culture. But you're right, I can't forget what the white race has done to my people in the name of Christ.

"Sometimes I suppose it makes me feel like my heart and mind are war zones. There is an inner reality of the spiritual life, and the outer reality of racial conflict. But I don't blame God, or Christianity for what the white man has done. We are all capable of atrocities in the name of our religion, country, or race. I still believe that Christianity is true."

Rachel sat with her arms folded, not looking at all convinced by his arguments. "So," she said, "is the white Christian war on Nature just another phase of the battle plan? I suppose most church people don't see out-and-out genocide as acceptable as it was in the Nineteenth Century. But they have to have something to conquer, so now they are wasting the environment, an action which is no more Christian than the genocide, if I hear what you're saying."

"Things are changing. There are a few organizations within the church that are taking a much more balanced stand toward environmental issues. There have been some good books written in recent years, too, that are well-thought out and in line with Scripture."

"But it isn't any different, Sam. The majority isn't changed, is it? No more than the majority of Christians stood up and protested the attempted extermination of the plains tribes, or the stealing of the ancestral lands of the Cherokee."

"Look, I don't know where these people get their theology of creation, certainly not from the Bible that I read. They have accepted the fallacy that everything has been created for mankind. But the Great Spirit did not make all this beauty so that man, any man, could pillage or use it in any way he wished. Now, I don't believe that every rock and tree has an individual spirit, like my ancestor's thought, but there is a spiritual essence to nature.

"I think that God created all of this for Himself, for His enjoyment, even. I know it when I am in the forest. And the parts of the Bible that I understand most clearly are those that speak of creation reacting to the majesty of God. David talks in the Psalms about the mountains singing with joy before the Lord, and Isaiah says that the trees clap their hands. Jesus said that not even King Solomon was arrayed as majestically as the simple wildflower, and Paul spoke of creation groaning, waiting for its redemption. I tell you, I've often heard the singing, the clapping, and especially the groanings. I believe truly that there is a degree of kinship between me, as a created being, and other creatures of nature. The trees are my brothers!

"But mankind, though also a created being like the fox or the deer, has an extra dimension, that of being created in the image of God, as a personal spiritual being, capable of reason and choice and creating, also. A being with a will. And because we are different, I think mankind was placed on the earth as a custodian, even as some of my people believe. But how many whites, especially Christians, have understood this? St. Francis of Assisi, yes. A handful who dared to transcend their cultural prejudices. Few others. And as you see, I am caught between two worlds, the white Christian's, and the Native American's, and I walk in a third of my own understanding."

"It's never easy to be a Christian and Anishinaabeg," said Mary. "It causes conflicts between people, and conflicts within, also."

"Well, to draw all of this together," concluded Whitefeather, "if humans are the custodians of the earth, from a Native American perspective, and the stewards from a Christian perspective, then we should realize that we care for the earth for someone else, and not simply for ourselves. There is no ownership in question, here. We, as humans, don't own anything, but we tend it for the Creator. We are allowed usage of its fruits for our sustenance, but what right have we to destroy it? None. No more than someone renting a house from any of us has the right to destroy that house. Then we have no right to overfish the lakes, no right to pollute the earth, no right to use it for our own personal gain if we, by that usage, destroy it beyond any hope of restoration.

"Some Native Americans believe that messiah is going to come back and provide for them. If all the fish are gone, then the Great Spirit will send more fish, and those people who have accepted this idea believe this is the Native way. It was never so. And many white Christians believe the same thing. Jesus will come back to clean up the mess they've made, as though they have been given no responsibility for that. I personally believe that, when Jesus does come back, we will be made responsible for our abuse of the earth. It's around this issue, the care of the earth, that I often try to communicate with my people. It is common ground. Most Ojibwe have retained their sense of kinship with the earth, even if they've accepted white ways for much else in their lives."

Rachel still seemed skeptical, much to Sam's disappointment. The subject turned to less serious topics, Mary made some more popcorn, and Rachel tried for the fourth time to call her uncle. He wasn't home. She tried once more before everyone retired for the night, but was still unable to reach him.

The following morning Whitefeather received a telephone call from Dan Roche, another member of the tribal council.

"Hello, Dan. What's going on so early?"

"It's what went on last night, apparently. Willie went to his boat this morning and found the nets slashed. Crane's and Boyd's , too. Cut to shreds."

"That's just what we need right now. Anybody have any idea who's to blame?"

"Lots of ideas. Could have been kids, could have been a crank, could have been members of the Wisconsin tribe. Crane's sure it was whites. Nobody saw or heard anything. The Tribal Police were all patrolling elsewhere because of the holiday."

"Well, I don't think it could have been the Wisconsin people. We've had our disagreements with them about territorial waters, but they would never do this. We'd better convene the Council as soon as possible so we can assess the damage and do whatever necessary to remedy the situation."

The meeting was held at one o'clock. No evidence had been found, and Whitefeather moved that a reward of $1200.00 be offered for information leading to the arrest and conviction of the person or persons responsible for the destruction. It was little consolation to anyone, but it was the best thing that could be done at the time.

He went right to the store from the council meeting. He had been spending much time away from the business, mostly on tribal affairs, and he felt guilty that Mary and their married son Jim had to assume so much responsibility for the place.

That evening after he arrived home he heard about Rachel's latest experience with Kohler. The girl was sitting in the living room with Jill.

"Sam, I hope your invitation for a place to stay still stands."

"What happened?"

"I thought he was going to hit me, this time. He said some really harsh things; accused me of shacking up with Rob. He was worse than he was the last time, and there is absolutely no reasoning with him."

Sam noticed that Rachel had freckles. They stood out very prominently against her white skin. Funny he'd never seen them before.

"You know you can stay here, and you're probably doing the smart thing, from the sound of it. Your uncle is a very bitter man, Rachel. I don't know why he is like this, but I know one thing. Bitterness is like a cancer. If it isn't removed from a person's life, it can end up killing them, and harming those they love."

"I hope you don't mind if I call my mother to give her your address and telephone number. She'll be so upset. Uncle John is her only brother."

Rachel made the call later. After a few minutes she called Sam over to the telephone and gave him the receiver.

"Hello, Mr. Whitefeather. My daughter has had such good things to say about you and your family, and I want you to know how much her father and I appreciate you taking her in at a time like this.

"I can't imagine what's got into that brother of mine. Rachel's not the sort of girl to make things up, so I know this is serious. I'm going to call him tonight and get to the bottom of this in a hurry, I'll tell you."

"Well, I'm really sorry that this has happened, Mrs. Johnson. Rachel seemed to have such a special relationship with her uncle, it's a real pity there are problems. But don't worry about her. Our whole family is very fond of her, and we are pleased to have her stay."

"Like I said, we sure do appreciate it. If there's anything that she needs, please do call us. This situation is surely a surprise to us, like I say, and it's good to know she's got somewhere to go safe and sound."

The next day after church Sam and Mary were driving home. Jill and Rachel were off on a picnic with some of the other young people.

"You know," said Mary, "the situation between Rachel and her uncle is really terrible. I confess, I don't like the man, but I hate to see such discord in a family. It's odd that all those years this never came up between them."

"Not much chance for it to come up, I suppose."

"I think we have to be careful that we don't make things worse."

"What do you mean?"

"Well, we mustn't give Rachel the impression that we think her uncle is a really evil man, hopelessly evil, I mean. The entire situation can become so polarized. You know what I mean, Sam?"

"I suppose, but that guy makes me so mad! I mean really mad! Sometimes it seems like he couldn't possibly be a rational human being…"

"But you don't say that about Crane, and he's just as prejudiced as John Kohler. You can see Crane's side. Don't you think that maybe you should take a step back and give Mr. Kohler a chance?"

Whitefeather was silent a moment. "I don't know. Maybe you're right. I can make excuses for a Native American bigot, but not a white one. Maybe I have a racial problem myself."

"I don't really think you do, Sam. It's just a problem of being able to identify with Crane easier. But you know I was thinking about those verses in Matthew that we read in Sunday School class today. 'Blessed are the peacemakers.' I think maybe you, and I also, should take that admonition a little more seriously."

"I try to. I mean, all that I do with the tribe and the community…"

"I know. But sometimes we get caught up in organizing and categorizing, and when something doesn't fit into the neat little boundaries, like 'the tribe', we aren't too peaceful about it."

"Hmm. You have a point. Where would I be without you to bring me back to the straight and narrow?"

"Isn't it the truth?" Mary replied with a mocking grin.

Whitefeather made a half-hearted swipe at her, which she adroitly ducked.

"But really, Sam, I don't think anything happens entirely by chance, don't you agree? We have a responsibility here, and I feel it's more than just providing Rachel with a roof over her head until she returns to school."

"Yes, and perhaps Rachel is meant to be some sort of catalyst in her uncle's life. He certainly needs to come to the realization of his own destructive tendencies. From everything Rachel has told us, she and Kohler have always shared such a special relationship, and I can't see how he would be willing to jeopardize that because of a prejudice against our people."

"Maybe this is John Kohler's chance to change. I always believed that when we go down the wrong path of life, truth pursues us, tries to make us see our mistakes. Maybe Rachel is part of that chase."

"Hmmm. You know what really bothers me about the whole thing, though? It's Kohler's blaming that Ojibwe midwife for everything. Rachel says that he's brought that up a couple of times as an explanation for his behavior."

"It is strange. I wonder who she was, and what on earth she was doing there?"

"Well, I'm sure she's long since dead, but maybe something could be found out about her. Maybe it would help to solve some of these problems."

* * *

But here it was, nearly the end of July, and nothing had been resolved between Rachel and her uncle. They still acted like night and day, and still were not speaking. Whitefeather pulled into the parking lot at the hardware store and went in.

"Sorry you had to open up again, honey. How's business?"

"Slow. What did Gerald want?"

He told her. "What do you think?"

"I think it's great, and don't worry about the store. We'll manage. This is the kind of opportunity you've always wanted, a way to explain our people to others."

Sam left early in the afternoon to go to the craft fair. George Elk had a display for the first time this year, and Sam was interested in seeing how he was doing. He also thought he would stop by John Kohler's booth. Sam had an idea.

He found Elk in a corner. Not an optimum spot, thought Sam. But the native craftsman seemed content. He talked to Elk for quite some time, then asked, "Have you seen John Kohler, here? I want to stop by his booth."

Elk just gave Whitefeather an odd look and pointed down the aisle. "Near the other end," he said, shaking his head.

Whitefeather immediately perceived that George had had some sort of altercation with the white man, but decided not to ask about it. Elk kept to himself in such matters. He was proud and independent, and let his craftsmanship do most of his talking for him. Sam walked down through the center of the big tent, beneath the naked light bulbs hanging over the aisles, past the various displays, and he felt a little nervous. He wasn't afraid of Kohler, but neither was he too sure of how receptive he would be to peacemaking.

When he found the booth the white man was sitting absorbed in a magazine. Whitefeather was about to greet him when he saw the carving of the white pine displayed on the table. He picked it up. The asymmetrical shape of the tree triggered a shock of recognition, and all the beauty and wildness of the north woods flooded in upon him with a burst of pleasure.

"This is beautiful!" he exclaimed.

Kohler looked up with a pleasant business-like expression that darkened immediately. His mouth formed a vicious dog snarl. "Take your hands off that," he commanded.

Whitefeather was under the spell of the artwork. He wanted very much to own it, to take it home and hang it somewhere prominent, someplace where it could always be seen; if only Kohler would sell it to him.

There is decency in this man, he thought to himself, *if he could create this*. Sam stood immobile as Kohler insulted him and continued to order him away from the display, but he hardly heard it, and it did not matter to him. He felt that he had seen a side of this man that was never shown to his people. The man was unveiled before him, and no matter what Kohler said or what actions he took, Whitefeather was convinced of another reality, an additional reality, about the white man.

"Rachel is staying with Mary and I," he said calmly, before he turned away. "She's quite well…"

Kohler refused to listen. Whitefeather shook his head and offered their telephone number on a slip of paper to Kohler so that he could call and talk with Rachel, but it was brushed to the floor. Whitefeather watched it float down and settle in front of the display table. He shook his head again. Such contradiction. He turned to go, but was compelled once more to try and communicate what he felt about Kohler's work. He then walked away, feeling as though he had been made privy to a revelation.

When he arrived home, still overcome by the image of the white pine carving, he discussed the results of his efforts with his wife.

"I was so moved by that carving," he said. "There is much more in this man than what meets the eye. If only he would give up this campaign of hatred against us."

"Well, Sam, it's still possible that he may never change. But you're right. The situation isn't good as it is, and perhaps we should actively urge Rachel to take a step toward reconciling their differences. Apparently John isn't receptive enough to start the ball rolling.

Later in the evening Whitefeather sat in his Lazyboy rocker reading a book on Hopewell archaeology that Rachel had brought with her. A pleasant blaze was crackling in the fireplace.

Rachel came in about 7:30 and greeted Sam, then stuck her head into the kitchen where Mary was baking a pie.

"Hi, Mary. What's cooking?"

"I thought I'd fix us some goodies. Sam got a new job today, so we're celebrating. Have you had supper?"

"I grabbed a bite out. New job?" She went back into the living room. "You give up the store, or something?" Putting her daypack down, she sat on the couch.

"Naw. I'm going to give lectures and tell lodge stories two times a day on Tuesday and Thursday as a part of the new program at the Tribal Center."

"Great!"

"I saw your uncle today at the Craft Fair."

Rachel shook her head and stared into the fire. "You didn't try to say anything to him, did you?"

"I told him where you were."

The girl looked up, startled. "I bet that went over really well."

"Not really. I guess he was typically John Kohler. But Rachel, he had carved the most beautiful plaque I've ever seen in my life! Suddenly I saw a part of your uncle that I'd never known, the part you knew as a child, the good and caring part. And I can't believe for a moment that he doesn't love you. You were so close to him when you were young, and even the first two or three weeks of the summer. He hasn't forgotten any of that, I'm sure."

Mary came into the living room, wiping her hands on a dishtowel.

"Sam and I have been talking, and we think you should make some attempt at reconciling with your uncle. We love you, dear, and we wish you could move in permanently and stay as part of our family. I hope you know that. But the reality is that John Kohler is a blood relation of yours, and no matter who is at fault, an attempt should be made to bring you two to some sort of understanding. Sam and I have a commitment to reconciliation between people, and we feel we have to urge this."

"And it doesn't appear that John will take the first step," added Sam. Rachel was silent a moment. "Look, you guys were the first ones to be glad that I left his house after the incident earlier this month. I guess I don't understand where you're coming from."

"We were concerned for your safety at the time," said Mary. "But I think Sam is right. Your uncle has had some time to think things over. We should always try to bring families back together. Or course, if he still doesn't want to iron out the problem, then you've done everything you can, and you'll know that."

"I appreciate what you're trying to do, and I even believe that what you say is probably right, but you have to see how difficult this is for me, too. You are some of the closest friends I've ever had in my life, even though we've only known each other for a short time. I feel as close to you as I do to my real family. So when Uncle John says something against Native Americans, I'm really torn up inside. I would be a traitor to you if I didn't defend you, and he wouldn't stand for it. How am I supposed to deal with those circumstances?

"I feel like everything has changed between he and I. I've seen a side of him that I never dreamed existed. And yet, I do love him. Not just because he's my uncle, but I love at least a part of who he is. I don't know. It's just turned into such a love-hate thing, but mostly I'm just angry with him. I don't think he'll ever listen to reason, ever change."

"I understand how you feel," said Sam. "But we need to hold forth a cautious hope that your Uncle John will change. Hope, but don't be crushed if the results are less than you'd like to see. Maybe John needs you to believe that he can change, or that he needs to. This attitude of his has got to be tearing him up inside too. Bitterness is most destructive to the one who is bitter."

"I'll think about it, but I just don't know if I'm ready to confront him."

It was a week later that Rachel brought up the subject again at supper. "I suppose I should try to call Uncle John, just to see how he's doing."

After helping to clean up from the meal, she went to the telephone, visibly nervous, Whitefeather thought. But then, who wouldn't be? Kohler could be so unpredictable.

The girl dialed the number and waited.

"Hello, Uncle John? How are you?"

Whitefeather tried to guess from her expression what was being said on the other end of the line. No look of hurt or shock, he thought. So far, so good.

"How's your work going? Have you been fishing lately?"

Sam started to relax. At least they seemed to be carrying on some sort of a normal conversation. He looked at Mary and she nodded her head.

"Sam said that the carving you had at the Craft Fair was beautiful. I never got to see it … Oh, come on, Uncle John, don't get insulting again … Why do you say such things? … Well, I'm really sorry you feel that way … I think we'd better hang up, now. Goodbye."

Rachel put the receiver into the cradle and sat down on the couch. She put her head back and closed her eyes. "He's one of the hopeless ones, Sam."

Whitefeather thought that perhaps they had been too hasty in insisting that the girl take steps to approach her uncle. He hated to see the disappointment on her face. Nevertheless, he said, "Nonsense, Rachel, we don't know that for sure."

"You should have heard the things he said!" she opened her eyes and lifted her head.

"It's not like I haven't heard them before. Sometimes a person fights the hardest just before they're going to go through a big change. Maybe all of this is making your uncle think seriously about himself and his attitudes. I'm sure he loves you, Rachel, and love is the strongest of forces."

"Pie in the sky, Sam. Hatred is a strong force, too, and if you look around you, you'll see more evidence of it than love. I don't believe that people can change." The girl made a disconsolate gesture with her hands. "I don't have an uncle, that's all. And my mother doesn't have a brother."

"So, you've lived so long?" asked Mary. "I'm not sure you could make that statement even if you were our age, and certainly I don't think a girl of twenty has enough experience to determine that people can't change. I've seen plenty of people change in my day. We just have to have some faith."

*   *   *

The summer was disappearing fast. Rachel was scheduled to return to the fall semester at school the Ninth of September, and the last big festival for the tribe was to begin on August Twelfth. Sam looked forward to the Pow Wow, a time of remembrance for the Ojibwe tribe. Recently such gatherings had become very popular with both Indians and whites. Sam supported the Pow Wows as events that contributed to the continuity of his people and spoke on it each time he gave his lecture at the tribal center, urging the whites to come and observe.

The Pow Wow began on a Thursday morning. In order that tourists could spend more time at the various booths and events available to them, Sam was scheduled to give only one talk each afternoon instead of the normal two.

At the end of his lecture Thursday on the history of the Anishinaabeg, he went to take part in two hours of dancing at the center of the tribal campgrounds. Most tourists expected to see the fast-stepping, fancy dances characteristic of most Pow Wows, but the Tribal Council had opted for history. The dance steps were slow, and methodical, that of the northern woodland tribes. Tourists raised on television, which showed only Cheyenne, Lakota or Arapaho, and then incorrectly, were introduced to the true heritage of the Ojibwes.

The leader, or caller, as the dancing got started was James Shohokia. There were three musicians; one drummer, and two men who shook rattles. Like Sam, they were all dressed in traditional Ojibwe costumes. Many of the other tribal members were clothed in varying degrees of tradition, but some felt quite comfortable taking in the affairs in their day to day attire.

The first dance was that named for the great bear. Shohokia had the responsibility of explaining to onlookers what the dance was, what it signified, and then chanting or singing any accompanying words. Women and men were not allowed to dance together, so the men lined up single file and waited for James to finish his introduction. Sam took his place in line, and when everyone was ready, Shohokia cued the drummer, who began the beat. The rattlers joined in, and the line began to move slowly forward. Whitefeather closed his eyes for a moment to focus on the rhythm, picked it up and let it fill him, and began to move his feet in a shuffle. Two steps, shuffle, his body swaying slowly from side to side in imitation of the bear, one of the tribe's most sacred animals. Most of the dances were named after beasts, though some honored the harvest, good fishing, the sun, the moon and the wind.

After three dances Shohokia stopped and said, "All right. Do we have any of our visitors who would like to volunteer to learn one of our dances?"

There were many white spectators in the audience. They all stirred around uneasily and looked at one another. No one said anything.

"O.k. How about you, sir?" Shohokia walked up to a blond young man in a powder blue polo shirt and navy blue slacks. The white boy looked startled, but his wife, equally blond, said, "Oh go on, Billy. It will be fun. I'll get a picture of you."

With much cajoling he stepped into the dance area, sheepishly moving from one foot to the other.

"Where you from, Billy?" asked Shohokia.

"Cleveland."

"Got any Indians in Cleveland?"

Billy grinned. "I think just the baseball team."

The onlookers laughed, and the white man seemed more at ease.

"All right, good," the caller said, grinning. "But believe it or not, there are more Indians in Cleveland than just the baseball team. There are populations of Native Americans in many urban centers all across the country. "Well, let's get started. You ready to learn the tortoise dance?"

Billy shrugged slightly and Shohokia nodded at the drummer, who began the rhythm. The men moved into the beat and Shohokia instructed the white man as they went along. Billy fumbled for a minute, and then began to get the idea. He soon joined the line of Indians, a fair-skinned, polo-shirted fellow in the midst of the darker set of dancers wearing bright, traditional regalia.

Whitefeather was thinking that Billy would never see an old western on television in the same light again. He would remember that he had met some Indians, and they weren't at all like the stereotypes made in Hollywood.

Midway through the dance someone shouted and shoved some onlookers out of the way. Thomas Crane, red-shirted and flailing his arms, forced himself into the dance area.

"Shame! Shame!" he cried, then stopped to pick up some dust and flung it into the air. The drummer ceased and the line stopped.

Crane walked up to Shohokia. "Shame!" he said again, and turned toward Billy.

"Hey, white boy, you come to see the spectacle? You get out of here."

Shohokia had gently taken Crane's arm and was speaking to him in a low voice. Sam moved from the line of dancers, also. Crane wrenched his arm free from the caller's grasp.

"Shame! You let a white man share in a ceremonial dance of the Anishinaabeg! You defile the traditions of our people and dishonor our ancestors. But then, why not? Most of you are half-breeds anyway."

The crowd murmured among itself and Billy returned to his wife, guiding her quickly away from the area. Some of the whites were stepping back, others hung on every word spoken by the Natives.

"Come on, Thomas." Whitefeather approached the traditionalist leader. "This is no time for this discussion."

Crane spit into the dust at Sam's feet and looked at him in blank hatred. "You're a dog, Whitefeather. A dog of dogs. You're a traitor, and you'll be the first to go in the coming judgment upon those who call themselves by the Anishinaabeg name, but have forsaken the Anishinaabeg ways." He spit again, and stalked back through the crowd.

"That guy is single-handedly going to drive away all of our tourist business," said Shohokia.

"Not necessarily," said Sam. "You'll notice that some people feed on this type of thing. Unfortunately, it's not the sort of image we'd like to project, but it does draw a crowd."

"Yeah, well I have some real mixed feelings about Crane. He's done a lot for our people in the area of pursuing treaty rights, but he doesn't know when to stop. He's a fanatic. Right now I'd like to take a club to him."

"He doesn't live in the white man's world, James. In his world Manabozho still walks and the Mediwiwin holds great power. To react to white participation in our pow wows with anything less than outrage would be to negate his entire belief system." The two men were talking in low voices as people milled about in the aftermath of the confusion caused by Crane's intrusion.

"Well," said Shohokia, "nevertheless it's affecting us here. I still say he needs a good talking to."

Sam and the caller reorganized the dance, and Shohokia apologized for the disruption. Sam overheard a white man and his wife discussing the incident. They were convinced that the entire affair had been staged by the Indians to give an added Wild West flavor to the benign nature of the pow wow.

They think that the whole world is one big TV script, thought Sam.

The interruption caused by Thomas Crane's protest of the dance did not ultimately hurt the pow wow. Things went on smoothly, and at the end of the day the coffers showed a good profit from the sale of craft items and food. The following day was without incident during the ceremonies and activities.

In the evening Sam was walking in the campground area, intending to check in on one of the women's weaving exhibits. He saw Dan Roche striding swiftly toward him.

"Thank God I found you," Roche said. "We got big trouble, and got to get over to the center right away. Willie Barnett's boat has been impounded by the DNR, and him and Crane were jailed. They caught them overfishing the legal limits."

CHAPTER ELEVEN – NIGHT CONFLAGRATION

The days passed in a blur for Kohler. He worked as though weights were tied to his hands and feet, and he found himself mis-measuring and having to discard valuable pieces of lumber. His mind wandered often. His stomach was worse than ever, and he awoke every day with a burning flame in the center of his belly. He finally went to the doctor, something Kohler had rarely done in his life. The physician told him to calm down and watch his diet. He was developing an ulcer that could kill him.

"What do you mean, calm down?" Kohler yelled. "I live in the woods and work for myself. I'm very calm!"

"Well, something's wrong somewhere," the doctor said. Kohler left the practitioner's office in a huff.

Rachel had called around the first of August. Kohler was glad to hear from her. He had told her that work was coming along as well as could be expected, and that he hadn't been fly-fishing in weeks. Then the stupid little girl had to ruin the conversation by bringing up that filthy Indian and the white pine carving that Kohler sold to the Governor's assistant. The afternoon in the tent came back to Kohler in a rush of rage, and he purposely said things to Rachel designed to hurt and anger her. Who needed someone around that was mixed up with those savages, anyway? A new wave of wrath swept over him each time he thought about it. His own flesh and blood living with the scum of the earth, filthy beasts that should have been exterminated long ago. He tried not to dwell on it, but he dreamed a lot, and awoke to recall the faces of Whitefeather, Rachel, Crane, and his sister Grace, as they floated in tatters through his mind.

One afternoon near mid-August he returned from a trip to Marquette where he had driven with a few pieces of furniture. Though he wasn't hungry, he fixed himself a supper of canned tomato soup and a few stale crackers and sat down in front of the television to watch the evening news. Might as well catch up on what's happening in the outside world, he thought, and turned the channel to the Marquette station. Kohler sat sipping his soup from a mug and watching the newscasters as they told about the latest bill in the House of Representatives in Lansing, and a trailer fire in Michigamme. Then the announcer began to cover a different story.

"The situation continues to heat up in the treaty rights battle in the Upper Peninsula," he said. "The DNR today towed in a fishing vessel belonging to members of the Keweenaw Bay area tribe of the Chippewa Indians for fishing beyond the limits agreed to in negotiations between the tribe and the State of Michigan. Taken into custody were Willie Barnett, the owner of the trawler, and two companions, Teddy Strong and Thomas Crane. The boat is temporarily held tonight at the L'Anse harbor Marina. Tomorrow it will be taken to a DNR impound facility in Houghton."

Kohler got up and snapped off the television. He paced the floor in the living room shaking his head. "A slap on the hand," he said aloud to himself. "Tomorrow those savages will be out of the hoosgow and walkin' around big as life. And Crane! He'll use this to make himself the big hero and just get more and more of them on his side. They'll have that boat back in a couple of days and off they'll go. Pretty soon there won't be a whitefish left in Lake Superior." He kicked at the coffee table, missed it, and nearly lost his balance. It just made him angrier. "Let them go and there won't be a grouse, a deer, a trout, nothin' left in the north woods. Nothing!"

He stomped into the kitchen, poured the rest of his tomato soup down the drain, and began to do the dishes. He had allowed them to pile up the past few days, and there were several cereal bowls with dried, hardened pieces of food stuck to them. He took out his frustration on the crusted vessels. While he was working the telephone rang.

"Hello!" he shouted into the mouthpiece.

"Hey there, buddy. You don't need to shout at me. I'm not deaf."
It was Presslein.

"Sorry," said Kohler. "Guess I was thinking about something else."

"Did ya hear about the DNR hauling in the red boys' boat today? Looks like the rangers are finally doing what they're paid to do for a change."

"Don't make any difference," Kohler said sullenly. "It's just a slap on the hand. They'll just go right on doing what they've been doing."

"Well, you might be right, but I don't know. I think the law is finally starting to hear the people in the matter. Whites have been getting shafted all along, and I think with our organization doin' as well as it is, the powers that be are gonna see that we're fed up. They're going to start helping us, and not the redskins. By the way, ain't seen you at any of our meetings. How come?"

"Been busy. And besides, you're just fooling yourself if you think your little club is going to stop those red devils from anything they're up to. It's going to take more than politicking."

"You mean like our little escapade here a while back."

"And more, if needs be. More! One thing I know, a lot of those old Indian fighters back in the 1800's were right. They should have slaughtered the whole bunch of the scum altogether. But no, they ended up leaving some for us to deal with. It'll haunt the white man for the rest of time because they didn't exterminate them."

"We didn't live back then, John, we live now, and nobody wants to necessarily exterminate anybody. Just keep 'em in their place. I think we're gonna make some headway on that these next few months. We've got a meeting here on Tuesday night at the Buckhorn Bar on 41. 7:30, if you'd like to drop by. We got some real good ideas for making money, kind of like the Pact Beer, but styled for us Yoopers. You ought to get out and see some of the boys involved. Lot o' trout fishermen there. They'd sure like to see some of your flies. New market, Kohler."

"I got too much to do," he answered gruffly. "And I don't feel like playin' cowboys and Indians."

"What's the matter with you, John? I thought you wanted to stop them."

"It's stupid. Everything is stupid. I won't waste my time. Now I got to go. Goodbye."

Kohler hung up the telephone before Presslein had the chance to answer. He felt hot and a bit nauseated, and he wasn't thinking quite clearly. The words of the newscaster kept running through his mind in fragments. *Boat impounded. L'Anse Harbor Marina. Tomorrow to Houghton.*

He went back to his dishes and a glass slipped from his soapy hand and shattered in the sink. He cursed loudly. Everything that went wrong in the world could be blamed on a certain few races, he thought. And around where he lived, everything wrong could be attributed to a particular breed. Everything.

Later, he sat at the kitchen table with his fly tying equipment spread before him, working on a Kohler's Dun Special. The thread had a mind of its own, knotted, and refused to go around the shank of the hook smoothly. The hook slipped from the tiny vise and implanted itself in the ball of Kohler's index finger. "Ahww!" He leaped from the chair and clutched his injured digit. The hook had sunk past the first barb and he let loose a steady stream of profanity while he removed it. The finger, freed from the point, bled profusely.

After bandaging it, he could not accomplish the precise work on the flies, and gave it up in disgust. Twilight was approaching, and he had been awake since dawn. It wouldn't hurt to just go to bed, he thought, so he retired to his room, undressed and lay down.

Kohler's eyes closed, but his lids were diminutive movie screens. In his head the newscaster's voice narrated the picture of the Indian trawler bobbing peacefully on the water in the L'Anse Marina. Kohler flipped to his side from his back and squinted his eyes hard, but the image of the boat stayed on the back of his lids. He ran through the newscast again and was overcome with indignation. Then he thought about Crane, Barnett, and Strong walking out of jail, scott free, and all the stupid people who would say that they were persecuted because of their race, and the other stinking Indians that would proclaim them as conquering heroes. Kohler angrily thrashed about in his bed. And how long would that trawler be impounded, anyway? They'd hire some hot shot lawyer to tell some empty-headed judge that the impounding of the boat was an affront to the Indian people, and causing them undue hardship, and the white race should seek ways to make amends for the atrocities perpetrated on the Native Americans, blah, blah, blah. Yes, he'd heard that litany a dozen times. The boat would be out and underway by afternoon the next day. Back out in the lake, taking more fish illegally. That is, unless someone stopped it. And on the back of his eyelids Kohler saw himself walking up to the trawler anchored in the harbor. He had a kerosene can in his hand. He boarded the boat and splashed the fuel everywhere, everywhere. And then he struck a match, and as he jumped away from the craft, flicked the small dart of light into the fuel-drenched deck and watched while the flames roared up and engulfed the structure.

He derived tremendous satisfaction from this scenario, and played it over and over in his mind, each time tasting the vengeance anew, and the sweet fulfillment as the fire licked up the sides of the Indian boat. He lay in bed with his fists clenched, wide awake, tossing from side to side, replaying the destruction and letting the hatred wash through him in angry waves. Finally he sat bolt upright and ran his hands through his damp hair. "If there was only some way to do it!" he said aloud.

Then, like a revelation, an image pervaded his mind, an image of his canoe, turned upside down behind the house, unused since last year. "From the water! Yes! No, how would I explain being out in the middle of the night with a canoe if somebody saw me?" he thought some more, and the image of the boat, engulfed in flames, kept playing upon his mind.

After a few minutes he clapped his hands together and rose from the bed. He began to dress quickly; the nights were cold this late in the summer, so he put on thermal underwear, a flannel shirt and a jacket. He glanced at the clock. After midnight and time a'wasting. He pulled on his heavy woods boots over wool socks and left the house by the back door. A small shed located where his back yard met the woods showed a faint grey in the darkness. He fumbled with the lock and the door swung open. Groping carefully along the right inside wall, he traced the location of machines and tools in his mind. In the far corner was a two-gallon can of kerosene fuel for a small heater he used in the winter. He picked it up and followed the wall back to the doorway and outside.

Kohler stopped after he locked the door of the shed and stood stock still in the night, listening, feeling. His senses told him the winds were calm; there was only a pale quarter moon hanging in the sky among the carpet of stars. He carried the can of kerosene around to the front of the house and put it in the pickup. In the back again, he hefted his aluminum canoe upon his shoulders and carried it to the truck, sliding it along until only two feet of the length was hanging past the end of the bed. Paddles. He swore softly. They were in the shed. More wasted time. He went back to the small building, retrieved the wooden paddles, and carried them to the pickup.

Kohler was hot with excitement and he undid his collar and opened his jacket to let in the crisp air. Now for the final preparations. He went back into the house and opened the closet that contained his fishing tackle. Instead of reaching for the fly equipment, he withdrew two heavier rods with open-faced reels attached. Rummaging further, he took out a tackle box that contained lures and baits for bass, pike and muskie. A drawer in the kitchen yielded several books of matches, which he stuffed into his jacket pocket. The last item was the ice chest, which he placed near the front door with two frozen half-gallon milk cartons of water in it.

He stopped for a moment and thought, ticking off items in his head. Satisfied, he went to the bathroom, then carried the rest of the gear to the truck. It was 1:00 when he left the driveway and headed north toward L'Anse. On the way he rehearsed the plan again in his mind, but mostly the part where the trawler burst into flame. Kohler was perspiring profusely and had to open his shirt several more buttons.

It was nearly fifteen minutes after the hour when he arrived in L'Anse. He wanted very much to drive to the marina and see the boat, but he knew he shouldn't. "I'll see it soon enough," he said to himself. Instead, he drove up Skanee Road, past the Post Office, and then turned left toward the bay. The street took him to Bay Shore Drive and he turned north once more, and followed the water.

Kohler's hair prickled beneath his collar with the knowledge that he was on reservation land, completely surrounded by his enemies. But there was a certain irony that presented itself to him, too. He would use their own facilities to hurt them. The thought appealed to him. He drove two miles and began to slow down and peer hard at the left side of the road. A few more yards and he saw what he was looking for. A break in the brush and grasses gave away a narrow lane that led toward the water. Kohler turned in. Only at that moment did it occur to him that he might not be alone. What if someone else had decided to spend this chilly night fishing on the waters of Keweenaw Bay? People did it, though fishermen primarily used this drive during the day. The Tribal Council had cut the lane down to the water's edge and constructed a crude boat launch to accommodate anyone who desired an entrance to the bay for simple sport fishing. On many summer days up to five vehicles could be found parked in the area, the owners out on the lake in rowboats or motorboats, plying their lines for the big game fish.

Kohler breathed a sigh of relief when his headlights revealed nothing but trampled grass and rutted gravel, however. He cut the lights and brought his pickup to a halt beneath a pine tree. Within a few minutes he had the canoe half in the water and the rods, tackle box and paddles situated. The last item to go in the bottom of his craft was the can of kerosene. He climbed into the stern and pushed out into the lake, pointing the bow south, toward L'Anse.

The conditions are favorable, thought Kohler. The water was almost glassy calm. There was enough light from the stars and sliver of moon to see to do what he had to do, but not enough to recognize faces or letters on a boat. It was a night of shadows and obscure forms. His paddle cut the surface of the bay cleanly and silently as he propelled the canoe slowly toward the marina, about two miles from the boat launch. It wasn't necessary to hurry right now; he wanted to make sure that most people would be asleep and unable to give an immediate alarm. He stayed about twelve feet from the shore and glided along quite comfortably. He could see the trawler in his mind's eye, moored at the end of the marina docks, bobbing just slightly on the face of the water.

It was about forty-five minutes later when Kohler could see the street lights in the marina parking area and the forms of several boats anchored in the harbor. He slowed his paddling and looked about cautiously. All was quiet as he neared the largest vessel, tethered to the end of the dock nearest him. It was the Whitefish King, Barnett's fishing trawler.

The night was still. Kohler could hear nothing but the barking of a dog in town, and the faint sound of an automobile some distance away. He concluded that the area was entirely deserted, and he drew close to the trawler until the bow of his canoe gently scraped against its side. Kohler waited quietly again, listening and watching, then tied a length of rope through the hole in the bow of his craft and looped it securely through the anchor line of the trawler. He reached for the can of kerosene and gently lifted it to the fishing boat's deck and, grabbing hold of the edge, pulled himself up after it.

The boat was one of the same ones that he, Presslein and Behrendsen had vandalized, and he had already decided how to go about firing it. He went to the nets at the back and poured some of the gasoline on them, then made a trail to the outside of the small wheelhouse, where he splashed the majority of the fuel. He made sure that any wood was doused, then made a puddle with the remainder right above his canoe. Placing the can in the middle of the small pool of fuel, he lowered himself back down the side of the trawler. Kohler was sweating profusely, but the night had turned quite cold, and he shivered almost uncontrollably from the air hitting his damp clothes. He had difficulty untying the knot in the rope that held his canoe to the larger vessel, but once free, he rolled the rope and placed the coil beneath the bow seat. Fumbling in his jacket pocket, he withdrew a book of matches. Once more he sat very still and listened. There was only the occasional creaking of the boats rubbing against the docks. He waited some more, with bated breath. The cold thoroughly penetrated Kohler's clothing, and his teeth began to chatter. *This is it*, he thought. *Do it*. He struck one match from the open book and held it against the rest of them. Fssst. The sudden glare startled him. It died as the sulfur was expended and the book of matches began to burn steadily. He half kneeled in the canoe, then tossed the small flame up and over, into the area where he had left the pool of kerosene.

There was a hollow-sounding "whomp" and an orange glow that spread quickly. Kohler had dropped to his seat and grabbed the paddle as soon as the matches left his hand. He turned the canoe north and paddled as quickly as he could, following the shore a few yards out. The prow cut through the water at such a speed that small white caps formed beneath it. He wanted to look back, but knew he didn't dare. He just kept his arms moving, two strokes on the left, two on the right, bending his body toward the gunwale in front of him to even the center of gravity, and lessen the wind resistance. After about five minutes he heard a small explosion in the distance behind him, and then a larger one that sent shock waves rippling through the air. A lurid glare briefly illuminated the water, but Kohler forced himself to continue paddling north, faster, faster. A few seconds later he heard the faint whining of sirens, and he realized that he had already traveled more than a half mile from the marina. Though his muscles were screaming, fear began to grow at the center of his chest, so Kohler kept punishing himself to continue at top speed. In his mind he calculated the events taking place back at the harbor. Someone awakened by the explosions had called the fire department. It took them about two minutes to get three blocks from the firehouse on Main Street. Those were the sirens he had heard. The police would get there a couple of minutes later. How long would it take them to decide the fire had been set? Surely they would think it was arson. Then they would begin to cruise the streets of town, stopping anyone who was driving this late at night. Almost no one in such a small town stayed up this late, not on a work night. It might be hours before they suspected that the boat had been boarded from the water. No one heard an outboard. No one could possibly have seen anything.

Kohler suddenly stopped paddling, gasped, and gripped his right shoulder. A cramp tied his muscle into a painful knot, and he was forced to allow the canoe to float while he kneaded the shoulder. The night seemed darker than when he had started out. The shadows beneath the trees on the shore were as black as the inside of a cave. There was no sound but the sound of the lake. The sirens had stopped; there was no vehicle along the Bay Shore Drive, which was hidden from his view by the trees, just a few yards to his right.

The muscle finally relaxed and Kohler picked up the paddle quietly and began moving again, this time slower, but still steadily toward the place where his truck was parked. After some time he distinguished ahead a break in the shoreline foliage. He drew closer to the overhanging tree limbs, stopped, and sat motionless and nearly breathless, waiting for a sound; the scrape of a boot on gravel, the click of a cigarette lighter, the low murmur of voices of men lying in wait. He heard nothing, but stayed still for ten minutes, then fifteen. Surely if they were there waiting they would have given themselves away by now. More time dragged by, and finally Kohler slipped his paddle back into the water and silently nosed the canoe back out into the lake.

He headed directly away from the shore, then north, and paddled until he was about a half mile past the parking area. There he stopped and opened the tackle box. He withdrew a small flashlight, which he used to choose a muskie lure. Attaching it to the line on one of the rods, he cast it far out into the water, and began to reel it in slowly. For the next two hours he sat quietly and fished while the canoe floated about, carried by the currents. He caught two good-sized muskie, an extra bonus for the night's work, he thought. His body had relaxed somewhat, and his clothes had dried so that he was as warm as could be expected, sitting out in Keweenaw Bay in a canoe at an ungodly hour. He thought about how nice it would be to go home, slip into his comfortable bed and drift off to sleep. But he couldn't. Not just yet.

A breeze started off shore, ruffling the water and causing the canoe to bob about like a cork. It signaled the approach of dawn, and Kohler strained his eyes toward the east. He could see a slight difference in the blackness; the sky was turning a faint charcoal color. He reeled in the lure, gathered the gear together, and began to paddle slowly south and toward the shore. I'd better be careful, he thought. The canoe has probably drifted some, and I could miss it altogether. He found that it had drifted toward the south, and was much closer to the truck than he anticipated. It took very little time to gain the shore. He approached with a great deal of caution. The shadows were not as deep as they had been; dawn would break soon, and other fishermen would be coming to launch their rowboats and outboards.

The prow of the canoe scraped the gravel and Kohler got out quickly, pulling it up near the truck. There was no one around, and he loaded the craft in the pickup bed and stowed the rest of the gear in after it. The two muskies were placed in the ice chest.

The cab of his truck had never seemed so good to him. Though it was cold, it was comforting, and a flash of joy shot through him as he turned the key in the ignition and the engine caught. He grinned in the semi-darkness. Got away with it, he thought to himself. He was on the road before he turned the lights on, then he headed back toward L'Anse.

A few people were driving to early jobs, but the city was still asleep for the most part. He passed through town and turned onto 41. He looked forward to stashing the fish in the fridge and going to bed for a while. They could be cleaned later.

About three miles before the turnoff to Wolf's Lodge Kohler was startled to see the red flashers of the State Highway Patrol in the rear view mirror. Panic seized him, and for a moment he had the urge to stamp on the gas pedal and try to escape. Then he laughed to himself and slowed the pickup. It was fruitless to try and outrun the state cop in a truck with a canoe hanging out the back. They had caught him. It was over, and he

would go to jail. But how did they know?

Kohler pulled over to the berm, stopped, and watched in his side mirror as the patrolman got out of the cruiser and walked up to the driver's side window of the pickup. Kohler rolled it down, his hands so sweaty they slid on the handle.

"Yes, sir," he said. "What did I do?

"Do you know you have a tail light out back here?" the officer asked.

"No, I sure didn't," Kohler said, feeling some relief.

"Left one. Early to be out and about." The patrolman's blue uniform was black in the dim morning light, but the badge stood out over his heart with a glaring brilliance. "Where you been with the canoe?"

Kohler's throat tightened and he thought that perhaps no sound would be able to escape it. He was surprised, then, at his calm reply.

"I been fishing all night on the bay."

The officer walked to the back of the truck and looked at the canoe, then came back to the window. "Where abouts?"

"Up at Pequaming," Kohler lied. The tale came out easily, like melted grease poured from a skillet.

"Catch anything?"

"Only two muskies for the whole time. Want to see them?"

"Yeah."

Kohler climbed out of the truck, walked around to the back, and drew out the ice chest, which was lashed to the side so it wouldn't slide out of the open tailgate. He unlatched the lid, grasped one of the big fish by the gill, and hung it before the officer's face. It gleamed a flecked iron grey in the dawn.

"Nice catch." The policeman glanced into the ice chest at the other muskie. "All night for two, huh? Well, I've been out longer than that and had nothing to show for my effort. Glad you came up with something."

Kohler put the fish back in the chest and secured it in its place. The patrolman tipped his hat.

"Better get that tail light fixed as soon as you can."

"I sure will. I'll stop into the gas station today and have it checked out."

"You have a nice day, now." The officer got back into his cruiser and left.

Kohler walked stiffly to the open door of the pickup and got in. He started it up right away and pulled onto the highway. The band of his cap was sweat-soaked and his chest constricted. *Had the cop suspected anything? Why did he ask where I had been?* Kohler wondered. *Why did he want to see the muskies? Certainly he must have thought it strange that I was out in the bay in a canoe instead of an outboard or even a rowboat. Maybe I should have gone up towards Huron Bay for a couple of days, driven up on the back roads before light, and camped by Big Eric's Bridge. By the time I'd got back the whole thing would have calmed down. That cop probably took my license number. It could be run through the computers and they'll find out who I am, and maybe start asking around. It's no secret about how I hate the redskins. They'll find that out, too. They probably have that on a computer somewhere, just like Big Brother. The government has records of everybody these days, and everything about them. What if Sam Whitefeather says something to them?* Kohler envisioned Whitefeather walking into the police station as soon as he heard about the firing of the trawler. "I know who it was," he'd say. "John Kohler. Check it out." Or maybe even Rachel. *She's so taken with the savages,* he thought. *She could do it easily. My own flesh and blood might turn against me!*

By the time Kohler turned into his driveway he was soaked through again with sweat, and feeling strangely weak. He climbed out of the truck slowly. *If they come for me*, he thought, *I have to make a run for it. I can go to the woods. If they don't have dogs they'll never be able to find me. Maybe I could even go back to Oregon. But I'm so tired.* He dragged the canoe from the back of the truck. It seemed to weigh three times what it did before. Evidence. What could he do with it? But he found that he couldn't think straight about it, he was so exhausted, and his mind so sluggish. He carried the craft to the back of the house and turned it over where it had been before, then returned to the truck and unloaded the rest of the gear. *I'll just put these fish in the freezer like they are,* he thought, *just to prove I was really fishing.*

It was full light when he was finally ready to retire. He peered out of the windows in the living room and pulled down the shades. As an after thought he carefully locked all of the doors, something he rarely did. When he darkened his bedroom, grogginess nearly overcame him before he could undress and get into bed. He fell asleep immediately.

Kohler couldn't tell what time it was when he smelled smoke, acrid and strong in his nostrils. He thought he was back in Oregon, for the trees all about him had girths of enormous proportions. Then he was nearly deafened by a roar like five diesel engines, running full throttle down a mountainside, and he looked up and realized that he was in the midst of a great forest ablaze. There was fire in the crowns of the trees, a hundred feet up, with the flames leaping from the top of one tree to the next like fiery circus animals.

Each time one of them leaped, the new tree would burst into an aerial blast furnace. The crackling of the branches as they split open and were consumed sounded like rifle shots. *How in God's name did this get started?* He wondered as he looked around. Then he saw a book of matches lying by the trunk of one huge tree, and recognized them as some he had picked up in a restaurant over by Houghton a while back. It dawned on him that he had begun this great inferno, but how? Certainly not on purpose!

He had to find a way out. The smoke was filling his lungs and it was very difficult to breathe. The heat parched his body, and he thought his skin would curl up and drop off like a leaf under the blast. He crouched down and tried to crawl along the ground to escape the worst of it. But which way should he go? He finally scuttled straight ahead and managed to gain several feet before a great limb, all ablaze, dropped in front of him, cutting off his retreat. He quickly reconnoitered and crawled in the opposite direction, but again the fire prevented him. Each time he took another tack, he was cut off, until he was entirely hemmed in by the inferno of his own making. Kohler cowered, choking and gasping, and waited for death to overcome him.

He awoke on his stomach, swathed in the blankets of his bed, clawing at the sheets, which were in piles where he had stripped them from the mattress in the throes of the nightmare. He was burning with fever, and felt like his body was composed of skin stretched over a volatile liquid, a sort of human water balloon. He raised his head and immediately dropped it again to the pillow. An anvil seemed connected to his neck. But even in the midst of his illness Kohler felt thankful that he was not among the blazing trees of his dream.

He threw off the blankets and lay for some time, trying to gather his strength.

Images of the previous night intruded upon his mind, but he wasn't sure that any of it had happened. Perhaps he had gone to sleep at 10:00 and everything had been a dream; the night on the bay, the trawler, sitting in the darkness fishing for muskie. He thought about the fish. If everything were a dream, then the fish wouldn't be in the freezer. He would know for sure, and would get up and see as soon as the weakness passed.

The heat in his body suddenly turned to ice, and he shook violently. He drew the covers back over himself, but they were not enough to stop the freezing hands that enveloped him. He became so cold that his teeth chattered and he wondered if he was dying. He found that, try as he may, he could not regulate his body. His thought processes, also, were going about their own strange business, with odd bits and pieces of conversation long past combining with weird images and nonsense syllables in his brain.

In mid-afternoon Kohler opened his eyes and felt stronger and more coherent. There was something that he had to find, something he needed to check on. He tried hard to remember, and then the image of the two muskies, wrapped in foil in the freezer, projected itself onto his mind. That was it. He had to see the fish, to see if they existed, and if he had gone to the marina and burned the trawler.

He struggled out of bed and stumbled to the bathroom, then to the kitchen, where he had to lean against the counter when a wave of weakness suddenly swept over him. When he had recovered somewhat, he opened the refrigerator door and looked into the freezer. Lying across frosty packages of hamburger and stew meat, and a bag of mixed vegetables, was something long and foil-wrapped. He took it out and closed the door. When he tore back the foil, there were the two muskies, their eyes glazed over in death, and their mouths slightly agape, revealing rows of tiny needle-like teeth.

Kohler stared at them for several minutes, and the fears of the previous night began to crowd in upon him again. It was all true. He had set fire to the Indian fishing boat, and someone would surely suspect him. That cop who had stopped him would keep thinking about the canoe in his pickup and eventually put two and two together. Kohler put the fish back in the freezer. It's best to act normal, he thought. I need to get dressed and get to work.

He moved quickly toward the living room, but stumbled and nearly fainted. He was very hot again, and weak. *I can't be sick*, he thought. *If I have to run, if I have to leave, I can't be held back. What if they come to get me for burning that stupid savage's trawler?* But Kohler's body would not cooperate, and he barely made it to his bed, where he collapsed.

He slipped immediately into a sort of delirium, a half-consciousness plagued by bizarre images. He was in his canoe on the bay, paddling very fast. His shoulders ached with excruciating pain, and when he turned around he saw the highway patrolman in his cruiser, with its red light flashing across the water, just a few feet behind his craft. Kohler could see the face of the cop, the sharp chin and nose, beneath the mounty-style hat. The cop was craning his neck through an invisible windshield and screaming, "Your tail light! Your tail light!"

The scenes kept changing, and shards of his life would fling themselves into his mind; Rachel's face, what looked like a bunkhouse from his Oregon days, Merle in his sauna, but wearing a woolen Mackinaw. Nothing made any sense, but twirled around before him like the colored glass of a kaleidoscope, then passed on and disappeared. That evening he awoke with a burning thirst and managed to lurch to the kitchen for some water, then to the bathroom. He was extremely weak, and went directly back to bed. The night was spent alternating between the bizarre dreams and periods of semi-consciousness, and either freezing cold or parching heat.

The following morning the ringing of the telephone in the next room awakened him. At first he thought that it belonged in the dream he was having, but he finally realized that it was a part of reality. Surely it was the police! They were calling him to come in for questioning. He lapsed for a second back into the semi-delirium and then surfaced from it, like a piece of driftwood riding storm waves, gaining the crest, and then washing under. The telephone rang many more times, until he was commanding it to stop, to cease and leave him be. When it finally did stop, he became more fearful, certain that uniformed officers would be at his door in twenty minutes. They would drag him out in his underwear and throw him into Lake Superior, which never gave up its dead. And what if the tribal police came? They would scalp him, and burn him at the stake. He was so hot, so hot now.

The telephone seemed to jangle again, insistently, in the afternoon, but Kohler couldn't separate it from the lurid visions that had consumed his bed. In late evening, just before sunset, he thought he heard a pounding at the door and a voice calling faintly, but he couldn't distinguish what it said. In his nightmare world he imagined it to be Thomas Crane, with a firebrand in his hand, coming to set the forest around him ablaze.
Then there were voices in his room and he opened his eyes. Rachel was bending over him, a worried expression on her face. Kohler couldn't remember when he had last seen her.

"Uncle John, how long have you been sick? I tried to call you several times today, and when I wasn't able to get an answer, I decided to come over."

Kohler groaned, and had to think what the string of words he had heard meant. Their meaning eventually became clear and he managed to say, "Nice of you." Somehow things seemed better with his niece there. "What day is it today? I was fishing…" The image of the trawler flashed into his mind and he stumbled over his words. "Fishing," he said again weakly, "the other night. I don't know what night it was. Not last night."

"This is Wednesday."

"Wednesday." Kohler tried hard to remember. Everything was hazy, the events of a thousand lifetimes ago. "Monday night? Fished on the bay all night. Must have caught a bug." He paused, swept back into the semi-dream state for an instant. "Are they coming?" he asked.

"Who, Uncle John?" Rachel turned away from his bed and he heard her voice directed toward the doorway of his room. "He's pretty sick. Do you think I should get him to the hospital?"

A deep voice answered behind her, a voice that sounded vaguely familiar to Kohler. "It might be a good idea. Looks like he's running a bad fever."

Kohler raised himself weakly on his elbow and squinted at the doorway. A dark face with a crown of iron-grey hair met his eyes. Whitefeather! A protest rose from Kohler, but he collapsed onto his pillow, too feeble to utter it.

"We're going to get you to a hospital," Rachel said.

"No," he said weakly. "No hospital." He paused, gathering more strength. "I'll never get out alive. Please don't take me there."

Rachel turned away and said, "What do you think I should do?"

"See if you can find a thermometer to take his temperature, and then we'll decide. If he's coherent enough to refuse treatment, it might just be a waste of time to take him, anyway."

Rachel left for a few minutes, and when she returned she stuck a cold thermometer under Kohler's tongue. It tasted vaguely like rubbing alcohol.
"101.5" she said after she withdrew it.

"I would have thought it to be higher," Whitefeather said from the background. "That way he's talking, it seems he's really sick. Well, why don't we see how he is in the morning, and then decide. Jill could stay here with you tonight to help out. Do you think you girls will be all right?"

Another feminine voice outside of Kohler's doorway said. "We'll be fine, Daddy."

"O.k. How about if you give me a call at 8:00 and let me know how things are."

Kohler wanted to feel incensed that these Indians were in his house, but he couldn't gather up sufficient strength. He felt so terribly tired, and wished simply to sleep. If only the strange images would leave him alone!

He saw Rachel leave the room and heard the soft murmur of the two female voices, then she returned.

"Can I get you anything, Uncle John? Would you like some water?"

Kohler nodded, and in a few moments he was sipping ice water through a straw. He soon slipped back into the stupor that had characterized this strange illness, and he knew no more until during the night when he found himself once more in the midst of a dream where he was being threatened, by whom, or what, he could not tell. He was screaming in the dream and then he felt a cool cloth on his forehead, and a voice softly calming him, a voice like a mother's saying, "It's all right, everything will be fine." He opened his eyes to see the round face of an Indian girl by his bedside.

"Please don't kill me!" he cried.

"I'm not going to kill you, Mr. Kohler. Don't be frightened."

And he was immediately embarrassed that the words had slipped out of his mouth, but he had still been in the half-dream state. She took his temperature and studied the thermometer.

"Hmm. A little better." She had a soft, melodic voice, and the sound of it soothed Kohler. He took some more of the ice water and fell back to sleep.

In the morning Rachel appeared again and took his temperature. "How are you feeling, any better?"

Kohler's mind was clearer, but the strange weakness still weighed down his body.

"Yeah, but I feel like there's half of the Upper Peninsula sitting on my carcass."

"Well, your temperature has dropped a little more."

He was able to get up to go to the bathroom, then Rachel came with some Cream of Wheat sweetened with maple syrup. He ate a few spoonfuls before he felt nauseated.

"I still think you should go to the doctor," she said.

"No need. I'm getting better." With his head clearer, Kohler was able to reflect on the fact that Indians had been, and probably still were, in his house. But he lacked the strength to become angry about it.

"Who was that squa… ah, girl, from last night?" he asked Rachel.

His niece looked hard at him, and Kohler saw some fight come into her eyes.

"That's Jill Whitefeather. She came to help you, and she happens to be one of my best friends."

"Humph," Kohler replied.

He discovered that Jill was still there, in fact that it was she who had cooked the cereal he had eaten. *It's a wonder she didn't put rat poison in it,* he thought to himself. Kohler became very tired after a short time, and dozed off. He didn't wake up again until early afternoon, when he heard a man's voice. Immediately he thought about the trawler, the fire, and the state cop. A bolt of fear shot through him and he broke into a sweat, but as he listened he knew that the voice was Sam Whitefeather's. *What's he doing here again?* He wondered. *This place is getting to be a regular reservation.*

"Well, if he's feeling better, maybe Jill should come on home. I know how John is, and once he's able to think straight, he'll not take kindly to her presence here."

Kohler could hear Whitefeather walking past the entrance to his bedroom, and on the spur of a moment he raised himself up on his elbows and called out the Indian's name.

The footsteps stopped and retraced their way to the bedroom door, and Whitefeather entered the room. His face was severe, not with hatred or fear, but with a severity the meaning of which Kohler could not discern.

"How are you feeling, John?"

Kohler immediately recognized that Jill's voice was a feminine reflection of her father's, and the knowledge surprised him. Suddenly he did not know what he wanted to ask the man, and he balanced in his bed shakily on his elbows, feeling somewhat perplexed.

Finally he said, "You doing this for Rachel?"

Whitefeather shook his head. "No, not just for Rachel." He began to say something more, then paused. "Well, I hope you're up and about soon," he said, and turned away.

Kohler collapsed back into the bed and stared at the ceiling for a few minutes, overcome with confusion. He wanted to generate the feelings of hatred that he knew should have been there, but rather he felt a void, as though his chest cavity had been scraped clean the way you prepare a Thanksgiving turkey before the stuffing. He was tired again, and presently fell back to sleep.

Rachel stayed on and Kohler continued to improve physically. The fever disappeared in another two days, but he still felt exhausted and sometimes dizzy, so he spent most of his time in bed. He slept much, and still dreamed, but these were not the dreams of the fever, vivid and terrifying, but rather shadowy and menacing. He awoke from them with a vague feeling of foreboding.

He and Rachel talked little. She was dutiful in her care of him, and he was thankful, but he found his thanks nearly impossible to express.

Within a full week of his night on the bay, Kohler had recovered. But instead of feeling robust and energetic, he slipped into a deep depression, a sort of resigned waiting. It was with difficulty that he returned to his wood working and fishing flies, though he was behind on orders for both. He felt that he should be doing something, acting in some way, perhaps setting off into the woods, to avoid the sure retribution over the firing of the Indian fishing trawler. He was still convinced that they would finally discover that it was he who was guilty. But he was weighed down by the sensation that somewhere, for him, a clock had stopped, and the normal forward progression of living had been suspended indefinitely, leaving him in limbo.

He carried on, though, as soon as he was able, working without spirit on his cabinets, and finding the wood uncooperative in his hands. The flies took forever to construct, and then looked hideous. *No self-respecting trout would be seen striking such a shoddy-looking contraption*, he thought. Yet he worked on by sheer willpower.

About nine days after the night on the bay he turned on the evening news, which he had watched faithfully from the time he could get out of bed after his illness. There had been silence concerning the fishing boat in the past few days, until this night. The newscaster reported on a plane crash over by Seney, then said, "More news in connection with the burning of the Chippewa fishing boat in L'Anse on the fourteenth of this month. Thomas Crane, who was taken into custody on that boat when he and his companions were caught exceeding state fishing limits, has once again refused bail and remains in jail tonight in Houghton.

"Mr. Crane states that he will stay behind bars as long as it takes to, quote, 'stir his people from their lethargy in relation to the violation of their treaty rights'. He also mentioned that he is considering a hunger strike with the purpose of forcing the state to allow unlimited rights for native fishing and hunting everywhere in Michigan.

"The police continue their investigation into the burning of the fishing trawler, but have uncovered no suspects at this time. Some Chippewas are accusing the State Police of dragging their heels due to the fear of TOMBS, the new white activist group in the area. TOMBS stands for Treaty Outrages Must Be Stopped, and is composed of an undetermined number of local sportsmen and commercial fishermen dedicated to putting a halt to all treaty fishing and hunting rights for Indians. They contest that the numbers of wildlife have fallen drastically since the tribe began winning concessions several years ago. The recent arrests of the three Chippewa commercial fishermen, they say, is a result of their efforts to bring the public and authorities' attention to the extremes in Indian behaviors that are leading to the decimation of fish populations in the Great Lakes. If these behaviors are not halted, TOMBS contends, all commercial fishing, and fishing and hunting for sport, will come to an end in the Upper Peninsula.

"In other news…"

Kohler clicked off the television. So, Crane was going to starve himself. He was surprised that the Indian was still in jail. He had imagined him to be out hunting for the person who set fire to the boat. Hunting for Kohler. He knew he should feel relieved that Crane was incarcerated indefinitely, but he didn't. He felt pursued, like the cottontail among the ferns at Estivant Pines, and nearly too exhausted to continue the flight. And Kohler knew that the coyote must eventually overtake him, there beneath the ferns in the midst of the forest, and that it would be merciless when it brought him down.

CHAPTER TWELVE – ANISHINAABEG STOCK

It was late August and the forests and skies were displaying the season's age. Clouds hovered closer to the earth and trooped by in slate grey platoons before a brisk wind. The maples had already begun to discard their green garments for the glowing vermilion that made them stand out like lanterns against the darker pine and spruce. The nights clearly threatened frost.

Rachel had remained in Wolf Lodge after Kohler was up and about, and continued on her way each day with her studies and research. He gathered from overhearing a telephone conversation that this met with Whitefeather's approval, and he wondered if Rachel had offended the Indians in some way and made herself unwelcome in their home. That did not seem to be the case, however, since there continued to be close contact between the Whitefeather family and his niece.

He was secretly glad that his niece had returned to his home, though he spoke not a word of this to her. Rather, he kept her at arm's length. But the depression that blanketed his every moment was easier to bear knowing that another human being was near, even if there was no exchange of conversation.

He dreaded the day she would leave to return to Saginaw. The prospect of the approaching winter held a terror heretofore unknown to Kohler. The bitter and bleak whiteness had always possessed a fascinating beauty before, but this year he believed it would be the cold of death. The girl was scheduled to leave in a little over a week.

On this particular evening she arrived home early and prepared supper in a brooding silence. Kohler watched her and noted the sighs escaping now and then while she worked. He said nothing.

Uncle John," she spoke as they sat down to the meal, "I've been thinking."

Kohler grunted in reply. Since their falling-out in July he had not felt entirely comfortable enough to talk candidly with her, as at the beginning of the summer. Rachel acted cautiously toward him, but nevertheless, appeared to have forgiven him for his trespasses. Perhaps that was what bothered him, he thought to himself. So now, realizing that something important was troubling her, he kept a non-committal distance.

"I think I am going to transfer to Northern Michigan in Marquette."

Kohler raised his eyebrows in reply, but felt a small gladness steal into the center of his bleak depression.

"It's not that I want to be away from my family, I mean Mom and Dad and the guys. I love them. But something strange has been happening to me up here, something that I certainly wasn't prepared for, and couldn't have expected.

She paused, and Kohler thought her freckles stood out against her pale skin very prominently again. She bit her lip and brushed her short hair from her eyes.

"There is something so … spiritual about this area. I can't really describe it, but I felt it when we were trout fishing that day, and since then many times. I feel like I've come home, and to leave and go back down below would be to leave a place where I really belong."

Kohler smiled a little when she used the phrase "down below". She had assimilated the feeling that many residents of the U.P. had, that the two peninsulas of the state were in reality two different countries, and somehow separated by much more than the Straits of Mackinac.

"What about your studies?"

"I think it would be o.k. Central and Northern are both state colleges. I checked it all out and I see no problems in transferring credits or anything."

"What about your mother?"

"Well, I'd be near you. It's not like there's no family up here."

Kohler laughed bitterly, and wondered why he did so. A strange reaction, and Rachel gave him a startled look.

"I haven't talked to your mother lately," he said quickly. "I doubt she'd be glad." He thought about the telephone conversation the night that Rachel moved to the Whitefeathers.

"Mom's pretty resilient. Maybe we've all had our disagreements, but I think they can be ironed out, don't you?"

"But I ... no, I don't know that is," Kohler stuttered. "If they're ironed out, as you say, what does that mean? That I have to turn into an Indian lover? I can't. I won't!"

Rachel looked crestfallen. "Maybe I shouldn't have mentioned this, if it's going to start another war. I thought you had changed a little since Sam and Jill were here. I thought that at least you'd be thankful for their kindness."

Kohler made a helpless gesture with his hands and then let them fall like lifeless birds into his lap.

"It was Sam's idea that I come back here again. I don't want to make it sound like I hate you, Uncle John, because I don't. But you hurt me, and you insulted some people that I've come to love and respect greatly, and I'm the type of person who will take just so much, and then figure I've done my share. I felt so frustrated with you, I just couldn't deal with it. Sam and Mary kept urging me to call you, and when I tried several times and you didn't answer, I got worried, so I came and saw your truck here. I guess I got scared that something had happened to you, but I probably wouldn't have actually had the courage to come in if the Whitefeathers hadn't insisted I check on you." She paused and looked at Kohler long and hard. "I guess I don't know how you can go on hating someone that, despite the way you have insulted him, can still find enough human compassion to go out of his way to help you."

Rachel's words were stinging barbs, and Kohler found little strength with which to defend himself against them. He sat motionless, and finally gathered enough bile to say, "Whitefeather's a crazy old guy. I don't know why. He just is. Now I can't talk about this anymore." He began to concentrate on forcing food into his mouth as fast as possible, even though he had lost what little appetite he had possessed.

Kohler spent the days following in much consternation. He believed himself to be weak of will, and continually analyzed and chided himself for indecision and cowardliness. The fear of being arrested by the police for the destruction of the fishing boat still haunted him, and he was angry because he allowed it to paralyze him. Setting fire to that trawler was one of the best things he had ever done in his life, he thought to himself, and it was small payback for the agony that the red man had caused white people, himself included.

He mentally argued with Rachel, striking down her contentions that Whitefeather or his dirty family could be anything but vulgar beasts. He spent much time reviewing what Merle had related to him concerning the death of his mother, and imagined further debate with his sister Grace.

"What about Merle's feelings for Mother?" he heard her ask. "He just made up the story out of grief, because he didn't know who else to blame."

"No," Kohler insisted. "Merle was there. He wouldn't have lied to me. My whole life has proven out the truth of what he told me about that filthy race. They're a plague on the face of the earth…"

And so he continued, dredging up from deep within himself every drop of hatred he ever felt for the Indians, stirring it around, and tasting it again. But a battle persisted within him. To hate the Indians was to distance himself from his niece, and he could not do so easily. He loathed to admit that he was glad to have her back in his home, and that her possible transfer to the university in Marquette, an hour or less to the east, was good news to him. He concentrated on convincing himself that she was an immature child, one to be pitied for her naïveté. She sought the noble savage, but there was no nobility, just savagery.

Kohler had not been away from Wolf Lodge since the night he fired the fishing boat, and he knew he must venture out again. He had allowed Rachel to do all of the grocery shopping, fearful of going out, but if he wanted to continue to eat, he must eventually take care of things himself. It would also be necessary to drive to Marquette with some small items of furniture.

His first trip was to the Amoco station in L'Anse to have the taillight fixed on his pickup. The day was cloudy, with a chill north wind. He turned the collar of his jacket up against it as he stood on the oil-stained cement by the gas pumps while a blond kid checked the light.

"Only a bulb, mister. Cost ya fifty cents."

Kohler was staring down the street toward the harbor, where the water was flat and slate grey.

"Sir?"

"What's that?"

"Fifty cents for a bulb. Getting more like fall, isn't it?"

"Yes, sure is." Kohler dug into his pocket and counted out the change. "Seems colder than usual." He was trembling.

"We're due for a bad winter. Golly, last year it took near the whole winter for ice to even freeze on the bay, and hardly any snow, either. I hope I can get some cross-country in this season. Don't like winter without plenty of snow, 'specially in the North Country."

Kohler thought the kid rambled on too much, though a few weeks ago he would have been pleased to stand and chew the fat with him. Now he felt pressured and a little ill physically.

"Thanks for the bulb," he said, and went around to the driver's door of his truck. He drove around to the Superette to pick up some groceries and his hands tightened on the steering wheel when he passed the police station. He was amazed that he hadn't been arrested yet for his crime. Surely they must know! He was stopped by a cop within hours of its commission; he had to be their only suspect. *What if they never catch me*, he wondered? *What then*? But the waiting. The waiting!

Kohler wandered through the supermarket aimlessly, forgetting some of the items he needed to purchase, and bumping into a display of paper towels, sending the packages to the floor in a heap. He was glad to finally leave the store and be on his way home.

I can't go on like this, he told himself. *I've got to get back to normal pretty soon, and stop acting like a fool. I'm going back and finish my work, and I'm going to begin living like I've always lived, with the opinions I've always had, and the devil take the police, the redskins, and the rest of creation, if need be!*

Through sheer willpower Kohler kept himself occupied. He reasoned that if he simply kept busy, kept his hands moving, measuring and sanding and using the tools, the strange depression would eventually go away of its own accord. And maybe he would never be arrested! Maybe the State patrolman believed that he had been on the bay at Pequaming fishing all night. Maybe he was a dumb cop stationed up here from Detroit, and he didn't know that most folks don't fish the bay in a ten-foot canoe. Kohler marveled now that it had seemed like such a good idea to him that night. *But a dumb cop, for sure! Lucky I caught those two muskies, too.*

He drove to Marquette the next day with a load of small bookcases and coffee tables and took them to Galway's Gallery of Fine Furniture, where he had arranged to sell them on consignment. Several times during the trip Kohler had to force himself to surface from the deep pool of depression that overcame him. He talked to himself often, and told himself to not act like an old woman. *Buck up, man*! By the time he returned to Wolf Lodge he was feeling almost normal.

Rachel had stuck to her studies as the summer wound down. She also took a trip to Marquette to talk to admissions counselors at NMU concerning her transfer. Once he was back on his feet after the illness, Kohler saw very little of her during the day. Two days after he returned from his selling trip he put in some very good time in his shop, and decided to spend the evening with the fishing equipment. It was the first time he had felt entirely right-minded in several weeks.

He sat at the kitchen table, carefully tying a fly of pale green tinged with bright yellow on the tip of its gossamer wings. The area before him was strewn with feathers of every color and description, spools of thread, bits of cork, and several tiny fishhooks. The front door opened and he bent around in his chair to see Rachel enter, her daypack slung over her shoulder and the rays of late afternoon sun streaming in behind her. Kohler reached up and flicked on the light over the table.

"Howdy," he called as he struggled with a tiny knot on the fly.

His niece came and stood in the kitchen doorway, saying nothing.

"Been studyin' our noble Indian friends, I suppose?"

Rachel gave him a disapproving look. "Uncle John, I have something to tell you." He grunted as he fumbled with the last knot on the fly. "As long as it's good news I'd be glad to hear it. Wouldn't happen to have anything to do with your transfer up here to school, would it?"

"No." Rachel pulled a highback chair out from the table and sat down. "It's about Grandmother Rachel."

Kohler looked up quickly. "Your grandmother? You never came within thirty-five years of knowing your grandmother. I never even got to know her," he said, then under his breath, "thanks to your red friends." He finished the last touches on the fly. "So what do you think you're going to tell me about my mother?"

"Well, you were delivered by a Chippewa midwife, right?"

"Yeah, the one that killed my mother as she was birthing me." He turned to look pointedly at his niece, accusing her in his mind. "So?"

Rachel took a deep breath. "Uncle John, she was there because Grandma asked for her to be there. She was a relative."

"Of who, Whitefeather? Or some worse red scum? Figures. That's great. You're hanging around with the direct descendants of your own grandmother's murderer."

"No relation to the Whitefeathers," she answered, her voice reticent.

Kohler tensed up involuntarily.

"Her family was Rising Cloud. The same as Grandmother's. The same as ours."

Kohler shoved his chair back violently. "What kind of shit is this?" he shouted. "My mother's name was Delatour, and you know darn well that she comes from French-Canadian and Scandinavian blood, just like most of the folks around here. I told you all that before. What's the matter, weren't you even listening?" Kohler was furious. "And you know damn well that my daddy's side is all German and Scotch-Irish. How you get any filthy Chippewa blood out of a pure white group of European stock is beyond me, girl. I should never have allowed your mother to talk me into letting you stay here this summer. I knew it couldn't come to any good, dealing with those savages. You've gone crazy mixing with them!"

"Listen to me, Uncle John, please!" Rachel brought out a sheaf of papers from her daypack. "As part of my research I've had to go through a lot of old records from newspapers and things from Mr. Swensson's historical collection. Some of the stuff I've picked up from people like Sam, it's true..."

"I knew it," Kohler spit out. "He's never been anything but trouble to me, and now he's turning my own flesh and blood against me with his lies."

"You know that's not true! And what I have to show you is not something I got from Indians. It's documentation from county records and newspapers. I'm not making this up!" she turned to a sheet that bore a family tree.

"Look. Grandma Rachel was born to Paul Delatour and Helen Keleva in August of 1908. Great-Grandma Keleva came from a Swedish family that moved here to farm around the turn of the century. Paul Delatour, her husband, was born to a man named Louis Delatour, an old French-Canadian family, as you said. But Louis' wife was named Marie Rising Cloud, and she was a full-blooded Ojibwe." She paused, and Kohler sat very still. "We're Anishinaabeg stock, Uncle John."

"That's bull crap." Kohler was looking stonily through the window at the deep green of the pines in back of the house.

"We're of Ojibwe lineage," Rachel repeated. "Marie Rising Cloud was pure-blood, which makes her son Paul a half-breed, Grandma Rachel one quarter Indian, and you and my mom one eighth. I'm only one sixteenth." She added the last words with a note of caution in her voice. "I wondered if I should tell you, the way you feel about things, but I felt that you should know the truth. Maybe…"

"Shit!" Kohler turned from the window, completely composed, and feeling a calm that bordered numbness. He picked up the coffee cup from the table and went to the sink and washed it out. "It's a lie. Just another lie. The kind of crap they make up all the time."

"But Uncle John, it's true! I have a photo copy of everything I used…"

"It is a lie!" He returned to the table and began to pick up the hooks and place them carefully in his box. "Now, I'm going fishing, up on the Huron. In fact, I'll spend the night at Big Eric's Bridge so I can catch the early light on the river. You can have this place to yourself. Just don't ask any of your vermin friends over here."

He finished putting the fly materials away and stomped off to his bedroom, emerging a few minutes later with a rucksack and sleeping bag, which he threw in the pickup along with his fishing gear. He provisioned himself for the trip and placed the food items in the truck. Rachel sat the entire time watching him, saying not a word.

"I'm going now," he said as he closed the door behind him.

He drove north into L'Anse, then caught Skanee Road north and east from town. He stepped heavily on the accelerator and sped past the boundary of the reservation, past the Bingo Hall and the general store and the Indian Cemetery Road. He concentrated hard on the Marquette radio station he was listening to as his pickup traveled into the hills in the early evening light. At the crest of one of the highest elevations he glanced back in the rearview mirror at the strip of road behind him. It looked like the track of a roller-coaster running back toward L'Anse. Then he was out of the reservation, still speeding on, and through the village of Skanee. "Don't blink or you'll miss it!" he cried in a jolly voice, to no one in particular. A mile further, and the road turned into a wide ribbon of gravel full of bumps that shook the pickup as though he were traveling over railroad ties. Behind the truck there rose such thick clouds of acrid grey dust that the road and forest were entirely obscured. A song came on the radio and he began to sing along.

"You make me feel like such a fool,

Sittin' around, playing the clown, while you're out breakin' the rules.

And I sit here while you play around.

I'm a fool," he howled the song out, stepping harder on the gas pedal and watching the dust billow up behind him like the smoke from a gone-crazy forest fire, "to be waitin' for you,

But don't kid yourself, I might find another,

And when I do, I'll be gone forever.

I'm your ace in the hole, the card up your sleeve,

When you heart gets broken, you've still got me…"

He just barely made the Y-split where the Skanee Road turned right toward Big Eric's Bridge and the Huron River. He barreled into the state forest campground and pulled the truck into site number five. The area was deserted, as usual. Kohler hurried to set up camp, hungry, now that it was evening. After the tent and sleeping bag were in place, he put the stove together, emptied a can of beef stew into a pot, and placed it on the flame. "Guess I'll go down to the river and see how the water flows," he said to himself. The shadows were long beneath the trees, so he walked out the campground path to the gravel road where the sun still shone, hanging low in the west. Kohler went to the bridge and his footsteps sounded hollow and lonely, echoing off the surrounding forest. He watched the river for a few minutes, judged the water levels, and decided to go downstream in the morning. He concentrated very hard on the riffles and small whirlpools of the stream, and allowed nothing else to intrude into his thinking.

A chill crept across the back of Kohler's neck as he stood watching the water, and he pulled his collar up and jammed his hands in his pockets. Rachel's face flickered into his mind and her voice saying, "Anishinaabeg stock." His face became hot, and he kicked the sole of his boot angrily against the wooden floor of the bridge. He muttered an oath and swatted viciously at a lone mosquito that dove for his ear.

"Best get back to camp so I can be sure to catch the early morning fishing," he said aloud. He was reassured by the sound of his own voice.

Back at his site he dragged some chopped firewood from the pickup bed and tossed it into the firepit. In a few moments he had a blaze going. He ladled out a bowl of stew, ripped open a bag of potato chips and fetched a slice of bread from the half loaf he had in a box.

The fire crackled and spit and threw lanky shadows behind him as he sat and ate, pre-occupied, staring into the flames. He attempted to think about the flies he would try in the morning, but Rachel's voice continued to intrude into his thoughts, and then his own answering her, "It's a lie. It's a lie!"

A wind sprang up with the onset of darkness, and it moaned through the sugar maples, black spruce and birch that surrounded his campsite. The voice of one of the long-dead loggers from the Iron Pine spoke in his mind. "Yep," he said, "sometimes when I'm out in the woods and I hear the wind a'wailin' through those trees I think it's the spirits of them giant white pine we logged outta here back in '99. The Injuns say that everything's got a spirit, and that the forest grieves for it's dead, same as human folks do."

Kohler jumped up from his seat at the picnic table and looked at the huge, rotted stump of the white pine that stood next to his site. The woods around Big Eric's Bridge were full of these remnants of the virgin forest. And for the first time in his life, John Kohler felt fear while alone among the trees. He shook himself and tramped around the campfire, kicking at it and making the sparks fly up and the flames grow brighter. He slapped his arms around his sides to stave off the intensifying cold of the late summer north woods night.

"This is crazy," he muttered. "Am I losing my mind? Getting senile at fifty-five."

He finally dowsed the fire with dirt and water, entered his tent, and hurried to get into the sleeping bag, trying to fight the numbing chill. "It can't be this cold," he said to himself. "Feels like the last of October." He zipped up his goose down bag around him, then reached into the small compartment in the front for a tiny flask of liquor, which he kept in that spot for just such times as these. A few sips and he felt much warmer. In fact, he felt much better altogether and, bringing the mummy top around his head, he soon fell into a deep sleep.

Sometime during the chill night the dream began. The dream. The terror. The unknown. And, struggle though he may, Kohler could not wake up. He found himself in the forest, as he had so many times before. The cathedral pines rose one hundred and fifty feet tall all around him and the lush ferns were like a carpet beneath the roof of the trees. Spears of light hurled through the needles to strike the understory. The cold sweat was running down his back and arms and chest, and streaming down his face and the rasping sound of the breath was in his throat and the pounding of his heart … And there was a strange familiarity in the rhythm of the beat, and the rasping. It seemed to swim about him and take form, then fade away, then it came nearly into focus. He could see the clearing far off beyond the trees, with its promise of safety from the nebulous something that pursued him among the fronds of fern and trunks of pine, from the something he feared … where? The something seemed to swirl, and settle closer and closer to him, and closer, and in him, within himself, that which he feared. It had come out from among the shadows of the deep woods and could not be separated from himself.

He began to struggle frantically through the ferns and small trees, toward the clearing, and he realized that the beating wasn't that of his heart after-all, nor the rasping his breath, but that it came from the direction of the clearing. The beating, rhythmic, and the rasping, the rattling, accompanying it, growing stronger and louder as he made his way toward it. He was running, now, toward the light, and found his progress less and less impeded, and he could hear Rachel's voice echoing the truth in the ferns whipping past him as he raced toward the clearing in the midst of the forest. The fear was ebbing from him, then flowing, then bursting away from him like the water in an ice-jammed river when the jam is broken. He reached the edge of the clearing and the beat and the rattle were distinct. The air shattered around him in a million scintillating fragments as he walked into the bright, hot sunshine. There was a man standing in the light, his back turned toward Kohler, but the form of his body, and the grey hair, were familiar. Then the man turned, and John Kohler met the outstretched hand and smiling face of Sam Whitefeather.

Made in the USA
Charleston, SC
30 July 2012